GIVEN

A DJINN WARS NOVEL

CHRISTINE POPE

DARK VALENTINE PRESS

GIVEN

Copyright © 2024 by Christine Pope

ISBN: 978-1-946435-76-7

Published by Dark Valentine Press

Cover design by Indie Author Services

Ebook formatting by Indie Author Services

Prologue

THE GROUND RUMBLED UNDER KHALIM AL-Usar's feet. He paused in his endless ramblings and glared down at the rocky soil, which in this particular section of the outer circles was tinted an odd, bilious shade, not quite red, not quite yellow, but some sickly hue in between, like vomit that had been heaved up from the belly of some particularly noxious beast.

Not that anything lived in this part of the otherworld...other than him. That was the entire point of the outer circles, to serve as a prison that somehow managed to be even less hospitable than the other parts of this plane where his people had been banished for countless centuries.

Or at least, where they'd been forced to live until recently. Khalim had spent his own time on Earth, had seen its beauties...and sampled its women...for himself. To lose the chance to enjoy all that after countless centuries of suffering seemed an even crueler slap in the face.

And all for a single minor transgression.

True, the elders had not deemed it so minor, which was the entire reason why he'd been living in torment here in the outer circles. They had decreed that no djinn might lift a hand against another djinn's mortal partner, their Chosen, and Khalim had done that very thing. He had scarred the partner of his former lover, leaving the human male's once-perfect face in ruins, and had taken Martine, the Chosen of another djinn, for his plaything.

Once, the elders would not have interfered in such doings. But after the Heat was set loose upon the world and everything changed, the elders had made it very clear that they expected everyone to obey an entirely new set of rules.

He simply hadn't thought they would be quite so strict in upholding them.

There was even less of a sense of time passing in the outer circles than there was in the sections of the otherworld where his people had built their palaces, so he had no good idea as to exactly how long he had been here, forcing himself to eat the few sickly plants that grew in the blighted space, wandering from place to place because he had nothing else to do with the endless, grinding days. He'd grown thinner during his imprisonment, but he knew he would not expire from such a limited diet.

It took far more than that to kill a djinn.

In all that time, he had never caught even the slightest glimpse of the others who had also been banished here. But that was the way of the outer circles, and perhaps the reason for their name— anyone sent there was relegated to his own private circle of hell, for being left there with anyone at all for company might make the experience at least slightly bearable.

He knew one thing, though—his fury toward the elders and those miserable djinn in New Mexico who had thwarted him and allowed him to be caught in the first place would never abate.

The ground shook again, and Khalim's scowl deepened. Such tremors were something he had never before experienced in this forsaken place. Overhead, the sky might have boiled with colors just as bilious as the ground beneath his feet, and a cold, bitter-scented wind might have blown endlessly, but the earth itself had always seemed stable enough.

His gaze swept the area, but he saw nothing of note, just more harshly colored dirt and a few stunted plants, the source of the acrid smell on the wind. Certainly no sign that a fault line might traverse this piece of territory, nothing to show why the ground had suddenly decided to shake.

Was this some new torment dreamed up by the elders?

Perhaps, but he somehow doubted it. Once they had cast him away here, he had been forgotten, left behind like a small coin abandoned in a worn-out piece of clothing tossed in the trash. It was clear the elders believed banishment here was punishment enough, and would see no reason to invent new forms of torture.

No, this was something else.

Another tremor, but gentler this time, as if whatever deeply buried fault line that might exist here had expended most of its energy. All the same, he decided to begin walking again, hoping that if his strides were swift enough, they might bring him quickly away from the area affected by the minor quakes. After so much time spent here, he knew there was no chance of ever reaching the end of this particular circle, for it seemed to go on forever, vast and trackless, with nothing more than a rocky outcropping here and there to give the landscape some dimension.

However, he had only taken a few steps before the ground began to shake again, harder this time, as if some giant hand had taken hold of the world and begun to rattle it like a child's toy. Khalim did his best to maintain his equilibrium, but soon enough he found himself thrown to his knees, palms spread against the pebble-strewn earth in an attempt to maintain some kind of balance. The shaking intensified, and now he was flat against the ground, desperately doing his best to hang on, as everything seemed to tilt.

He was sliding, sliding into blackness. It enveloped him, and he was gone.

Chapter 1

OLIVIA RASKIN LIFTED A HAND TO SHIELD her eyes from the glaring sun, still almost impossibly bright even though the world had now passed through most of autumn and there was only a week or so left until December began.

Or at least, she thought it was almost December. With so much time elapsed between the bitter now and an almost impossible-to-remember then, she couldn't say for sure. She'd found a five-year planner in one of the abandoned houses here in Cedar Crest, but there had been days here and there when she'd forgotten to draw a line through the date, so she knew her count of the passing time wasn't entirely accurate.

All she knew was that the days had grown shorter and colder, although the New Mexico sun still blazed down clear and bright the way it almost always did. Several weeks ago, an early storm had dropped a ton of rain on her hideaway here in the small settlement off Highway 14, but this far south, it hadn't snowed, even though the peaks of the Sandia Mountains to the west had picked up quite the dusting. A few months from now, it would be a lot more than just a dusting...and she was very, very glad she'd come down from the mountain all those years ago rather than try to stick things out where she'd been when the world ended.

She hadn't been living there, though. No, what she'd thought of as a demanding but decent-paying part-time job at 10-3, the restaurant perched on the highest peak's western side, had turned into a nightmarish prison after the Heat began making its rounds in Albuquerque. Even in their five-star eyrie, the horrible fever had struck, turning patrons and employees alike into little piles of dust in only a few hours.

Well, it had been no more than ten or twelve hours at the most, even though at the time, Olivia had thought she'd been consigned to an unending, nightmarish hell.

When it was all over, she was the only person left alive in the place. The power failed soon after, leaving her with very few choices. The restaurant was usually reached by the Sandia Tram, which swooped its way up the rocky peaks to the combination of scenic lookout and fine dining experience located at 10,300 feet above the valley floor...hence its name. With no electricity, though, there was no way she could get back down on that side, over a mountain face that might have made even an experienced rock climber think twice about making the descent.

There was another way out, though, down the eastern side of the mountain. Olivia had never used that route, but several of her fellow servers had once been forced to hike out on foot via a rough gravel road that eventually wound down to Highway 14 after the tram had experienced some kind of mechanical failure. And after a few days of living on bottled water and scrounging what she could from the restaurant's stores, she'd had no choice but to make her escape along that same badly maintained road.

That wasn't the worst of it, though.

No, the worst of it was worrying the entire time whether she was going to get scooped up and eviscerated by a djinn.

A few days earlier, before the Heat had turned everything upside down, she would have laughed at the idea of those elementals from storybooks being real.

Problem was, she'd seen one for herself, not long after she heard one of those frightening transmissions from a scientist in Los Alamos warning any survivors who could hear him that there were even worse things than rampaging microbes to worry about. She'd been walking back from the tram station—where the radio was located—to the hiding place she'd made for herself in the restaurant's break room when a dark shadow came barreling down toward 10-3.

No conscious thought in that moment, only a pounding *Hide, hide, hide* reverberating through her brain. There was no way she could make it inside without the djinn seeing her, so she'd dropped to the ground where she was and huddled behind a pair of boulders that the landscapers had left next to the pathway that connected the tram station to the restaurant, probably because they thought the oversized stones would add to the scenery.

They were attractive...but much more importantly, they provided plenty of cover.

The djinn hadn't seen her, had drifted his way around the front of the restaurant, peering inside the enormous plate-glass windows, presumably to look for survivors.

But there hadn't been any, so after a few minutes, he flew away to the south and west, where she guessed he would find plenty of hunting in Albuquerque's empty streets and sprawl of suburban neighborhoods.

Even though her eyes had told her he was gone, she'd still remained crouched behind the sheltering boulders for what felt like an hour, until her abused thigh muscles began to scream at her that she needed to move or at least stand up.

When she had, nothing attacked her, so she'd known she was alone.

For now.

And that had decided things. Maybe her luck wouldn't be any better farther down the hill, but she knew she was a sitting duck up here.

Not much to take with her, only bottled water and a few snacks she'd scrounged out of purses and backpacks belonging to people who wouldn't need them any longer. All the food in the refrigerators and the freezers had begun to spoil as soon as the power went out, and she knew she needed to leave it behind. However, she'd taken one of those backpacks and put a few bottles of wine inside, the high-end stuff she would never have been able to afford on her own.

It wasn't as if anyone else was going to need it, and if this was truly the end of the world, she might as well allow herself one small indulgence on her way out.

The trip down the mountain was something she still revisited too often in her nightmares, but she made it to the highway without incident, emerging not too far from the small settlement of Cedar Crest. Her first thought had been to scrounge what she could find there and then keep going, and yet she realized once she got to the town that it would be stupid to head to Albuquerque, even if it was the only place she'd ever lived. If the djinn really were trying to kill off what remained of humanity—and the visit by the one who'd peered into the restaurant's west-facing windows seemed to indicate that was the situation—then going home would only result in her being killed as well.

And what would she have to go home to? The cramped house she'd shared with two roommates, the only place she'd been able to afford while working to get her nursing degree and hustling two part-time jobs on the side?

No family to speak of, no boyfriend. Her father had walked out when she was only a toddler, and her mother, barely hanging on through numerous addictions, had told Olivia to leave the house after she turned eighteen—probably in retaliation for her daughter's insistence that she give rehab another try.

Some friends and classmates and her roommates, sure, but after seeing how everyone else at 10-3 had succumbed within hours to the Heat, she wasn't holding out hope that anyone in her social circle would have survived a disease with such an insane mortality rate. Why in the world she'd turned out to be immune, she had no idea, but that was something she'd worry about later.

In the meantime, it had seemed much smarter to focus on survival.

That was why she'd carefully scouted Cedar Crest and its environs, looking for any signs the djinn had come this way. All she found were those awful little piles of gray ash left behind when something died of that awful fever, which told her no one in the small community about a half hour outside downtown Albuquerque had been immune.

Whether or not the djinn she'd spotted had already come by to make sure, she couldn't tell, but maybe he'd come here before flying over the mountaintops to scout the restaurant. She hadn't seen which way he'd come from, only that it looked as if he was heading into the heart of Albuquerque once he was done prowling around 10-3.

So she'd done her best to scuttle from property to property in Cedar Crest, trying to use trees and outbuildings and anything else she could find to conceal herself from unfriendly eyes. As she did so, she attempted to evaluate every house she passed to see which one might serve as at least a temporary shelter, until she found one on the outskirts of the settlement that seemed just about perfect to her. Built in the New Mexico territorial style with a tin roof and porches that wrapped around the house, it sat on four or five acres and had solar power, propane, and its own well. Sooner or later, the propane would run out, but she figured she'd deal with that problem when she had to.

And that was where she'd been for the past four years. She knew it had been that long because it was easy enough to mark the changing of the seasons, even if she couldn't recall the exact date. As she'd feared, the propane had run out after a while, but it had helped her survive the first winter, and that was enough.

From time to time, she wondered if she should leave, and yet this isolated little corner of the world seemed a much better prospect than anything else she could think of. Albuquerque was off limits, and although she knew Miles Odekirk, the scientist she'd heard on the radio, was in Los Alamos… presumably with other survivors…it seemed like such an impossible distance to cover that she'd long ago abandoned the idea of going there. Besides, he'd stopped broadcasting after a while, so there was no way to know for sure whether he was even still alive.

Better to hunker down here and let the day-to-day focus on survival do its best to banish the hideous realization that she might be the only person left alive in the world.

And there was always a lot to do. She'd scrounged all the nonperishable food she could find in the houses and ranches in the immediate area, and was very glad that Cedar Crest had a small general store that helped beef up her supplies immensely. All the perishable food was a total loss, but she had lots of cans of just about everything she needed to live, plenty of fresh water, and, after that first winter, several gardens where she grew lettuce and tomatoes and zucchini and beans and just about anything else that would prosper in this part of the world, thanks to a bunch of seed packets she'd found at the local feed store. Before then, her gardening experience had been confined to keeping some houseplants alive, but it was sort of funny how motivated you could get when you were trying prevent yourself from starving.

Even her worry about attacking djinn began to taper off. She hadn't seen a single one of the murderous elementals since that one memorable day at the restaurant, and it seemed to her they must have dismissed Cedar Crest and the other tiny settlements up and down Highway 14 as not being worth their time. And a month or so after she came to live in the house on the edge of town, a big male tuxedo cat had decided to come and hang out with her as well. The tag on his collar told her his name was Zorro, which fit him perfectly, thanks to the mask-like patches on his face.

What had happened to all the other dogs and cats in the neighborhood, she couldn't say for sure. She hadn't seen any roaming the area, although a week or so after Zorro showed up, a couple of goats appeared at the property as well, as if telling her they were tired of wandering and wanted a place to settle down.

That was fine with her. She didn't know the first thing about looking after goats, but since they kept the property free of weeds and the farm already had a stable that had probably once housed horses, they had a place to sleep and plenty to eat. Eventually, she learned how to milk the doe, and although she could never figure out how to make cheese, it seemed like the milk and butter helped to round out her diet and make the simple fare she was able to grow or catch that much more appealing.

She'd never cracked open the bottles of wine she'd liberated from 10-3, though. What she was saving them for, she didn't know for sure, but it didn't seem right to drink them with some canned chicken or a salad. As she was scouting for useful items in the other houses in Cedar Crest, she'd found plenty of other booze and had brought it back as well, although she'd only opened one bottle of pinot noir this whole time and nursed it along for almost a week, allowing herself a half glass each night in the days between Christmas and New Year's the first winter she'd been here.

Her mother's drug of choice had been pills and not alcohol, but Olivia had never wanted to tempt fate.

Now, as she walked from the fallow vegetable garden to the back porch of the house, she thought she saw something moving in the distance, and her entire body tensed.

Almost as quickly, however, she found herself relaxing. Yes, something moved out there, black against the dun-colored grass on the hillsides about a mile away, but she realized it was only a raven. They were huge in this part of the world, easily bigger than Zorro, who wasn't exactly what you could call a small cat.

Not that any of the ravens would have dared to take him on. That cat had some serious attitude. She'd never had to worry about mice or rats around the property, that was for sure.

Just as Olivia moved to step onto the back porch, the ground lurched under her feet. At once, she reached out to grab one of the support beams that flanked the steps, even as she looked around in confusion.

We don't get earthquakes in New Mexico, she thought, although she shook her head at herself immediately after that notion passed through her mind.

No, this part of the country wasn't seismically active the way the West Coast was, but that didn't mean you wouldn't still get a minor shaker every once in a while. True, this was the first she'd felt in years and years, although maybe that just meant they'd been due for one.

A glance around told her the tremor hadn't been strong enough to do any damage—the flowerpots on the porch hadn't moved even an inch, as far as she could tell, and when she went inside, the only thing that looked noticeably disturbed was Zorro. He sat on the rug in front of the hearth, black tail going to and fro, green eyes slitted in annoyance.

"Just a little earthquake," she told him. Almost as soon as he'd appeared, she'd started talking to him like this, more to make herself feel better than because she thought he actually understood what she was saying.

Or maybe he did. That was one smart cat.

In response to her attempt at reassurance, his tail flicked again. Then he went to the front door, which she'd just shut behind her, and gave an imperious *meow*.

"As you wish," she said with a grin. At first, she'd worried about letting him roam at will, but then she'd reminded herself that he'd survived for more than a month on his own and obviously knew what he was doing.

So she opened the door and let him out, and he headed off toward the barn, where he tended to do some of his best mousing. If the earthquake had rattled him at first, he seemed to have bounced back right away.

A quick survey of the house told her everything was fine there, except for a couple of pictures that now hung a little crooked. Olivia righted them, since she knew leaving them like that would start to drive her bonkers, then headed into the kitchen. Tremor or no, it was time to get dinner started.

It was a minor shaker, nothing more, and she knew in a few days' time, she'd forget all about it.

Chapter 2

Almost a month had elapsed since Omar al-Qadir had confronted his brother and that mewling human woman he'd fallen in with, and yet anger still burned within him, a flame so strong that he wondered why he'd been born an earth elemental.

Fire seemed far better suited to his nature.

Unfortunately, he had to work with the hand he'd been dealt. And that meant retiring to his home in Placitas, a town that once had been an upscale hillside community just north of Albuquerque and was now entirely his.

The house the elders had given him was spacious, some six bedrooms and an equal number of baths, all contained within a sprawling Southwest-style home that sat on a ridge and had a commanding view of the Rio Grande river valley some five miles away. While he had to admit that sometimes he enjoyed the scenery—especially in the autumn, when the cottonwoods that grew on the river banks turned it into a ribbon of gold slashed through the countryside—now he felt confined here, trapped in a human house he hadn't even been able to choose for himself.

How could his brothers have betrayed him? How could they have thrown away the bonds of family to pair themselves with those simpering human females?

If he hadn't been so angry, he might have been able to acknowledge that he was now the odd man out, as they were both happily living in Santa Fe with their mortal partners, while he languished here in Placitas on his own. However, that notion would have only served to further fuel his fury.

Instead, he stepped out into the yard, a large space enclosed by a high adobe wall and with wide green lawns that should have been somewhat foolish in this arid landscape. But it was easy enough to use his djinn powers to ensure they were well-watered, and he had to admit there was something soothing about viewing that expanse of green, bordered by low shrubs and flowers that provided a riot of color in the summer.

Or at least, they would have been soothing under normal circumstances.

Now, though, with the first of December come

and gone, even those green lawns had begun to yellow a bit, and the blooms of the warm season were only a memory. The place didn't look precisely desolate—it was too well manicured for that—but at the same time, he had to admit it didn't provide the same soul comfort it once might have. He could have used his elemental powers to bring the grass and the plants back to life, although doing so would have gone against the natural order of things, depriving the flora in his garden of their necessary season of quiet and rest.

Best to leave it alone.

Once upon a time, he and Aamir and Jamal had spent the winter months together, taking solace in the presence of family...and, oftentimes, planning how they might continue with their plan to eradicate the few pitiful remainders of humanity, despite the elders' more recent decision that the two races should learn to live in harmony from now on.

Harmony. As if there could ever be peace as long as humans...despoilers of this earth and its riches...still walked upon its surface.

Among djinn, he and his brothers were something of an anomaly, as most of their people had only one or two children at most, and even if they had more than one, they were often separated by decades or even centuries in age. With only three years between him and Jamal, and that same number between Jamal and Aamir, they were far closer than most djinn generally were with their siblings.

Which made Aamir and Jamal's betrayal all the more gut-wrenching.

How could they have not considered what taking a Chosen would mean for their family?

Of course, Omar did not much wish to admit that Jamal might not have done such a thing...if he had not been goaded into it by his younger brother's threats against the woman he'd discovered living alone outside the small town of Las Vegas in northern New Mexico.

But the thing was done, and they would all have to live with it...one way or another.

If djinn were more inclined toward visiting—and if Omar had worked harder to cultivate friendships among his people—then perhaps he would have had someplace to go. At the moment, a change of scenery seemed as if it would be the only thing to improve his foul mood.

Well, that should be easy enough to accomplish, even if he had no friends whose homes might welcome him. Although he had thought from time to time that it would have been much better to be given a home on a beach or a lake, he had to admit that New Mexico offered its own beauties, ones that were easy enough to see simply by stepping outside his property.

And, while the elders may have decreed that each djinn should occupy the home they had been given, they had never said it was not allowed to get out and explore as well.

For some time, he'd been curious about the abandoned restaurant that sat near the top of Sandia Peak, so he thought he would make it his destination today. Although he was no elemental of the air and therefore could not fly to the place directly, he could still make his way to the base of the mountain and then use his gifts as an elemental of the earth to propel himself along the rocky crags until he reached the summit.

A series of leaps down the empty highway that had once served as the main artery between Albuquerque and Santa Fe, and then he moved along the road that led to the tramway complex at the foot of the mountain. Multiple cars still sat in the parking lot there, now beginning to rust after years of exposure to the sun and the elements. They provided mute testimony of the souls who'd perished in the restaurant and the tram, but Omar cared little for that.

After all, they'd been dead for a long time.

He mounted the stairs that once would have led to the tram, although he had no intention of taking it. No, this was merely the easiest way to gain access to the mountainside.

A jump, and he landed on the rocky ground,

feeling its strength like a pulse of energy through the soles of its feet. Yes, these mountains had endured for millennia and would be here for millennia more. They would guide his way.

Anyone watching would have seen a dark blur moving with impossible speed along the mountain face, ascending in seconds what would have taken a human rock climber at least an hour, if not more.

But there was no one to see him now...and he was most definitely not human.

Soon enough, he reached the top, where the observation deck still stood, although it also showed signs of decay, the wood faded and beginning to splinter after enduring season upon season with no human intervention to ensure it maintained its structural integrity. The boards creaked under his booted feet as he walked across the deck and mounted the steps that led to the restaurant, but he could tell they would hold.

For now.

The doors to the restaurant weren't locked... not that it would have mattered if they had been. As he entered, he saw that off to one side was a bar, a spot that had probably once served as a moodily lit introduction to the restaurant itself. Now, though, bright, pale winter sunshine streamed in, revealing an empty space.

But what else had he been expecting?

Some sign that people had died here, he

supposed. Even after all these years, those telltale piles of gray dust should have remained, since none of the windows had been broken and the building appeared intact.

Well, perhaps those afflicted with the Heat hadn't had the time to pour themselves one last drink before the fever took them away from this world forever.

He moved past the bar and into the main room of the restaurant. As he'd expected, the space offered breathtaking views of the city below, and he guessed it must have been even more spectacular in the evening with thousands of lights twinkling in the darkness.

Those lights had been extinguished, however, and he couldn't say he was particularly sorry for that.

In here, just as in the bar, the place appeared to be free of the gray dust, and Omar found himself frowning as he surveyed his surroundings.

Was it possible that someone here had been immune, and had cleaned up the remains?

He supposed it wasn't outside the bounds of possibility. If there had been a survivor, though, they would have left this place years earlier.

Still, his theory merited some closer inspection.

A doorway at the far end of the room appeared to lead into the kitchen, so he headed in that direction. Sure enough, he soon found himself in what had once been a large and well-appointed commercial kitchen, with multiple refrigerators and freezers, and enough cooktops and prep tables to accommodate an army of chefs.

No sign of their remains, either, although the faintest whiff of spoiled food told him no one had bothered to clean out the refrigerators or freezers.

Instead, he moved deeper into the room and went to a door he found on the far wall, a door that opened into what he guessed had once been a sort of break room for the employees. One wall held a series of lockers, although the doors stood open and several backpacks and purses sat on the floor nearby.

Although he could only guess what had actually happened here, it looked to him as though the survivor who'd cleaned up the ashes had also taken whatever they needed from the personal belongings of their coworkers. They must have been desperate and afraid, trapped up here thousands of feet above any possible help.

Not that help would have been available. As he recalled, the power grids had failed less than a day into the heart of the crisis, and anyone still alive in the restaurant would have been fully trapped.

Had they attempted to descend along the route the tramway took? Omar had followed its path fairly closely, but he was a djinn, and the insanely steep, rocky passage had been no problem for him.

He supposed it was remotely possible that one of the people trapped at the restaurant had been an experienced mountain climber, but he somehow doubted it.

Which meant there must be another way out.

The break room had a door that opened onto a walkway that appeared to pass behind the bar. Omar went outside and followed it to a small parking lot that held a few rusting, dusty cars, as well as a Shamrock Foods truck that also looked much worse for wear after so many years in the open.

Of course. Perhaps the guests and the majority of the employees had come and gone using the tram, but the restaurant would still need to accept food deliveries by truck, and that meant there must be a road around here somewhere.

A quick inspection of the parking lot showed a narrow gravel lane that wound away from it down the eastern side of the mountain. Surely that was the way the sole survivor must have gone.

More than four years ago, Omar told himself. *Whoever it was would be long gone by now.*

Had they tried to return to Albuquerque? If that was the case, then they would certainly be dead, for the reavers had remained in the state's largest town for quite some time, glad of the easy hunting there.

But then he thought of how Jamal had found a

woman living alone, how she'd managed to survive in an isolated location by escaping detection by the djinn...and he assumed sourly, by using her wits, even if he would have preferred not to make such a concession to human ingenuity.

Still, if one had survived, then he supposed others might have, here and there.

Most likely, he would find nothing at all. And if that turned out to be the case, so what?

It was not as if he had anything else to do with his time.

The going down the gravel lane was not nearly as rough as the climb up to the restaurant had been, so Omar made good time of it, estimating that it was a descent of a couple of miles to walk down the eastern side of the mountain to the spot where the road widened and a signpost pointed him toward Highway 14.

The Turquoise Trail, according to the sign, although he wasn't quite sure what that meant. Had there been turquoise mines around here, once upon a time?

Perhaps. The name of the highway wasn't important, though. No, in this case, it was all about where it led.

He made his way along the street until he came to the highway, not anything more than a glorified two-lane road stretching roughly north and south. There, he paused, not sure which way would be best to go. The signage indicated that a place named Madrid lay north of here, while something called Cedar Crest was supposedly several miles to the south.

Better not to go north. Omar had a feeling that Madrid was probably a good distance from Santa Fe, but still, he saw no point in traveling toward the town where some of the One Thousand lived with their Chosen.

Including his brothers and their women.

Mouth compressing to a flat line, he turned right, heading south. The land around here resembled much of what he'd seen in northern New Mexico, dry yellow chaparral studded with junipers, with a bare cottonwood or oak every once in a while to break up the landscape a bit. Here and there, rows of fencing indicated the boundary line of a ranch or farm, but whatever cattle and other livestock had once lived here were now gone.

Perhaps they had gone south in search of more comfortable temperatures. True, it was warmer here than in Santa Fe or, he supposed, the hated Los Alamos, home of the only human community in this post-Dying world, but, as he'd discovered at his home in Placita, snow still fell at this latitude if a storm was strong enough and cold enough.

He passed a church, its parking lot crowded with abandoned vehicles, and his lip curled slightly. Had people flocked there, seeking succor from their God as the Heat stole their lives from them? Most likely, although he could have told them none of it would do them any good. Perhaps God had once sheltered humankind, His creation, but He had turned His back to allow the djinn to do what they willed.

A restaurant on the other side of the street, then a tire shop, and what looked like a small general store. Just enough to provide some amenities for the people who lived in this isolated spot so they wouldn't have to drive into town for every little thing. It was hard to remember that a sprawling city of nearly a million people had lain on the other side of these hills.

The place felt utterly deserted, and yet...

...and yet he wasn't sure if it was as empty as it appeared on the surface. Several roads branched off from the highway and headed up into the hills to either side, which meant there were plenty of places where a single survivor might have gone to ground.

Omar paused on the front porch of a small restaurant on the east side of the highway to consider his options. If he'd been an elemental of the air, he could have simply taken to the skies and continued his search that way, but, although he could hover in place like any other elemental, he did not possess the gift of actual flight.

And that meant he had to be methodical about this.

Although some of the properties he'd passed had butted right up to the highway, he doubted anyone who'd been hiding around here would have chosen something so conspicuous. No, they would have done their best to find something well away from the main route in and out of here, probably something "off the grid," as humans had liked to say, with solar power and a well, perhaps land to grow food. After all, even though he knew the local reavers would have passed this way in the early days following the Dying, he doubted they would have had any reason to return to a place where there was no real chance of finding any easy prey.

Then his eye caught a faded sign in the restaurant's window.

Dine In, Pickup, Delivery.

Delivery. Was it possible there might be a map of the town somewhere inside? Omar guessed that was something of a long shot, since humans had seemed fixated on using their so-called "smart" phones for everything, but he supposed it was worth a look inside.

It wasn't as though he had anything but time.

Like the restaurant on Sandia Peak, this one was also unlocked. Because of its remote location in this small backwater town, however, Omar wasn't certain whether that had been a normal state of affairs for the establishment or whether, as with so many other human buildings in the aftermath of the Dying, it had been left that way because no one remained to lock up and make sure the place was secure.

He went inside. A layer of dust covered the tables in the small dining room off to his right—dust that he could tell had mingled with the remains of those who had expired there—but the dining area was not his destination. No, he guessed that if there was a local map anywhere in here, it would be in the kitchen, or perhaps at the hostess station near the entrance.

A quick peek inside the faux-wood lectern told him it was empty except for a stack of menus. Very well. He'd just have to keep going.

The kitchen here was much smaller than the one at the restaurant at the top of the tramway, which was what he'd expected. This was a small local diner, not a facility intended to feed more than a hundred patrons willing to go to the top of the mountain for views of the city lights while they ate.

But there was an old landline phone fastened to the wall near the back door, and beside it was a map of Cedar Crest and its environs, probably taken from a larger survey of the area.

As he'd hoped, he'd struck gold.

He moved closer, eyes scanning the map. The town was long and narrow, straddling Highway 14, and appeared to encompass more territory on the western side, moving up onto the shoulders of the Sandia Mountains. It seemed several neighborhoods resembled the tightly clustered developments found in more suburban areas, but there were an equal number of country roads that led to properties sprawled over several acres.

Omar's eyes narrowed as he pondered the grid of streets. Once more, he had to believe that the person—or persons, although the likelihood of more than one person in such a small sample of humanity surviving the Heat was very low—would have taken refuge on a property with the mechanisms to sustain them, if only for a few weeks or even months before they decided to move on. Therefore, the houses in those neighborhoods with lots of only a quarter of an acre or so wouldn't have made a very good choice.

But all those ranches or homes that sat on multiple acres...those seemed much more likely hunting grounds.

No reason to pull the map from the wall and stow it among his clothing; having studied it like this, he knew he would hold it in his mind for long enough. And while there were at least fifty or sixty properties here that met his criteria, he thought he would start at the southwest edges of the town and work his way up. Cedar Crest was wider at the bottom than at the top, which meant the homes located in the countryside there would be farther away from the highway, more isolated.

What better place to go hide from the world?

He headed back outside and began to walk down the middle of Highway 14, altering course every once in a while to avoid a vehicle that had been left in the middle of the road. Up near Santa Fe, of course, there were no such hazards, for the djinn in the former capital had made sure to clear the streets so it would be easy for their compatriots in Los Alamos to travel back and forth as necessary.

His lips thinned. Bad enough that those traitor djinn had taken human partners. Far worse for them to be friendly with the mortal scum in Los Alamos.

But as much as he would have liked to possess the power to change the situation, he knew he did not. In the meantime, he might as well do his best to discover where the mountaintop survivor's hiding place was located.

If, he was forced to admit, it was here at all. Perhaps they had somehow learned of the sanctuary in Los Alamos and had made their way there, or gone to Albuquerque and perished at the hands of reavers.

Or they simply could have died of starvation or illness as the years following the Dying wore on. Immunity to the Heat would not prevent a human from perishing of dysentery or tetanus, after all.

The air was chilly but the sun bright, making for pleasant conditions as he walked along the highway, gaze scanning the area for any signs of movement. All he could detect, though, was a few ravens circling near one of the hillsides to his left, and the wind moving through the evergreen branches of the junipers that dotted the landscape.

An impulse made him turn off onto one of the streets near the southern border of the little town, one that shifted to gravel almost immediately as it wound its way past more juniper trees and the occasional piñon pine. Private lanes connected to the country road, but because he could see the houses there clearly when he paused to look at the properties, he guessed they wouldn't have provided sufficient cover to be deemed safe by his unknown survivor.

As he went, his nose detected the scent of wood smoke, and his eyes narrowed. He doubted what he smelled was a forest fire, for he hadn't seen any signs of one and besides, enough rain had soaked this area in the recent past that a wildfire would have had a hard time taking hold.

But would someone take all the trouble to hide themselves back here, only to give their location away with a careless fire in a hearth or a woodstove?

Perhaps. After all, it had been years since any reavers would have passed this way, and it was possible the person who'd lit that fire had deemed themselves safe.

Well, he thought as anticipation stirred within him, *they are about to find out it is never a good idea to let one's guard down.*

The gravel road ended at a set of gates made of black metal, while above them, a five-pointed star made of the same metal had been placed at the apex of an arch from which hung a metal sign proclaiming the place to be the Miller Farm.

He doubted it was the Millers who lived there now, but he supposed he would find out soon enough.

A single leap was enough to send him over the gates, and soon enough, he was making his way along a narrow lane that wound through open fields to a large house with a metal roof and white-painted siding—siding he guessed wasn't as shiny and bright as it used to be—as well as an expansive porch that he thought would provide a fine place to sit and listen to the world's sights and smells. It was empty now, though.

But smoke pulsed up through one of the home's two chimneys, telling him someone was there. Past the house was a large red barn whose doors stood open, and in front of the door, a pair of goats nosed around on the ground, apparently preoccupied with the dry grass that grew there.

Everything appeared neat and tidy, as though

whoever lived here had taken care to preserve the property as best they could in these years since the world had changed. No sign of any other livestock, but he thought he spied a small greenhouse and some raised garden beds behind the main house.

And then more movement made him shift his gaze back toward the barn, where someone had just emerged from within.

A woman, her dark hair pulled back in a ponytail.

Omar's heart sank. He had been so ready to kill, so ready to rid this place of the human who had taken it for his own and, no doubt, had congratulated himself on escaping the wrath of the djinn. But....

While he and his brothers had looked upon the act of removing human survivors from the face of the earth as something close to a holy mission, they had also agreed that they would not kill children or women, for it was largely the actions of men that had brought the world to the brink of destruction. And he and Jamal and Aamir had never wavered from that pact, even as they took grim pride in adding more notches to their already worn belts.

Fists knotted in frustration, Omar watched as the woman went up to the goats and patted them on their heads, submitting to their head butts with a smile, even though it was difficult to discern her expression clearly from this distance. She looked to be in her middle twenties or so, slim but not overly tall. No way to make out her eye color from here, but...

...but he was forced to admit that she was attractive.

Not that it mattered. Unlike his brothers, he was not one to be swayed by a pretty face, especially a face belonging to a human woman.

As soon as she'd emerged from the barn, he'd moved back off the path so the nearby junipers might shield him, which meant he doubted that he'd given his presence here away. Sure enough, after patting the goats one more time, the woman crossed over to the house and went inside. If she'd caught a glimpse of him, he doubted she would have been quite so casual.

But now what? Logic stated that he should simply walk away and return to Placitas, as women were not his prey and he had no reason to disturb her in her solitary existence.

Simply leaving felt far too anticlimactic, though.

Perhaps it would be better to stay a while and observe her. It seemed as if she was alone, but if she wasn't...if some male survivor was holed up here with her...then perhaps Omar would be able to strike after all.

He might as well have something to show for all his efforts in finding this place.

Chapter 3

FOR SOME REASON, OLIVIA COULDN'T quite rid herself of a creepy-crawly sensation, as though someone was watching her. Which, she told herself, was ridiculous, because she knew that she and the goats and Zorro...well, and a few chickens...were the only living things in this isolated spot.

Well, except the birds, but even though there were plenty of them in the area, they didn't come close to the house very often. In the early days following the Heat, she'd fed them with birdseed she'd found at the feed store a mile or so up Highway 14, but that had run out years ago and they now didn't have much reason to come near. Hummingbirds were an exception, as she still had enough sugar to make nectar for them, but the tiny, fascinating hummers wouldn't be back until the end of April when they deemed it warm enough to move north.

It was just the earthquake, she thought. *It's put you on edge.*

That seemed the most rational explanation, because even though everything in the house had survived the temblor just fine, she knew her nerves were still a little rattled. After surviving the Heat and managing on her own here for so many years, the last thing she wanted was for the very earth to betray her.

Besides, Zorro came in a while after that, looking pleased with himself, which told her he'd probably caught another mouse while wandering around the barn. He hadn't brought his prize into the house, though, because even from the beginning he'd seemed to understand that she wasn't a fan of those sorts of feline "gifts."

Anyway, if someone or something had been lurking around the property, she doubted the cat would be so nonchalant. Of course, he wasn't the same as having an actual guard dog, but one time when a mountain lion had come prowling around not too long after she'd taken up residence in the farmhouse, the cat had gone crazy, hissing and spitting, hair on end, tail standing up like an illustration on a Halloween postcard.

So she had to believe if anything threatening lurked nearby, he'd let her know.

Or maybe she was finally starting to go crazy from the isolation.

Winters were always the worst, even though it was only the beginning of December. Still, her garden had yielded everything it could except for some butter lettuce, and with the cold months closing in, she wouldn't have nearly as much to keep her occupied. There were always her occasional forays into neighboring houses to glean what she could from the items their residents had left behind, but she had to admit that the pickings were starting to get pretty slim.

One thing she could do, though, was crochet. She'd tried knitting, too, but hadn't liked that nearly as well, so she fell back on the other kind of needlework, gathering all the yarn she could find and making it into throws and shawls and even a couple of sweaters, although she had to admit those were a lot more difficult and the results a little lumpy where the sleeves attached to the body of the garment. The farmhouse also had a well-stocked sewing room, and she'd used the machine there to repair a hem or a torn sleeve, or even make a new set of curtains for the kitchen window.

But the hobbies gave her something to do, especially since she knew she wasn't artistic, didn't paint or sing or write or make pottery. Even before the Heat, her world had been focused on survival, and she'd never had time for those sorts of things.

No, she had planned to keep her head down and get her degree, but not so she could work in a doctor's office or a hospital. Instead, she'd wanted to get certified as a nurse practitioner so she could run her own business, could have a clinic where people who couldn't afford regular medical insurance could still talk to a health professional and get their necessary prescriptions and bloodwork and other kinds of basic care.

Maybe it had all been a pipe dream, but she'd never know how things might have turned out if the Heat hadn't struck. She'd been one year away from getting her bachelor's degree in biology and still had many years of school ahead of her, which had been fine. She'd had a goal, and that was the important thing.

Or at least it had been, once upon a time. Now her only goal was to get through yet another day.

Even though common sense told her there was nothing to see out in the yard, she set aside the afghan she'd been working on, laying it over an arm of the couch so she could go on the porch and take a look around. The day was certainly bright enough that there wasn't much shadow to distort the landscape, and she had to lift a hand to shield her eyes even with the shelter of the porch roof over her.

As she'd expected, she couldn't see a damn thing. Sure, Billie and Willie, the two goats, had meandered away from the barn and were now munching on the dry grass in a pasture that had been meant to support far more animals than a single pair, but nothing else was moving out there. Every year, Billie had babies, but once they were grown, they wandered away from the farm and never returned. Where they'd gone, Olivia had no idea, although she was pretty sure wild animals hadn't gotten them, since she'd never seen a single trace of that kind of slaughter. It was more as if, after they were old enough to survive on their own, they'd decided to move on.

After that near-miss with the mountain lion, though, Olivia had thought about putting up some kind of defenses around the house, maybe deadfalls with sharpened sticks at the bottom like she'd read about in a book when she was in high school. However, she'd abandoned the idea, mostly because she couldn't think of a way to keep the goats out of the pits without putting up fences that would have advertised the sticks' presence to anyone in the vicinity. Instead, she kept a shotgun in the hall closet downstairs and had another one leaning up against the wall near her bed, and after practicing with them for the past couple of years, she figured that should be enough for home defense.

Well, unless some djinn came creeping around. She hadn't heard enough from Miles Odekirk to know for sure whether a djinn could even be injured, but she had to believe that an immortal being with supernatural powers might not care if you pumped them full of buckshot.

But she lingered on the porch a moment longer than was necessary, gaze still scanning the perimeter. For the first few months after the Dying, she couldn't prevent herself from hoping that maybe another survivor would be able to find her here, that maybe she wouldn't have to be alone at the farm forever. She'd even harbored a few wistful fantasies about what it might be like to have that other survivor be around her own age, a man who didn't necessarily have to be handsome but who would be strong and kind and resourceful.

That way, she wouldn't have to do this all on her own.

But the perfect stranger had never appeared, and she'd done her best to reconcile herself to living out the rest of her days alone. At least she'd never gotten sick, had never injured herself. Her first aid skills were definitely up to a variety of mishaps, although she didn't know if she would have been able to splint a compound fracture of her tibia, if such a thing were to occur.

It didn't, though, and so she managed as best she could with her gardens and her crochet, and evenings spent reading or watching one of the DVDs she'd gathered during her scrounging of the local houses. The ranch's solar had been new and extensive, with multiple batteries mounted to the wall in the detached garage, so she probably could have watched TV all day without ever having to worry about draining the system. Squandering electricity that way felt far too indulgent to her, which meant she allowed herself one movie a week, usually on Sunday night, as a special treat.

Otherwise, she most likely would have already run through them all.

A final visual sweep of the pasture and the goats who still cropped at the dry grass there, and then she shook her head and went back inside.

No point in manufacturing ghosts. The world had enough of them as it was.

The dark-haired woman went back inside her house, and Omar permitted himself a sigh of relief. For just a moment there, it seemed as if she had spotted him, which would never do. No, if he were to approach her—and he wasn't sure he would, as he didn't see the point—he would do so on his own terms.

All the same, he had to wonder what had made her linger on the porch for so long. It seemed she had been looking for something, although what, he couldn't say. Her goats had been in plain view, but it seemed she had been looking past them, gaze moving over the split-rail fence that marked the perimeter of the property.

Was it possible she might still be hoping for survivors to come along?

No, that was a foolish notion. If she had been resourceful enough to live here on her own for more than four years, then she must have sufficient intelligence to realize there would never be anyone else.

He waited in the shelter of the junipers for a moment more, wondering what he should do next. Returning to his house in Placitas didn't appeal to him very much, but he had very few other options. It was not as if he could visit Aamir in his stately home in Telluride or Jamal in his place in Jackson Hole the way he once had been able to when he had something on his mind that he wanted to discuss. No, his brothers were now lost to him, buried in Santa Fe with the rest of the traitors against their kind.

Well, at least he had solved this particular mystery. If the other reavers had still been active, he might have informed them that a survivor dwelt here in Cedar Crest, so that one of their kind who did not scruple at killing females could come and dispatch her.

But they had all lain down their swords as well

at the behest of the elders, so there was no one left to handle such messy business.

Out of nowhere, his brother Aamir's voice sounded in his mind. Omar was startled, for while his brothers had always been able to speak with him thus, he hadn't thought he would hear from one of them this way, not when they were so clearly estranged and should have had no reason to reach out and make contact.

A terrible thing, Aamir said. *Khalim al-Usar has escaped the outer circles.*

Omar could not quite keep his eyes from widening. *How is this possible?*

We do not know, Aamir replied. *We only know that the elders came to inform Zahrias al-Harith of this development, and they passed the word along to us. All djinn are to be on the lookout for him. At least it seems as if he was the only one to escape, so we will not have to hunt all of his followers down.*

A good thing, Omar supposed, for those followers had numbered more than twenty, all of them proud and vicious and caring little for the rules of the elders... or much of anything else, for that matter. Perhaps he would not have been in any danger from them, considering how their goals aligned somewhat with his, but he most certainly did not care for their methods.

The elders are particularly concerned about New Mexico, Aamir went on, *seeing that it is here that*

Aldair al-Ankar was able to return to the world when he also escaped the outer circles to the place called Madrid.

Omar blinked. He had heard something of Aldair's escape, which had occurred several years earlier, for it was certainly a singular event, but he had not realized the rogue djinn had landed so close to where he currently stood. Madrid was only some fifteen miles up the highway from here.

However, lightning rarely struck in the same place twice. There was no reason to think Khalim was lurking anywhere near here.

And what do you expect me to do about all this? Omar asked. *It is not as if I am in any danger from this man.*

Perhaps not, Aamir returned. His inner voice now sounded a bit annoyed, but he only added, *It is more that this is a direct request from the elders, to watch out for Khalim. And you know it is never a good idea to ignore a request from the elders.*

Well, that was true. While they did not precisely rule the djinn, they still had no issue with letting their feelings on a particular subject be known.

Before he could reply, Aamir went on, *Is all well with you, brother?*

It is well, he said, those words stiff, stilted. *But now that you have delivered your message, we have no reason to have further speech with one another.*

And he closed down the connection between their minds. Aamir could have tried to reach out to him again, he supposed, but had probably decided it would be better to leave matters as they were. After all, he had told Omar what he needed to say, and anything else would appear far too intrusive.

Even with that inner contact broken, Omar could not help feeling uneasy. No, he most likely did not have much to fear from Khalim al-Usar, but he could not prevent his thoughts from straying to the dark-haired woman in the house a few hundred yards away.

She was so very alone here...and Khalim had certainly not allowed scruples to prevent him from forcing himself on human women. True, he had used the djinn glamour on them, making them believe they were in love with him and desired his touch, but the whole situation was still utterly distasteful. Omar had never had any desire to be with a mortal female, and yet he had to believe that if a woman —human or djinn— did not desire a man on his own merits, then he had no right to trick her into thinking that she did.

And what if lightning truly had struck twice, and Khalim had emerged in this plane in Madrid?

Even if he had, Omar thought surely that must have been the first place the Santa Fe djinn would have looked. Clearly, they hadn't located him, or

Aamir would have had no reason to reach out to deliver a warning to his brother.

Which meant Khalim al-Usar might still be skulking somewhere nearby.

Or he could be on the other side of the world, Omar argued with himself. *There is no reason to approach that woman and give her a warning. You owe her nothing.*

True enough.

And yet....

No one—not even a human—deserved to be used in the way Khalim al-Usar had used the Chosen female he had stolen from one of the Santa Fe djinn.

Very well, then.

Omar set his jaw, then struck out in the direction of the cedar-sided farmhouse.

The chair where Olivia usually sat to crochet faced the front porch and the pasture beyond. She liked that position, not only because it provided lots of natural light, but also because it gave her a good vantage point to overlook the grounds and keep an eye on things—or at least, as much eye as she could spare from her latest creation.

And when she looked up this last time, she

couldn't quite hold back a gasp of alarm, even as her partially completed afghan fell to her lap.

A djinn was walking down the gravel lane straight toward the house.

Well, she assumed he was a djinn. He was very tall, with inky, shoulder-length hair nearly the same shade as the black garments he wore.

And he was heading in her direction.

At once, she tossed the afghan and skein of yarn and her crochet hook aside, then scrambled for the coat closet, where the Remington shotgun she'd liberated from a neighboring farm years ago leaned against the wall. With shaking fingers, she grasped it and then retrieved the box of shells from the top shelf, dropping several of them in her haste.

Despite her clumsiness, she had it loaded soon enough. Now that she was armed, though, she didn't know what to do next. Should she fling open the door, run out, and shoot him as he was approaching, hoping to catch him by surprise, or should she simply wait here and pray he had some other destination rather than the house itself in mind?

No time to dither. And, as they liked to say, fortune favored the bold.

Besides, after all those billions of deaths and all these empty years, she thought it might be time for a little payback...even if it might turn out to be completely ineffectual. After all, she still had no idea whether a djinn could even be harmed by a mortal weapon.

Shotgun in her right hand, she grasped the doorknob in her left and turned it, then strode out onto the front porch. He was much nearer now, so close that she could make out the strong, handsome features, the sensual curve of his mouth.

For some reason, she couldn't help being shocked.

Miles Odekirk hadn't said anything about how good-looking the djinn were.

Not that it mattered.

She raised the shotgun and pulled the trigger.

Chapter 4

OMAR SAW THE FRONT DOOR CRASH OPEN, and the woman he'd spied earlier standing there in its open frame. However, his brain didn't quite want to acknowledge what she did next, perhaps because she appeared too slight to be able to heft such a large gun and it didn't seem possible that she presented much of a threat.

Unfortunately, there was no mistaking the puff of smoke that emerged from the shotgun's barrel as she held it at her hip, though, or the accompanying *bang* that shocked his eardrums a fraction of a second later.

Or the horrible pain in his leg as he realized she'd hit him. Not dead on—her aim wasn't good enough for that, especially since it was clear she'd shot from the hip without much forethought—but enough that pellets ejected from the shell impacted with his left thigh, agony lancing through him as his leg gave way and he collapsed to the ground.

At once, she was running toward him, gun in one hand and an expression of utter shock on her pale face.

Was she coming to finish him off?

Before he could grit his way past the throbbing agony in his thigh to focus his powers so he might summon a minor earthquake to knock her off her feet and buy him some time, however, she'd dropped the gun and sunk to her knees in the gravel beside him, eyes wide with worry.

"Oh, my God," she gasped, frantic gaze going to the blood-soaked ruin of his trousers. "I didn't think it would hurt you. I just thought it would scare you off."

"Clearly, you were wrong," he gritted from between clenched teeth.

She shook her head, even as her gaze moved to the loose outer robe he wore. Once again, she moved quickly enough that he didn't have a chance to respond. However, this time she wasn't shooting a gun at him, but instead grabbing hold of his robe so she could tear off a wide section from the bottom.

"What the—?" he began, then stopped as she began to deftly wrap the makeshift bandage around his leg.

So...she'd shot him, but was now administering first aid?

"I didn't know djinn could be wounded," she said, hands still moving quickly, doing their best to staunch the bleeding.

She knew who...or at least what...he was. And yet she'd approached him anyway, even when she might have stood back and hoped he bled out.

"We can," he said, still in that strained voice that didn't sound much like his. "But we heal quickly."

"How quickly?" she asked, gaze fixed on the rough bandage that now encircled his leg.

That was a very good question. He'd never before suffered such a grievous wound, so he didn't have much frame of reference. However, he knew that minor bumps and breaks could heal themselves in a matter of minutes.

A shotgun blast that had taken out a good chunk of his thigh?

He had a feeling that might require a bit longer than a few minutes.

"I don't know," he replied.

The whole exchange didn't feel quite real. Here this woman had just shot him, and now she was crouching there next to him, her expression one of utter concern. Now that she was close enough, he could see her eyes were an unusual dark green, like nephrite jade, striking against her pale face and dark brown hair.

He didn't have much time to focus on her appearance, though, because she said, "Then we need to get you inside where I can tend to you properly. I don't know if djinn can go into shock, but I'd prefer not to find out."

Omar had a feeling that if djinn could experience such a condition, he would have already been suffering through it, considering how much blood he'd lost. However, he thought it probably a good idea to be someplace where he could lie down, even if he couldn't help but be struck by the incongruity of her offering him shelter when she'd just done her best to kill him.

"Can you get up?" she asked. "Otherwise, I can fetch the wheelbarrow from the barn and try to get you into the house that way."

Even while suffering a kind of pain he'd never before experienced in his long life, he did not want to suffer the indignity of being hoisted into a wheelbarrow like a sack of potatoes. "Let me try."

To his surprise, she came closer so she could slide an arm under his shoulders, then helped to steady him as he pushed up with his good leg. This maneuver made blood gush against the bandage in a new torrent, and for a moment, the world spun around him.

"Are you okay?" the woman asked, expression more anxious than ever.

No, he was definitely not okay. But those seconds of dizziness had passed, and with her propping him up—and surprising him with her strength, for he would not have thought she would be able to bear such a burden—he thought he might be able to walk, albeit very slowly.

"All right," he said. "Lead on."

———

Olivia had never thought that her morning would end with her helping a wounded djinn hobble into the house and into the main bedroom, but there he was, quilts pushed out of the way so he wouldn't stain them with his blood, face pale under its usual swarthiness. Or at least, she guessed he had a warm brown complexion when he wasn't drained of at least a few pints of blood.

Until her finger had spasmed against the trigger, she wasn't sure if she'd even have the guts to shoot someone. But then she had...and almost immediately, horror had struck her.

Once upon a time, she'd wanted to devote her life to healing people. And now she'd nearly killed a man.

Well, all right, not a man. A djinn. But her eyes

wanted to tell her he was a man, even if her brain knew he was something entirely different.

Djinn or not, he was wounded...badly. And although he'd told her that his people had healing powers that humans didn't possess, she knew she needed to intervene. Maybe a regular human would have already died of blood loss, but since she was dealing with uncharted territory here, she had to do whatever she could to help him.

Out came the first aid kit and the rolls of gauze bandages she'd stocked up years ago, along with the big bottle of Betadine and the bottle of amoxicillin she'd liberated from the local urgent-care clinic years earlier. The pills were already more than twelve months past their expiration date, but she had to hope they were still okay...and that medication designed for humans would even work on a djinn.

"I'll need to take your boots off," she said, a little surprised that she sounded so calm. But then, she'd managed to hold it together during her mother's numerous benders; keeping her head during stressful situations was still second nature to her, even though Maryanne Raskin had been out of her life for years. "And then those pants," she added, knowing they needed to come off as well so she could tend the wound in his left thigh.

Her voice had held steady the whole time, so maybe the djinn hadn't noticed the flush that touched her cheeks as she spoke those last words. Probably, he was just concentrating on not bleeding out.

"Do what you must," he said. Like her, he sounded calm, almost resigned. Was he reflecting on the irony of the woman who'd shot him also being the one intent on saving his life?

Because if he wasn't, Olivia knew she sure as hell was.

"What's your name?" she asked as she grabbed hold of one of the black boots he wore. They looked ordinary enough, simple black leather, reaching almost to his knees. But then, even though his clothing looked vaguely Middle Eastern, she could tell it was made of cotton and linen, nothing all that out of the ordinary despite it being something she might have seen someone wearing at the local Renaissance Faire.

Well, back when Ren Faires had still been a thing.

He blinked. His lashes were long and thick and black, making him look as if he was wearing eyeliner. "Omar," he replied. "Omar al-Qadir."

Also not that outlandish a name. Did all djinn have names that were Middle Eastern in origin?

Maybe she'd ask him at some point. Right now, she needed to focus on removing the makeshift bandage and discovering how much damage that shotgun blast had really done.

Beneath the boots were a pair of thin socks out of what she thought might be a blend of cotton and silk. She pulled those off as well, then allowed herself an inner breath, even as she did her best to keep her outward demeanor utterly neutral, just like the nurse she'd once hoped she could be.

There was no point in salvaging the billowy black trousers he wore; one leg was shredded and soaked with blood. In fact, they were in such bad shape that she realized the best thing to do would be to cut them off.

"I'm Olivia," she told the djinn. "Olivia Raskin. And I need to get a pair of scissors before I can go any further."

Was that an amused flicker in his coal-black eyes?

"The shotgun was not sufficient?"

Despite herself, her lips quirked a little. "Your pants," she explained. "They're such a mess that I need to cut them off."

His head tilted, almost a casual movement, but she could tell from the tightness of his jaw that he was in the kind of pain that would have made a regular person pass out to escape it.

But then, he wasn't a regular person, was he?

"Do what you must," he said, then closed his eyes.

Worried, she studied his face for a moment, looking for signs that he might finally be going into shock. However, he hadn't gotten any paler, and he didn't seem to be perspiring. No, he was probably just preparing himself for what would be quite an ordeal.

She hurried out of the main bedroom and up the stairs. From what she'd been able to tell based on the personal items left behind, this ranch had been owned by a husband and wife, a couple who were older, with their children long since grown and moved out.

And it seemed obvious enough that Molly Miller had been a quilter, because one of the spare upstairs bedrooms had been converted into a sewing studio, with an expensive sewing machine that did all kinds of fancy embroidery, not to mention an entire wall of shelves filled with bolts of fabric. It wasn't the fabric that brought Olivia here now, though, but the sharp scissors hanging from the rack behind the sewing table.

She grabbed them now and went back downstairs. Some part of her mind wondered if the djinn —Omar—would even be there when she returned. After all, he had the power to move from place to place as he liked, didn't he?

But no, he was still lying in the king-size bed in the master suite, eyes closed, when she returned. Maybe losing all that blood had affected his powers somehow.

"Once I'm done bandaging you up, I'll get you

a pair of sweatpants," she told him. Not an idle promise, since long ago she'd found several pairs in the dresser here in the main bedroom, one of them with the tags still on.

Omar's eyes opened then. "It is no matter," he said. "I will be able to conjure another pair of trousers when the time comes."

Just like that? But he'd sounded confident enough, and obviously, he knew a lot more about what he could or couldn't do than she did.

"Okay," she replied. "Time to get this taken care of."

Holding the scissors, she went to the bed and made a careful slice down the side of his pants, revealing a muscular leg dusted with dark hair.

More blood went to her cheeks, but she had to hope that with her head lowered like this, intent on her work, Omar wouldn't notice anything.

If he had, he didn't say anything. No, he lay there quietly as she cut the ruined trousers off him, working around the wounded area. Thank God he wasn't going commando, but instead wore a close-fitting black garment that looked like the djinn equivalent of boxer briefs.

And now it was time to cut away the blood-soaked bandage to see what lay underneath. Olivia hadn't been looking forward to this moment, even as she knew it had to be done. It wasn't as though she was overly squeamish, since she'd seen plenty of pretty gnarly stuff when she spent a summer working as a nurse's aide in a downtown hospital before deciding that she could make a lot more money while working as a waitress at a high-end restaurant.

Blood flowed from the wound as soon as she pulled the makeshift bandage away, but at least it wasn't pumping everywhere from his femoral artery. No, she hadn't hit him dead center, hadn't shattered the bone or severed an artery. Even so, the amount of damage buckshot could do was pretty impressive. As far as she could tell, she'd blown away at least half a pound of hamburger from his thigh, a wound that probably would have been fatal for just about anyone else.

Djinn, however, clearly didn't play by the same rules as regular people.

His fingers tightened on the sheet beneath him as she worked, although he didn't make any sounds but remained silent while she cleaned the wound and then began to stitch him up. This was the sort of operation that should have required a local anesthetic. Unfortunately, she didn't have anything like that on hand, only the sort of stuff she thought she'd need for basic emergencies. She'd certainly never imagined that she might have to perform surgery on one of the elementals who'd helped destroy the human race.

"I know it hurts," she said quietly. "But I should be done soon."

"It is—" He paused there, another of those halfway amused smiles touching his lips. "Perhaps I should not say it is fine, for it most certainly is not. However, at this point, I think the best thing is for you to keep going."

"I will." She allowed herself a brief glance up from her work, then added, "And I really should give you some antibiotics. Do you have any idea whether they'll work on a djinn?"

His brows, as inky black as his hair, drew together. "I have no idea," he said. "My people have never required the use of human medicines. But I believe that if it turns out to be something my body does not need, it will simply...ignore it, for lack of a better term."

Not exactly the answer she'd been hoping for, but at least it sounded as if she wouldn't have to worry about him having an adverse reaction to the amoxicillin.

"Okay," she replied. "Just a few more minutes, and then I'll be able to get this wrapped back up." She stopped there, wondering whether she should just let it go or whether she should attempt some sort of apology for her overactive trigger finger.

However, since she had no idea how long his convalescence might take, she hated for him to think she was the sort of woman who went around randomly shooting people whenever the urge struck her.

"I'm really sorry," she said as she tied off the last stitch, then snipped the thread with the scissors she'd brought from the sewing room. Not the most antiseptic of operation theaters, but she had to hope the combination of his djinn constitution and the amoxicillin she was about to give him would be enough to ward off any opportunistic infections. "I didn't mean to shoot you. I suppose I was kind of freaked out at seeing a djinn on my property."

One corner of his mouth lifted. "I suppose many people would say that sort of reaction was warranted. But if you did not intend to shoot me, then why the shotgun?"

"I guess I hoped it would scare you off."

Now the other corner of his mouth lifted as well, although she didn't see much humor in his dark gaze. "Djinn don't scare easily."

No, she supposed they wouldn't. It was easy to be fearless when you were all but immortal and gifted with all sorts of supernatural powers, wasn't it?

But djinn could still be wounded, as the stitched-up wound in his leg proved. Olivia could only hope that his djinn nature would allow him to heal without scarring, because he seemed too perfect to have to carry that kind of flaw on his body for the rest of his life.

Rather than reply right away, she picked up the roll of gauze bandages and began to wrap them around his leg, covering the ugly wound with its rows of stitches and the stain of Betadine on all sides. Omar's mouth tightened as she worked, telling her that, although she was doing her best to be gentle, even that light touch was enough to hurt.

She had done all she could, though, and excused herself to go to the kitchen and get a glass of water. Even now, she marveled a little at how seamlessly this place worked, how the Millers had made sure to set up their ranch so all of life's comforts could still be supplied by the well and the solar panels and their accompanying batteries. True, there hadn't been any way to replace the propane, but she'd had plenty of firewood, and had managed to stay clean and warm and dry the entire time she was here.

Glass of water in hand, she went back to the main bedroom and handed Omar the water, followed by a tablet of amoxicillin. "You'll need to take one of those twice a day for ten days," she told him, and one eyebrow lifted.

"Oh, it will not take me nearly so long to heal as that. I would be surprised if this wound was not completely better sometime tomorrow."

He sounded very confident, but Olivia wasn't

so sure. His injury was a messy one, the kind that would have kept most people off their feet for weeks...and quite possibly might have given them a permanent limp.

Omar, as she would have to keep reminding herself, wasn't "most people," which meant she had no idea what to expect next.

"I guess we'll just have to see," she responded, which she hoped sounded neutral enough. "But now that you're bandaged up, you can conjure yourself some new pants."

He glanced down at his exposed legs...and at the swath of gauze that wrapped one thigh. "Yes, I believe that would be a good idea."

Olivia wasn't sure what she expected to happen next—to have him bob his head like something from an old *I Dream of Jeannie* episode, she supposed, and for a new pair of those billowy trousers to hide the damage she'd caused less than a half-hour earlier.

To her surprise, nothing seemed to happen at all.

Omar appeared equally startled...and, for some reason, angry.

"What is this? Do you have one of those devices here?" he demanded, and she stared at him, nonplussed.

"What devices?"

"Those infernal devices that Miles Odekirk

created," Omar shot back, and this time Olivia could only shake her head, even as her brain worked away at the words the djinn had just uttered.

How could Omar al-Qadir have even heard of the scientist in Los Alamos, let alone accuse him of creating some kind of gadget?

"I don't know what you're talking about," she said. "There are no special devices here. Just the solar that powers the house, and the appliances in the kitchen. That kind of stuff."

He glared up at her from the bed, somehow menacing despite his wounded leg and obvious immobility. But as she gazed back at him, doing her best to show in her expression that she had no idea what had set him off, he seemed to deflate suddenly, leaning back against the pillows even as his angry stare shifted to one of puzzlement.

"Something very strange is going on here," he murmured.

"And I shall have to find out what it is."

Chapter 5

His powers were gone. Or at least, when he had attempted to conjure himself a new pair of trousers—a very minor feat, one he should have been able to accomplish in his sleep—absolutely nothing had happened.

Confronted by this unsettling conundrum, his first thought had been that Olivia Raskin must have one of Miles Odekirk's devices secreted in the house. What else could be causing such an obvious failure of his powers?

But she claimed not to know what he was talking about, and unless she was a very good actress, the expression of utter puzzlement on her face had been genuine. And, once his initial anger had ebbed, he'd been forced to admit that some other devilry must be at work here.

For while he had never experienced the effects

of the djinn-repelling devices himself, he knew they not only blocked a djinn's power but also conferred a terrible weakness, making it difficult to put one foot in front of the other, let alone summon the powers one had been born with. And he had certainly not experienced any such weakness, had felt entirely himself the whole time.

Even after being blasted by that damn shotgun.

Also, if a device had been affecting him while he was shot, he doubted he would still be alive. No, he probably would have bled out on that gravel drive before Olivia could even help him into the house.

As far as he could tell, he was still healing properly. Perhaps not quite as quickly as he would have liked, but at the same time, he'd never been hit by a shotgun blast before and therefore had no true frame of reference.

Then what in the world was going on here?

Olivia had left after providing him with the sweatpants she'd promised, saying she was going to fetch him some soup to help cushion the medicine she'd given him. Omar still did not know for sure whether the antibiotics were going to help at all, but he supposed they wouldn't hurt.

Right now, he was just glad to be alone so he could try to work his way through the puzzle that had confronted him.

Or rather, the two puzzles...one regarding his

apparently vanished powers, and the other being Olivia Raskin herself.

Who in the world would shoot an intruder, only to turn around and offer them first aid immediately afterward?

Someone who did not intend to cause that kind of harm, he told himself. *She only wished to frighten you away.*

Stupid, yes. A fool of a human who had thought a djinn would run at the mere sight of a firearm. Clearly, even though she might have known that djinn existed, she had no real idea of what they were...what they were capable of.

At any rate, he was not the sort who frightened easily, and even now he was more confused and annoyed than fearful as to what this sudden disappearance of his abilities might mean.

Could it be that the blood loss had somehow affected his ability to tap into his inborn gifts? Omar had never heard of such a thing happening before, but that didn't mean much. His people did not have a central repository of knowledge—well, unless one counted the djinn elders—and therefore the same sort of affliction might have affected a long-ago elemental and he would never have had any reason to hear of it.

But since he had no reason to believe that his wound...which he had to admit was grave, although even now he could sense that his body's healing abilities were working on knitting together the mutilated flesh...might not be the cause as to why he couldn't summon whatever he wished at the snap of a finger, he decided to put that conundrum aside for now.

Olivia Raskin provided an even deeper puzzle.

This house where she'd taken refuge—for he knew it could not be hers, not with someone else's family name emblazoned over the entrance to the ranch—seemed to have done an excellent job of sheltering her all these years. She had running water and heat and power, all in a place isolated enough that he doubted any djinn had come this way after the initial purge. Like the place where his brother Jamal's red-haired temptress had hidden herself, this ranch was just far enough off the highway that there would have been no incentive for any djinn to come here in search of prey.

And, for whatever reason, she had decided to stay in this place rather than venture out to locate any friends or family who might have survived.

Perhaps she was not quite as foolish as he'd first believed, or perhaps she had realized early on that the chances of anyone she cared about being immune to the djinn fever were very low. The way she'd tended to his wound, brisk and matter-of-fact and not at all troubled by the gore, coupled with the expert way she'd stitched up the damage, told him she had some experience with such things.

Too young to be a doctor—even Omar knew that profession had required years and years of study—but perhaps a nurse, or at least someone who'd worked in the healthcare field. If asked, he most likely would have said that he cared little about her background, and yet he knew he would be in far worse shape now if she hadn't possessed the skills to put him back together.

On the other hand, if she hadn't shot him, he wouldn't have been in this situation in the first place.

She returned to the bedroom, a wooden tray in her hands that bore a large bowl of soup and some kind of muffin, along with another glass of water.

"How are you feeling?" she asked as she set the tray down on the bedside table nearest him.

"Better," he replied cautiously, which was about fifty-percent true. His leg ached, but a certain itch that accompanied the ache told him his djinn powers were at work, doing their best to knit the shattered flesh together. Also, he didn't feel quite as weak, and that made him believe the blood he had lost was already beginning to replenish itself. All he needed now was time...and that was a resource all djinn possessed in abundance.

"Good," Olivia said, and some of the strain in her features appeared to ease itself somewhat.

Had she truly been worried about his well-being?

No, she simply doesn't want to confront the guilt of killing you, he thought, then shifted so he could look down at the tray more closely.

"It's nothing fancy," she said as she lifted the cloth napkin on the tray and handed it to him so he might spread it on his lap. "Just vegetable soup with noodles and a corn muffin. But it'll help cushion that amoxicillin, and you need to keep your strength up."

Omar couldn't argue with that assertion, although he thought he would have been able to heal better if she'd provided him with some protein.

Those thoughts must have revealed themselves in his expression, because she went on, "I wanted to see how you did with something light before I gave you any meat. There's some rabbit I caught yesterday that I planned to roast for dinner, but this should keep you going until then."

Well, that sounded like a better plan. All the same, he was feeling the lack of his powers even more at this moment, if only because if they hadn't deserted him, he could have snapped his fingers and conjured something a little more interesting than rabbit.

"It smells good," he said, a little surprised at how tactful he was being. He certainly did not owe this human any courtesy, not after what her people had done to this planet and definitely not after she'd shot him, but something in her expression...worried, with just a hint of pleading...made him more inclined to be on, if not his best behavior, then at least something somewhat adjacent to it.

The taut set of her shoulders seemed to ease slightly. "I hope you like it. But I'll leave you to eat —just call if you need anything. I'll be in the kitchen."

Was he disappointed or relieved that she wasn't going to stand there and watch him eat? Omar couldn't say for sure, but she appeared to take his silence as tacit agreement that he preferred to consume his midday meal alone, for she sent him a hesitant smile before heading down the short hallway that must have connected this part of the house to the kitchen.

Nothing for it. He picked up the spoon and began to eat.

Olivia couldn't say for sure whether it was the effect of the antibiotics or the makeshift first aid she'd performed, but whatever it was, she had to admit that Omar was already looking better, with that odd grayish tint to his skin completely gone and the shadows under his eyes disappearing as well. Maybe he'd never been in danger of dying...

although she thought he might have gotten closer than either of them wanted to admit.

Even if he seemed to be improving, she knew it would be a long time—if ever—before she forgave herself for shooting him like that. Some people probably would have argued that he was a djinn and therefore deserved whatever she could dish out, but her brain didn't work that way. Long ago, she'd decided she could either be angry about the life she'd been given, or she could move on and do her best to prove she didn't need anyone to tell her what to do or what to think.

And Omar hadn't seemed particularly angry with her. That could have been because he knew she couldn't permanently injure him, or maybe he, like her, wasn't someone who wasted his energy on grudges and pointless rage.

Hard to say, since she didn't know anything about him except his name and that he was a djinn. Hell, she didn't even know why he'd decided to wander onto her isolated homestead. It did seem a little odd that he'd come here now when so many years had passed without her seeing anyone at all, either human or djinn.

Well, maybe she'd ask him after she'd given him some more time to rest and heal up. The rabbit she'd caught earlier had been a big one, enough to feed them both as long as they had plenty of side dishes to accompany it. Rice, probably, along with a salad and bread and whatever else she could think of, like maybe some of that apricot chutney she'd made last summer. She'd gathered the fruit from a neighboring ranch, and the chutney had turned out much better than she'd expected.

Then she wanted to laugh at herself for worrying about whether the meal she planned for that night would be enough to fill him up and make him happy. Why in the world should she care what a djinn thought?

Because you pumped his leg full of buckshot, she thought, and shook her head. It was the sort of act that would probably require a lot of forgiveness.

And feeding someone often was an effective way to foster goodwill.

From the main bedroom, she could detect the occasional clink of metal against stoneware, telling her that Omar was definitely eating the soup and hadn't put it aside because he didn't care for it. Back in the before times, she'd been too busy to cook—not that she'd known how, since her mother had certainly never possessed the inclination to show her anything beyond how to operate the microwave. When she was in high school, she'd watched a lot of cooking videos on YouTube, thinking it was a skill she'd like to have, although adult life had taught her that going to school and working two jobs didn't leave much opportunity for burnishing her skills at making beef bourguignon.

Not that she could have afforded the ingredients in the first place.

Now, though...now she had plenty of time, and she thought she'd gotten pretty good at this cooking thing over the past four years. It would have been a whole lot easier if she could have just strolled to the local grocery store and gotten herself whatever she needed, but still, the garden provided a ton of different veggies, thanks to the seeds she'd liberated from the local feed store. And although she rarely ate one of the chickens she kept in one section of the barn, their eggs provided the basis for everything from vegetable quiche to fried rice.

Now that she had dinner planned, though, she figured she should go check on Omar.

He'd finished the soup and had set the empty bowl back on the tray. The cornbread muffin was gone, too, so it seemed clear enough to her that getting shot hadn't done much to affect his appetite.

"Was that enough?" she asked as she entered the room. "There's a little soup left over if you'd like some more."

"No," he responded at once. "I am quite full." A pause, and then he added, sounding almost startled, "It was good."

"Glad to hear it," she said, doing her best not to smile. "How are you feeling?"

"Better." Another pause, and he frowned slightly, as though a little surprised by his reply. "The food seems to be sitting well, and I can feel my leg healing."

"Really?" she asked, moving farther into the room, even though she'd only intended to stick her head in and get a quick assessment of his current condition. "You heal that quickly?"

He nodded, another of those flickers of amusement coming and going in his dark eyes. "If the wound hadn't been so severe, I would have already been up and walking by now. As it is, I see no reason why I shouldn't be completely healed by sometime tomorrow."

That was...incredible. True, she was dealing with a djinn here and not a human, but still, it was hard to get her brain to acknowledge that an injury that should have kept him in bed for weeks would disappear in less than twenty-four hours.

She wasn't quite sure what to think about a fully healed djinn being here under her roof. When he was bedridden and looking wan and pale, he didn't seem like much of a threat, but....

"That's good to hear," she said, doing her best to keep her tone light. After all, once he was all better, he would leave, wouldn't he? He would no longer be her problem.

But again, that begged the question of what he'd been doing here in the first place.

She did her best to set those concerns aside, instead adding, "Does that mean you might be able to get up when it's time for dinner? I can always bring you a tray again, but it's not as easy to cut up roast rabbit when you're eating that way."

"I think I can manage," Omar replied, this time with that same hint of a smile touching the corners of his mouth. "After all, I will have several more hours to heal before then."

"Sounds like a plan," she said lightly. "I'll come fetch you when everything is ready."

He nodded, and Olivia headed back out into the hallway. As she'd been speaking to the djinn, she'd thought of the perfect way to get him safely into the dining room. Yes, he'd leaned on her that first time as she helped him limp to the house, but she remembered how she'd seen a pair of crutches in the basement that must have been left behind by one of the previous residents of the house, a relic of a long-ago injury.

Right now, those crutches would come in very handy...even if Omar might not need them for more than a single night.

He stared at the pair of metal crutches she'd brought him. "You want me to use those?"

"Well, yes," Olivia replied. Her brow knitted ever so slightly, as though she wasn't sure why he would find the assistive devices problematic. "You look like you're doing much better, but you should still avoid putting any weight on that leg until you know for sure that it's healed all the way."

Her gaze met his, frank and slightly curious, and Omar's mouth compressed. He knew any arguments he presented would sound foolish to her, for he was forced to admit that they seemed somewhat specious to him as well.

All the same, he couldn't help thinking it was one thing to lie in bed with his wounds concealed under the blankets, and quite another to have to limp his way to the dining room while using a set of crutches, something he'd never imagined himself being forced to do. How could he? This was the first time he'd ever been injured at all, let alone suffered a wound that had driven him into bed.

Compounding the problem was the strange disappearance of his powers. If he had been fully himself, he could have simply blinked into the dining room and into a chair without having to confront the difficult task of walking the fifty feet or so such a trek would otherwise require.

No help for it, though. Not if he wanted to sit

down and consume his evening meal like a civilized person.

"Very well," he said, and reached for the crutches.

Olivia handed them over, relief clear in her expression. Questions crowded her unusual dark green eyes, but he could tell she did not feel comfortable asking them.

Which was just as well, for he would not have given her the replies she desired. She might have felt compelled to care for him until his body had finished the healing process, and he would certainly eat her food and accept the shelter she'd offered until then, but otherwise, he owed her nothing.

Not when she was the reason for his current incapacity.

Although he'd never used crutches before, they weren't too difficult to figure out. Padded rest in his armpit, allowing the aluminum structures to hold him up without putting any weight on his injured leg, and then he was pushing himself upright, wincing a little even as he did his best not to jostle the wounded limb.

Watching him, Olivia opened her mouth, then shut it abruptly.

Had she been about to offer him some help before deciding that might not be a very good idea?

Quite likely, although he would not have

accepted her assistance. It was one thing to allow her to treat his wound—she owed him that much —but he would never let her think he was incapable of something so simple as propping himself up on a pair of crutches.

And once he was balanced on the aluminum contraptions, he thought he should be able to make his way to the dining room.

"This way," Olivia said. Perhaps a slight hesitation before she turned and went out into the hall, as though she wanted to make sure he could manage a few steps before she started walking toward her destination, but Omar supposed he might have imagined it.

However, he could tell she deliberately slowed her pace so he wouldn't be too far behind her, and therefore, they entered the dining room only a moment apart. It was a large space with white-painted wainscoting halfway up the walls, which were a serene, misty shade somewhere between green and gray, while the furnishings were antique white as well, rustic and simple. An iron chandelier reminiscent of a wheel hung over the long table, big enough to seat eight people, although only two places were set at one end.

"Take the seat at the head of the table," Olivia told him. "I thought it would be easier for you to maneuver in and out of that spot."

True enough, since he wouldn't have to worry about working his way past any chairs on either side. He shuffled over to the place she'd indicated before settling himself down on the seat, which was upholstered in fabric that echoed the muted colors of the room. The crutches would have been awkward, but he propped them up against the unused chair to his right.

After seeing that he had managed to sit down on his own, she added, "Everything's ready. I'll have it out in a minute."

Toothsome smells were drifting into the dining room from the kitchen, and Omar's stomach gurgled. If Olivia noticed, however, she apparently thought it better not to react, because she only flashed him a quick, uncertain smile before ducking out to fetch their dinner.

Some might have been mortified by such evidence of fleshly weakness, but he didn't care that his body had just betrayed him. It was working as hard as it could to heal, and that meant it required extra fuel.

As good as the smells emerging from the kitchen had been, they were even better when the dishes were set on the table—a large roasted rabbit, a medley of vegetables, fresh-baked rolls. While not quite the feast he might have conjured if he'd had possession of his powers, he was forced to admit that it was quite the bounty for a meal produced by a human, especially one whose access to ingredients was limited.

Olivia returned to the kitchen a final time, then emerged with a bottle of wine in one hand. Glasses had been set on the table, but Omar hadn't been sure whether she intended to only fill them with water.

After seeing the bottle in her hand, he realized she had something much better in mind.

"Do djinn drink?" she asked, looking hesitant.

"Yes," he replied. "We quite enjoy human beverages."

"Then why—?" she began, then stopped herself. Possibly a brief head shake, and then she placed the bottle of wine on the table before at last taking her seat.

"Why kill all of you?" he finished for her.

Her dark, finely arched brows lifted, and then she gave a reluctant nod even as she picked up a corkscrew that had been sitting on the table and began to open the bottle—not very well, as she stopped after the first couple of rotations and began to reposition the corkscrew.

"Let me do that," he commanded, and she paused, frown deepening.

"I can manage," she said, her tone short.

A matching scowl pulled at Omar's brows. "You can manage to make a complete hash of that thing," he returned. "Give it to me, or we'll be picking pieces of cork out of our wine."

For a moment, she didn't respond, only continued to stare at him with narrowed eyes. Eventually, though, she handed over the bottle and the corkscrew.

"Can't you just use your djinn magic to remove the cork?"

Under other circumstances, of course he could. However, he had no desire to let Olivia know just how thoroughly his powers had deserted him. He should never have asked about Miles Odekirk's devices at all, but he'd been so rattled by being as powerless as a human that the words had slipped out before he could stop them.

"It is foolish to use our powers for something so simple," he told her as he extricated the cork, then poured a measure of wine into each of their glasses. Good thing he'd performed this same task many times before—not, as he'd just told her, because he didn't believe in using his djinn abilities for something as basic as removing a cork, but simply because he liked the physical sensation of it coming loose and the satisfying sound it made.

Her expression was dubious, and he halfway expected her to remark, *If you say so.*

But she held her tongue, instead reaching for her glass. No toast, of course, although she said, "I don't think the wine should interfere with the amoxicillin, but you should probably eat before you drink very much."

An admonishment that was just fine with him, since he knew the food would get cold if they continued to bicker. Again, something that wouldn't have been a problem if he still had full possession of his powers but which needed to be kept in mind now.

So he only nodded, and sat in his chair as she sliced off a generous helping of the roast rabbit and put it on his plate, followed by rice and vegetables. While she was busy with that, he selected a roll from the basket near his elbow, then cut off a slab of pale butter from the bowl next to the basket.

"It's goat's milk butter," Olivia supplied. It seemed to him she'd realized it was better for her not to pursue her former line of questioning, because she instead went on, "I actually like it, but if you've never had it before, it might be kind of a shock."

But Omar, like all his people, had tasted foods from all over the world and from centuries past, so it would take something much more adventurous than goat butter to shock him. "I have had it before," he told her.

She didn't seem to have expected that response, as she seemed almost taken aback before she nodded. "Then I guess you won't mind the goat's milk in the rolls, either."

No, he did not. They were delicious, light and flavorful, and the rest of the food was equally good. Not quite the same as something he could have conjured, but definitely much more than he had been expecting.

The wine was also quite good, and he wondered where she'd gotten it. This farm did not appear to be the sort of place where wine connoisseurs had resided, but he supposed Olivia had done a good bit of scrounging in Cedar Crest's abandoned homes and had found it in one of them. Or possibly she'd brought it down with her from the restaurant, if she truly was the person he'd been tracking.

Before he could ask about the wine's provenance, however, she spoke up again.

"Why did you come here?"

A reasonable enough question. Even having her shoot him in the leg hadn't quite made him forget the reason for his errand to the ranch, although some of the urgency had left him after he'd realized that Khalim al-Usar wasn't lurking in the barn or hiding in the farmhouse's basement.

He met her question with one of his own. "Are you the person who escaped the restaurant at the top of the mountain?"

For a moment or two, she only stared back at him, shock apparent in her widened eyes and suddenly pale cheeks. At last, though, she said, "How did you know about that?"

"Because I recently visited the restaurant and looked around, and it soon became clear to me that someone had survived the Heat there and then made their way down the east side of the Sandias. That made me wonder where you had gone to ground, so I kept looking and eventually made my way to this ranch."

Her expression turned hard, full mouth flattening as she continued to watch him without speaking. "So maybe it was smart to shoot you after all."

Omar allowed himself a grim smile. "If you hadn't been a woman, then yes, I most decidedly would have killed you. However, since you are one of the fairer sex, I knew I could not in good conscience do such a thing."

"Noble," she remarked, then reached for her wine glass and took a larger swallow than was probably necessary.

He shrugged and drank some more of his wine. "It has very little to do with nobility. It is a vow my brothers and I made to one another when we decided we would be among those who would finally rid this world of humanity."

Another small silence, and then she said, "Your brothers?"

Now he found himself wishing he had never

mentioned them. It certainly would not do to admit that they had lost their hearts to human women and were now dead to him.

"I do not wish to speak of them," he replied, his tone hard. "At any rate, I determined that this was where the person from the restaurant—you— had made your hiding place all these years. And, once I had seen you were a woman, I would have left and gone on my way. But I then received some troubling news and did not think it would be good to leave you alone without giving you a warning."

"'A warning'?" she repeated, now looking puzzled. "A warning about what?"

Omar broke off a piece of his roll and spread some of the tangy goat butter on it. While he knew he had intended to inform her of the threat presented by Khalim al-Usar, he did not know the best way of presenting it.

Well, no point in trying to conceal the gravity of the situation.

"There is a djinn by the name of Khalim al-Usar," Omar said. "He was held in a place we djinn use as our prison, but it appears he has somehow managed to escape. No one knows where he is. There was no particular reason to think he would be hiding anywhere near here, and yet there is also no way to know for sure where he has gone."

"So you came here to warn me about him?" Olivia asked, looking more puzzled than ever.

He could not really fault her for that. On the surface, it did seem rather odd that a djinn would care about protecting a human from another of his kind.

"I did," he said, then helped himself to some more rabbit. It had been seasoned to perfection, and, accompanied by Olivia's homemade spicy apricot chutney, was both delicious and unusual. "Khalim is...dangerous. He has shown that he cares little for the laws of our people, and he also...."

Omar let the words trail off as he tried to determine the best way to phrase the hard truth that the escaped prisoner was both vicious and rapacious, and no doubt would have enjoyed using the beautiful woman sitting across the table from him in the worst way possible.

Then he wanted to check himself. Beautiful? When he'd first spied Olivia Raskin from afar, he'd been forced to admit she was somewhat pretty, but he would not allow himself to raise his estimation any further than that. After seeing her up close, however, and noting the unusual beauty of her smoky green eyes and the porcelain purity of her skin, he had to admit she was much more than pretty.

For a human, of course.

"Khalim al-Usar is a rapist," he said harshly. "He has badly used human women, and there is no reason to believe he left those appetites behind simply because he was imprisoned in the outer circles for several years."

Olivia listened to all this, expression aghast, the hand that had been holding the remnants of her roll letting it drop to her plate. At last, she replied, words a shocked murmur, "That's terrible."

"It is," Omar agreed. "So I could not in good conscience go on my way without warning you that he was loose, not when you are so obviously alone here."

The pallor in her face only made the dark arches of her eyebrows and the natural rosy flush of her lips stand out that much more. "And then I shot you for your trouble."

That particular irony hadn't escaped him, so he only said, "Yes, you did. But I am healing quite well, and now you can consider yourself warned."

"Just like that?" she responded, and he shrugged.

"What else is there to say? Perhaps you would like to tell me that you would never have done such a thing if you had known why I was here. However, we cannot go back and change the past."

A thoughtful silence. Then she asked, "But... could you?"

Lying would accomplish very little. "No," he said. "Djinn have many gifts, but we cannot manipulate time in such a way."

She nodded, then reached for her glass of wine,

although she seemed content to allow her fingers to rest on the base, rather than lift it to her lips. At last she said, "Thank you for telling me about Khalim."

He shrugged. While she seemed genuinely grateful, he did not want her gratitude.

No, he only wanted to be healed enough to get away from here.

"It was nothing."

Chapter 6

AFTER THEIR MEAL, OMAR LIMPED BACK TO his bed while Olivia remained in the dining room to clear the table. The whole time, Zorro had been suspiciously absent, and she wondered if something about the djinn's presence had bothered the cat. But because Zorro had been roaming the property freely for the past four years, she knew he should be safe enough. Even the local coyotes seemed to know better than to tangle with the ranch's tuxedo cat.

Her head was still spinning. Bad enough that someone like this Khalim al-Usar person might be lurking around somewhere, but to realize that some djinn seemed to look at humans in a sexual way?

She had no idea what to do about that.

True, rape was about power and domination,

not sex, but still, if djinn had been physically incompatible with humans, then Khalim would never have used those poor human women like that.

At least Omar appeared to be utterly indifferent to her. Yes, they'd had a few conversations, but she'd never gotten the feeling that he'd noticed she was even female.

Well, except for the part where her sex appeared to be the one thing that had prevented him from killing her outright.

She set the last of the dinner dishes in the drainer that sat on the counter by the sink. The kitchen had a dishwasher, of course, but she didn't see the point in wasting all that electricity on a chore that could easily be done by hand. Much better to use the energy to keep the refrigerator running and the lights on.

After she was done with the dishes, though, she realized she'd boxed herself into something of a corner. She'd given Omar the main bedroom because it was the only one located on the ground floor of the house, but that meant she would have to sleep upstairs tonight...and it also meant she needed to go into the room where he was staying so she could fetch her nightclothes and get her toothbrush and toiletries from the *en suite* bathroom.

A peek down the hallway told her his bedside

light was still on, so at least he hadn't decided to go immediately to sleep.

If djinn even slept. It wasn't a topic that had come up at dinner, although she supposed they must get some kind of rest even if it wasn't exactly what humans could call slumber.

He had his eyes closed as she hesitated at the entrance to the main suite, but because he opened them right away, Olivia thought he must have only been resting, not truly asleep.

"Is something the matter?" he asked, and she shook her head.

"No," she replied hastily. "I just need to grab a few things from the closet and the bathroom. It'll only take a minute."

Those night-dark eyes narrowed slightly. "I am taking your room from you."

The words weren't a question. "Well, I wouldn't call it a matter of 'taking,'" she said. "There's no way you could've made it up the stairs with your leg in that kind of shape, so of course you needed to have the bedroom on the first floor. But since I'll be sleeping in one of the guest rooms upstairs, I have to get some of my stuff."

"Then take what you need," he said, and closed his eyes again.

Since it didn't seem as if he was inclined toward any further conversation, Olivia went ahead and hurried over to the closet, where she grabbed her flannel nightgown from its hook behind the door, along with a change of clothes for the next day— underwear, T-shirt and hoodie, a fresh pair of jeans. Luckily, the big oak dresser had been located in the closet when she stumbled across the farmhouse, and she'd seen no reason to move it.

Not that she could have managed the task on her own. That thing probably weighed a couple of hundred pounds.

When she emerged from the closet, Omar still had his eyes closed. A handy way of avoiding talking to her...or maybe he really was that tired. After all, even a djinn would have a rough time recovering from the gunshot wound she'd given him.

A quick stop in the bathroom to grab her toothbrush and toothpaste, moisturizer and lip balm, and then she hurried out of the main suite and up the stairs. As she went, she wondered what Omar would do about brushing his teeth...unless djinn didn't have to worry about dental hygiene.

Well, there was a pile of unopened tooth-brushes and boxes of toothpaste under the sink, everything she'd gathered while scavenging the local general store and all the houses in the community. From what she'd been able to tell, almost every household had had at least one brand-new tooth-brush or unopened box of toothpaste, which meant she had plenty to spare...for now. More than once, she'd wondered what she would do when her supply finally ran out, but she'd managed to push those worries aside, focusing on her day-to-day survival.

It was much colder upstairs since the heat from the woodstove didn't penetrate this far. However, her first winter here she'd gathered a bunch of space heaters and placed two in every room, thinking she should prepare just in case any survivors came this way. Of course, no one ever had.

Not until Omar, anyway. Olivia wasn't sure she wanted to reflect on the irony of having her first visitor to the ranch be one of the dreaded djinn.

He wasn't what she'd been expecting. Or rather, she hadn't known exactly what to expect, except to be struck down the second one of them caught up with her. Never in a million years would she have thought that a djinn might have issues with killing women and children.

So she was still alive, and was doing her best to figure out what she should think about Omar al-Qadir. True, he could be abrupt, almost haughty, and she got the distinct impression that he considered her much his inferior. After the way she'd been treated by some of the patrons at the restaurant—and the staff and residents at some of the assisted living facilities where she'd worked as an aide before that—this was nothing new. At least Omar had something of a justification for being a rude bastard, since he wouldn't have even been in his current predicament if it weren't for her.

Also, she had a feeling that all djinn considered themselves superior to humans.

Even those djinn who apparently had a taste for human females.

A shiver went through her at that thought, and she deposited the bundle of clothing and toiletries she'd been carrying on the bed so she could hurry over to the window and peer outside. It was nearly pitch black, the only illumination coming from the stars, but she just could make out the vague, blocky shape of the barn and the dark edges of the junipers and piñon pines at the edge of the pasture. As far as she could tell, nothing moved out there except the wind in the trees.

Still, for all she knew, this Khalim al-Usar was lurking nearby, waiting and watching.

She wasn't alone, though, not with Omar downstairs. True, he wasn't the most comforting presence in the world, and she didn't know how much good he could do with his leg not fully healed, but for some reason, she still felt a little better knowing he was there.

All the same, she thought she'd better head back downstairs and get the shotgun.

Just in case.

Omar heard the stairs creak and guessed that Olivia had come down from the guest room for some reason. However, since she didn't approach the main suite, and ascended the steps only a few moments after she reached the ground floor, he thought she must have forgotten something and had come to retrieve it, moving as quietly as she could so as not to disturb him.

Although he'd been resting his eyes when she'd come in to fetch her things, he hadn't been asleep. Slumber eluded him for some reason, even though he had a quite excellent meal in his belly and the ache in his leg had morphed into a small, nagging itch, telling him it would probably be good as new when he awoke the next morning.

He thought he could sense some faint, sweet scent clinging to the pillowcase, probably traces of whatever shampoo Olivia used, for of course she would not have had time to change the linens before she helped him over to the bed. Under other circumstances, he might have been annoyed or even disgusted that his flesh had to touch bedclothes that had been used by a human, but for some reason, he found he didn't mind so much. She had given up her bed for him, had gone to sleep some-place he guessed wouldn't be nearly as comfortable.

Out of guilt, he assumed. Still, he knew that if

she had been a different sort of woman, he might very well be dead right now. If she'd come to him while he lay there on the gravel path, leg nearly shattered, she could have lifted that shotgun again and blown his head apart like a ripe melon.

Even a djinn could not survive an assault such as that.

An oddly contradictory woman, this Olivia Raskin. Rather than finish the job, she'd done whatever she could to make sure he survived, and healed. And then she'd given him a hearty meal and made sure he had someplace warm and safe to sleep.

He would not allow himself to be grateful, not when it was her fault that he lay here with an itchy leg and not in his much more luxurious home some forty miles or so off to the northwest, but still, he supposed things could have been much worse.

Besides, tomorrow he would be away from this place. He might have to walk to Placitas under his own power if he could not determine the reason why his djinn gifts seemed to have deserted him, but there was no reason to linger here. Olivia had been given her warning about Khalim, and therefore Omar thought he had done his duty. More, really, because he certainly owed the human woman very little.

A small voice inside piped up then, telling him he should also let her know about the human community of Los Alamos, how she might be much safer there, although he did his best to brush that thought away. He was under no obligation to make her life more comfortable. Besides, she might not even want to leave her sanctuary here in Cedar Crest. The roads were not as dangerous as they once were, true, but with Khalim out there somewhere....

He is nowhere near, Omar reassured himself. *Even if he emerged somewhere near the place where Aldair came to this plane after his escape from the otherworld, Khalim would have made sure to get far, far away from anywhere so obvious.*

This all sounded logical enough on the surface, and yet Omar could not quite dispel some lingering doubts. For one thing, Khalim al-Usar was a capricious, vengeful djinn, and he would certainly hold plenty of grudges, both against the Santa Fe djinn and the elders themselves. Vengeance against the trio of elders was an impossibility, making the elementals in Santa Fe and their human partners much more of a target.

Or any other humans who had the bad luck to be living on their own, and vulnerable.

Well, Omar thought sourly, *she must only use that shotgun again...except if she shoots Khalim, it would be best for her to make sure he is dead. He would not be content to accept her apologies after such an act the way I have.*

Definitely not. And although she had shot him, Omar didn't think Olivia was capable of killing another sentient being, even one as despicable as Khalim al-Usar.

Which meant she might very well become one of his victims, should he come this way.

Damn.

Very well. He would tell Olivia about Los Alamos and Santa Fe, and offer to guide her as far as the city limits of the djinn sanctuary in the former capital city. That should be more than enough.

And if she should turn him down and elect to stay here, well, her fate would be of her own choosing.

———

Despite her worries that a murderous rapist djinn was hiding somewhere near the borders of her property, Olivia slept better than she thought she would. And when she awoke, the first thing she saw was Zorro asleep at the foot of the bed, purring loudly.

She smiled, but her smile faded as her gaze moved past the cat to the shotgun propped up against the wall on the other side of the nightstand.

Maybe it had been silly to bring it up here...and maybe knowing it was nearby was the reason she'd been able to sleep so well.

It felt strange to realize that Omar was downstairs, that they'd shared a roof last night. And even though she knew she shouldn't worry about what he thought of her, she still got out of bed quickly so she could shower and get dressed, apply some tinted lip balm, and pull her hair back in a French braid rather than the usual ponytail she wore. More than once, she'd thought it would be easier if she just cut off all her hair, but she could never quite bring herself to do that. She trimmed the ends about every six months or so and otherwise left it alone, and now it was much, much longer than it had been when the Heat struck the world, far past the shoulder-length cut she'd worn back then.

When she came downstairs, she was surprised to hear the shower going in the master bathroom. If he'd asked her—and obviously, he hadn't—she would have told him he needed to avoid getting his stitches wet and that he should try some other manner of getting clean.

On the other hand, she wasn't about to give him a sponge bath, and since it did seem as if he was healing very quickly, she decided to let it go.

Instead, she went into the kitchen, opened a can of food for Zorro, and then heated water in the kettle so she could make coffee with the French press. The house had an automatic coffeemaker, but, as with so many other supposed modern conveniences, she preferred a method that didn't tap into solar power that could be used for more important tasks.

Did djinn drink coffee? She had no idea, but since Omar had appeared to be just fine with consuming human food and wine the night before, she thought he might like a morning jolt of caffeine. And if tea was more his preference, well, she had plenty of that on hand, too.

He came into the kitchen then, black hair wet and combed back from his fine brow, wearing black sweats and a black long-sleeved T-shirt that had been among the clothing she'd gotten out for him the day before. She'd draped the over-robe he'd been wearing on a chair near the bed, but clearly, he'd decided he didn't need it today. The tunic itself she'd put in the hamper, since it had also been splattered with blood.

But then she blinked, and realized what his nonchalant arrival meant.

He was walking, so it sure looked like his leg had healed overnight.

As her gaze met his, he smiled. No doubt she'd been staring at him in astonishment.

"Yes, it is much better," he said. "Itches like the devil, but there was only a little scar this morning, and I have no doubt that will go away as the day wears on."

Olivia managed to close her mouth. "That's...amazing."

"I suppose it would seem so, to a human," he responded, tone completely casual. Then his head tilted, and he added, "Is that coffee?"

"It is," she said, glad that at least now she sounded relatively normal, and not as utterly gobsmacked as she'd felt only a moment earlier. "Want a cup?"

"Yes."

No mention of "please," but she supposed that was par for the course. Since she'd already put some goat milk in her cup, along with a little sugar, she fetched a fresh mug for him and filled it.

"Sugar or milk?"

"No, black is sufficient."

Well, at least that was easy. She handed the mug over to him, and for just the barest second, his fingers brushed against hers. They were warm but not overly hot, telling her he wasn't running a fever, had managed to avoid any kind of secondary infection.

Of course he had. He was a djinn, and their bodies didn't appear to play by the same set of rules as a human's.

And she wouldn't think about the odd little thrill that had gone through her at that brief touch.

Or at least if she did, she would only acknowledge it was probably because it was the first time she'd touched a djinn in such a way. She couldn't really count the surgery she'd performed on his leg the day before, since in those terrible moments, she'd only been thinking about how to keep him alive.

Omar didn't seem to notice her reaction. No, he only lifted the mug of coffee to his lips and took a sip, even though it should have been much too hot to drink.

"It's good," he said, sounding surprised.

"Thanks," she replied. "I found a huge stash of beans at one of the neighbors' houses a while back. He must have been a serious coffee fiend. But having that on hand made it a lot easier to make a decent brew, because now I can grind it fresh. Plus, there was all kinds of stuff—mocha java, French roast, Sumatran, things I'd never even tasted before." She paused there, then figured she might as well ask. "Do all djinn drink coffee?"

One of his eyebrows lifted, but he answered civilly enough, "Many do. Some prefer tea, but most of my people have been drinking coffee for centuries."

Centuries. How old was he, exactly?

Olivia guessed that would be a rude question to ask, so she pushed it aside as best she could. However, she thought a more general inquiry might not be quite as fraught.

"Do all djinn live for centuries?"

"Centuries, and more," he answered, now with a bit of a smile that could only be called condescending playing around his lips. "Many of us have been alive for millennia."

That was a difficult concept to absorb. What would it be like to have such a long life, to see the world change before your eyes over and over again?

But then, the night before, Omar had made a comment about something called the otherworld. Maybe that was where the djinn came from, and they didn't have much to do with the day-to-day life of planet Earth at all.

Which begged the question of why they'd wanted it for their own in the first place.

It all seemed like one huge puzzle, one that she doubted the djinn standing in her kitchen and calmly drinking coffee would want to answer any time soon.

"Good to know," she said lightly, and his smile disappeared, replaced by something that looked almost like confusion.

Was he wondering why she hadn't commented on how amazing it must be to live forever?

That sort of remark would never leave her lips. She'd seen way too much suffering in her own short life to believe that an endless existence was anything to envy.

However, he didn't say anything, but instead

took his mug of coffee over to the kitchen table so he could sit down. In true farmhouse style, the large kitchen had an eat-in area off to one side, where you could sit with your coffee in the morning and look at the barn and the pasture beyond before you got started with your chores for the day.

Letting the moment pass seemed the best thing to do, so Olivia only said, "Are you okay with eggs and toast? I'm afraid that bacon is a thing of the past."

A glint entered Omar's dark eyes. "Toast and eggs would be fine."

Good thing she'd made a fresh loaf the day before. Baking bread had been a real challenge, but she'd gotten good at it, just like making butter and milking goats and so many other skills she'd had to acquire during her time here at the farm. However, she'd tackled them all with her usual doggedness, knowing that practice would lead her to the desired result even if she failed miserably at the beginning. One thing she knew was that giving up was never an option.

And as odd as it was to have a djinn sitting in her kitchen, drinking coffee, it also felt good to have another person around, someone to talk to. Yes, she'd had Zorro all this time, and he'd been a great companion, but he wasn't very good at holding up his end of a conversation.

She cracked five eggs into the skillet, three for Omar and two for her, then cut several slices of bread from the loaf she retrieved from its box before putting them in the toaster. During these preparations, Zorro appeared, walked over to his bowl to ascertain that she'd placed his breakfast inside, then promptly went to the back door and meowed to be let out.

Not much she could do except set down her spatula on the counter and then go over to open the back door. At once, the cat disappeared outside, and she shut the door immediately. It might not have been freezing outside, but it was still cold enough that she didn't want to let in any more chilly air than she had to.

"The cat seems to be the one in charge," Omar remarked, and Olivia shrugged.

"Well, this was his house," she replied. "Or at least, I think it might have been, since he was hanging around here when I arrived and there was food and bowls for a cat. So I don't really mind if he rules the roost."

After delivering that comment, she turned back to the eggs so she could flip them. Omar didn't seem inclined to respond, which was fine. He could say what he wanted about her, but she was damned if she was going to let him run down the only companion she'd had for the past four years.

The toast popped, and she got it out and spread goat butter on it, then placed the slices on several plates and deftly slid the over-easy eggs onto them as well. A pause to get some apple butter out of the fridge, and then she took everything over to the kitchen table where Omar was waiting.

"This looks good," he said as she set a plate in front of him.

"Thanks," she replied, then sat down. "I suppose I should've asked you how you wanted your eggs, but this just seemed the fastest way to cook them."

His gaze flickered to the plate, to the over-easy egg with its slightly runny yolk. "I like eggs every way."

Well, at least he wasn't a picky eater. Olivia reached for her neglected mug of coffee and allowed herself several large swallows, even though it was barely hot anymore. Still, it tasted good in combination with the eggs and toast, and somehow comforting despite the djinn who sat across the table from her.

"And your leg is really all the way better?" she asked, and he nodded.

"Yes, it healed very well. As I said, a few scars, but I have no doubt they'll disappear soon. It certainly doesn't hurt to walk on."

Apparently not, because she hadn't noticed him limping when he came into the kitchen earlier.

Still, she couldn't help asking, "Any inflammation around the scars? Any redness?"

His mouth twisted in what could only be called a smirk. "Nothing like that. We djinn do not have to worry about such things. There is no infection. Within another day, there will not even be any sign that I was ever injured at all."

Must be nice. Olivia knew that she'd been lucky all these years, as she'd never suffered any injury any worse than twisting her ankle one time when she was hurrying across the pasture and not paying attention to where she was walking. But still, if she'd hurt herself badly, she would have had no one to care for her...and would have had to face the very real prospect of infection and even death.

"And that means it is time for me to move on," he continued.

"Oh, right," she replied, then realized that response had sounded inane at best. "I mean, you came and warned me about Khalim, so there's no point in you hanging around."

Something unreadable flickered in Omar's dark eyes. She didn't know him well enough to even guess what that flicker might have meant, though.

"No, there is not," he said, and Olivia experienced an odd little stab of disappointment.

What, did she want him to stay? That was stupid.

He wasn't even nice.

Before she could begin to sort out her disordered thoughts, however, he added, "But I am not sure whether it is wise for you to stay here alone. It would be much better if you went to Los Alamos."

"'Los Alamos'?" she repeated. "Isn't everyone there dead?"

"No," he said calmly. "It is the only human community left in the world. I haven't paid them very much attention, but I believe at least a thousand people live there now. Even someone like Khalim would give such a place a wide berth, especially because of the devices."

Olivia set down her fork. "That's the second time you've mentioned some kind of device. What are they, anyway?"

His mouth compressed in obvious distaste, and he deliberately reached for his slice of toast with its thick layer of apple butter and took a bite. "They are something the scientist Miles Odekirk invented. I do not know precisely how they work. I only know that they rob djinn of their powers, make us weak. That is why I said even Khalim al-Usar would not dare go near that place."

For a moment, Olivia couldn't reply, could only stare at Omar in astonishment. So that was why he'd asked her the night before if there were any devices in the house. He hadn't wanted to admit it, but something about his powers wasn't working properly here, and he'd leaped to the only obvious explanation.

Except...that wasn't it. She'd only just heard of the devices Miles Odekirk had invented, and she certainly didn't have any of them around here. Exactly what was interfering with Omar's djinn powers, she didn't know for sure, but it wasn't a device.

"It's not safe to travel," she said, her tone flat, even as her brain started to cautiously explore what it might be like to leave the farm, to pack up Zorro and go to Los Alamos. The very concept felt so alien to her that she wasn't sure she could get her brain to wrap itself around it.

A thousand people? What was that even like?

She didn't know. Back in the before times, she'd lived in Albuquerque, New Mexico's largest population center by far, and yet the concept of being surrounded by a thousand people felt far more overwhelming than it once had been in a place with nearly a million residents.

"For the most part, it is safe to travel the roads," Omar told her. "The days of the djinn hunting humans have been mostly over for the past several years."

Now she lifted her gaze from her plate and met his eyes directly. Again she thought she saw that glint in them, only this time she had a better idea of why he might be looking that way.

"'Mostly,'" she echoed. "Because you and your brothers were still out there looking for victims."

A lot of people might have glanced away. Omar, on the other hand, continued to match her stare for stare, although his jaw tightened ever so slightly as he did so.

"We were," he said after a long pause. "Even so, we would not have harmed you, would have allowed you to continue on your way if we had met you on the road. But otherwise, there is nothing to fear out there."

"Except Khalim," she said, and Omar gave a reluctant nod.

"He is the wild card. But the world is wide, and I would say your chances of meeting him would be very low."

Maybe Omar was right. Maybe it was time to go.

Olivia glanced away from him so she could let her gaze linger on her surroundings. She'd lived here longer than any place she'd ever lived during her childhood; her mother's substance abuse problems had ensured that they'd moved at least once every six months, sometimes even more frequently than that. And even after she was out on her own, she'd made sure to find places that rented month-to-month just in case something came along that would cause her to vacate an apartment before a full year was up.

This place was the only real home she'd ever known, even though she'd come here under the very worst of circumstances.

But going to Los Alamos would give her the chance to start over. Staying here meant living the rest of her life alone.

Still, she knew how reluctant she sounded as she said, "Then maybe I should go to Los Alamos."

Before Omar could reply, however, the back door was thrown open. Standing there was a tall djinn with wild black hair and an even wilder look in his black eyes. Those terrible eyes fastened on her.

"Oh, no," he said, in a hoarse rumble of a voice. "I do not think you will be going anywhere."

Chapter 7

OMAR DIDN'T REALIZE HE HAD LEAPED TO his feet until he heard the wooden chair where he'd been sitting fall over with a bang. Across the table from him, Olivia also began to rise, and he narrowed a warning look at her, hoping she would understand that she needed to stay out of this.

At once, she subsided, but he could tell from the sudden pallor in her cheeks that she'd guessed exactly who the intruder was.

"Khalim al-Usar," Omar said, moving so he stood between the human woman and the djinn interloper. "I do not recall you being invited here."

Khalim crossed his arms. It had been years since Omar had seen the other man, but even so, he knew the changes that had been wrought in al-Usar had everything to do with the place where he'd been imprisoned and nothing at all to do with the passage of time. He had never been as tall as Omar but had always been an impressive figure nonetheless, heavily muscled, broad of shoulder.

Now, though, he was nearly as lean as Omar himself, long black hair a mass of tangles and knots, the once-narrow beard that covered his jaw full and bushy. And although he had always been intemperate, he had a wild gleam in his eyes that did not bode well for anyone within his immediate vicinity.

Not that Omar intended to back down. He would have preferred not to be the defender of a human woman...but he was also damned if he was about to let such a madman anywhere near Olivia Raskin.

"I need no invitation, not to a human house," Khalim countered. It was not lost on Omar that the other man's gaze barely rested on him, but instead flicked past almost immediately so it could come to rest on Olivia, sitting motionless in her chair at the table, as though she feared their unexpected and unwelcome guest might lunge at her suddenly, like a rattlesnake or a rabid dog.

Come to think of it, that was not such a bad comparison.

All the same, Omar knew he needed to do whatever he could to defuse the situation. If his powers hadn't been blocked for some unexplained reason, then he would have made the ground shake and hoped the unexpected temblor would be enough to knock Khalim temporarily off balance so he could make his escape with Olivia.

Unfortunately, Omar realized he now had nothing to protect her except his wits, and a frisson of unease moved through him.

"Then go ahead and sit," he said easily. "We can provide you with food and drink, something I am sure you desire after your long imprisonment."

This offer, however, was met with an angry furrow of the other djinn's brow. "That is not what I desire, and you know it as well as I do. For while I was able to summon food for myself after coming to this plane, there was one thing left I required to meet my needs. It has been uncounted days since I have been with a woman, and this one sitting here pleases me very well."

At those words, Olivia stood up, eyes flashing green with anger, her chair making an angry scraping sound against the wooden floor. "Well, you don't please me—" she began.

Omar cut her off at once. Khalim was already balanced on a knife edge, and the last thing they needed was for her to provoke the escaped prisoner. He thought the other djinn had mastery of flame, and there was no reason to believe he wouldn't strike out with a fireball or some other nasty manifestation of his talent if properly provoked.

"I do not see why you would want to sully

yourself with a human," he told a bristling Khalim. "Not when there are so many beautiful and willing women among our own kind."

At once, Khalim sent him a scornful look. "And have them possibly let the elders know that I have escaped? I cannot say we are well acquainted, Omar al-Qadir, but I still never thought you a fool."

There was that. Omar was quite certain that no matter what he said, Khalim would come up with some argument to counter it.

And that meant there was only one thing left to do.

"Olivia, run!" he cried out.

To her credit, she didn't hesitate. No, she took off for the back door like a doe that had been startled by a rifle blast, moving so quickly that Khalim didn't have time to react.

Or at least, she was too far away for him to physically grab her by the arm, but that didn't mean he didn't intend to take her, one way or another.

His hands raised, and Omar tensed, knowing the fire elemental was about to fling his weapon of choice at him.

But then...nothing happened.

"What devilry is this?" he demanded, his words an echo of Omar's own only the night before.

Olivia paused by the back door, expression

puzzled, questioning, as if she could tell something odd had just happened. But Omar sent her a violent head shake, and she seemed to understand that they could puzzle this out later after they were both safe.

She hurried outside, and Omar turned back to Khalim, who had taken several threatening steps toward him, hands clenched into angry fists at his side.

"What have you done to me?"

"Nothing," Omar replied calmly. Only the truth, after all. This was no magic of his own, even if he couldn't say whence it had come, or why.

Now he thought he might be able to settle this. Once upon a time, Khalim would have far outweighed him and might have prevailed by sheer mass alone, but his years of captivity had stripped the muscle from him. And while he might have made sure to procure food for himself after arriving on this plane, he still looked lean and half-starved.

Djinn, as a general rule, did not engage in hand-to-hand combat. They used their elemental gifts to fight one another, often in heavily super-vised duels governed by a particular set of rules. Omar, however, had had the singular opportunity to grow up in a household with two brothers, and therefore had a childhood and adolescence where they had often tussled with one another.

Without thinking, he raised a hand and made

sure to keep his thumb outside his fist before landing a heavy punch on Khalim's jaw.

The other djinn staggered backward, dark eyes wide, shocked. It was obvious that he hadn't been expecting a full-on physical assault, although he gathered himself after the original blow and rushed forward to attack with his fists as well.

Omar had been expecting such an assault, and neatly stepped out of the way so Khalim's punch met empty air. At the same time, he brought up his other fist to drive a blow straight into his enemy's solar plexus.

He let out a *whoof* of shocked air, and Omar continued his attack, hitting Khalim again in the jaw, this time so hard that he staggered backward, connected with the chair Olivia had left sitting a few feet away from the kitchen table, and went down like the proverbial ton of bricks.

No time to lose, however. Omar looked around the kitchen, noted the heavy cast-iron pan sitting on the stovetop, and lunged for it. Just as Khalim began to stir, trying to disentangle himself from the chair, Omar grasped the pan and heaved it with all the strength he could muster against the other man's head.

At once, Khalim went still. However, a faint twitch of his mouth told Omar that the fire elemental was only knocked out, which was what he had expected. It would take far more than a blow like that to kill a djinn.

But he was certainly down for the count, as the humans might say. A quick search of the kitchen and the laundry room found a coiled rope on the shelf above the washing machine, possibly for Olivia to hang her clothes when the weather allowed.

It would do just fine for the task at hand.

Soon enough, he had the rope tied around Khalim's wrists and ankles. Just as he was finishing the task, Olivia cracked open the back door and peered inside.

"What happened?"

"Our friend here met the wrong end of your frying pan," Omar replied dryly.

To his surprise, she actually grinned. "I guess all those cartoons I watched when I was a kid had it right after all."

Omar knew very little about cartoons—he thought they might be some kind of moving comic strip to amuse children—but if they depicted frying pans used as weapons, then he supposed they must have some truth in them. "Possibly," he allowed. "The important thing is that we now have this man restrained, and he should not give us any more trouble."

"Well, until he wakes up," she replied, expression dubious. "I mean, I assume he will eventually, if he heals anywhere close to as quickly as you did. What do we do with him then?"

A very good question. The logical thing to do would be to alert Zahrias al-Harith, the leader of the Santa Fe djinn, and let him know that Khalim had been captured. Then Zahrias could turn the escaped prisoner over to the elders, and he could be sent back to the outer circles...preferably, a circle far more secure than the one where he'd previously been imprisoned.

But Omar was not sure whether that was the best idea. After all, Khalim had escaped once. Who was to say he might not accomplish such a thing again?

And if he did, then he would most certainly have revenge on his mind.

"I—"

He only got that one syllable out of his mouth before Khalim sat up with a roar, straining against the ropes that bound him.

And then they tore, and he was free.

A very quick recovery passed through Omar's mind, but he could not allow himself to pause to absorb what had just happened.

No, they needed to get out of here.

Now.

Just as Khalim lunged for him, Omar ran for the door, grasping Olivia by the wrist as he went. A startled gasp escaped her lips, but she didn't reprimand him for being so brusque, only fled the house at his side, the heavy work boots she wore tearing into the dry grass. Omar himself was barefoot, as he hadn't thought he would be doing anything more strenuous than remaining indoors until he was certain his leg had fully healed.

In fact, it gave an angry twinge, but he did his best to ignore it, even as he tried to ignore the rough grass and the pebbles biting the unprotected soles of his feet. Behind them, heavy footsteps signaled Omar that Khalim was giving chase.

A glance over his shoulder told him that although the other djinn had certainly bounced back quickly from being hit in the head with roughly ten pounds of cast iron, he appeared to wobble a little as he ran, clearly not completely recovered from the blow.

But then, Omar was also not as fleet of foot as he might have liked, thanks to his nearly healed leg and his bare feet.

It had to be enough, though, for he was not sure how he would fare in a repeat bout with their furious pursuer.

If only he had his powers. Then he could take hold of Olivia and blink them away from this place, away to the safety of his home in Placitas. Only a temporary shelter, of course, for she would not be able to stay there for any length of time, but at least it would get them away from Cedar Crest and the furious Khalim.

"Persistent, isn't he?" Olivia panted at his side, and Omar could not help sending her a fierce grin.

"Yes," he said. "We can only hope he runs out of steam before we do."

Indeed, Khalim appeared to be flagging somewhat, the distance between them beginning to increase. However, Omar could not take that as a sign to slow down as well, but only kept running, doing his best to ignore the pain in his feet. Yes, they would heal very quickly, and yet he needed to get away from here, needed to be in a place where they wouldn't be injured over and over again.

He thought of the gracious Spanish-style home he'd been given in Placitas, how he had once thought it small and plain compared to the houses the elders had bequeathed upon his brothers but now would consider it the most beautiful place in the world.

If only he could be standing in front of the fireplace there, allowing its warmth to soothe his battered limbs.

As soon as that thought passed through his mind, the scrubby junipers and pinon pines that had surrounded him disappeared, and he was standing in the very place he'd imagined only a moment earlier.

What in the world?

Your powers have returned, he thought then. *Whatever was blocking them seems to be gone.*

He could not allow himself a second of jubilation, though.

Not when he'd left Olivia behind, prey to a furious and relentless Khalim.

Only one thing to do.

He blinked himself back to Cedar Crest.

One moment, Omar was running at her side, and in the next instant, he was just...gone.

He got his powers back, she thought.

Which under other circumstances might have been good news. Now, though, cold dread gripped her belly as she realized she was alone here, with no one to shield her from Khalim. Yes, he wasn't running as quickly as he had when he first burst out of the kitchen door, but she'd paused as she realized Omar was no longer next to her, and now the gap between her and the furious djinn wasn't nearly as wide as she would have liked.

She increased her pace—only to collide with Omar, who had appeared out of nowhere directly in front of her.

Before she could even start to ask him where he'd gone, his arms went around her. Not in a true embrace, but a tight grip that told her he meant business.

"Hold on," he said.

She wrapped her arms around his waist, and in the next instant, the world around her disappeared, replaced by a whirling darkness flecked with odd lights here and there, not cold or warm, and yet still with something wrong about it that sent a chill into her very bones.

The unpleasant sensation only lasted a second or two, however, and in the next moment, they appeared in the living room of a house she'd never seen before, a place vaguely Spanish in style, with its bright white walls and accents of black wrought iron. A few feet away, a warm fire flickered in a large plaster fireplace, and floor-to-ceiling windows on the other side of the room allowed a breath-taking view of the Rio Grande valley.

"Where—where are we?"

The words came out way too breathy, making her sound more like a frightened little girl than a grown woman of twenty-six. Then again, Olivia figured most people would forgive her for being just a bit off-balance right then.

Omar had released his hold on her as soon as they emerged from that frightening, whirling dark-ness, and he now stood a few feet away. Somehow, in that single instant he'd gotten rid of the sweat-pants and long-sleeved T-shirt, and he now wore the same sort of black robes and baggy pants he'd had on when she first encountered him on her property. His battered feet were covered in black boots, and she hoped whatever healing powers that had fixed his leg were also at work on those feet. They hadn't been in very good shape.

He didn't sound in pain, though, as he replied, "This is my house in Placitas. I thought it the best place to come."

She certainly hoped so. "Does Khalim know where you live?"

"I doubt it very much," Omar said. His expression didn't reveal any concern that she could detect, so maybe what he'd said was the simple truth. He added, "We were never anything close to friends, so there is no reason for him to know the location of this house. Being here should give us a chance to regroup."

Regroup. That sounded like a very good idea. Her legs shook, and she doubted that was only because of the way the two of them had fled the farmhouse.

A couch covered in soft beige leather stood only a few feet away from her, and she stumbled over there so she could collapse on it. Omar watched her but said nothing, although she detected the faintest frown touching his brows, as though he'd expected her to ask permission before sitting down.

Annoyance flickered through her, even as she reminded herself that this was his house, after all. When he spoke, though, he sounded solicitous enough.

"Some water? Or tea?"

"Water would be great," she replied at once, realizing then that her mouth was parched from running all that way in the cold, dry December air.

She'd never seen a djinn in full possession of his powers, so it startled her a little to watch a glass of water materialize out of nowhere, resting on one of the stone coasters that sat on the copper-topped coffee table. However, she did her best to act nonchalant as she leaned forward to pick up the glass, then took a long swallow.

"Thank you," she said.

Another glass of water appeared in his hand, and he sat down on the matching couch that faced hers. He drank before responding, "It is nothing. But now I think we must decide what to do next."

What she wanted to do was sit here on this heavenly couch, drink water, and try not to think too hard about what a narrow escape she'd just had.

If Omar hadn't come back for her....

"You didn't leave me there," she said, and although she hadn't phrased the words as a question, Omar appeared to take them as such.

"No, I did not," he replied calmly. "Since I was

willing to face down Khalim on your behalf, I certainly couldn't leave you behind once my powers returned. I would not leave a dog to deal with such as he."

The remark about the dog made Olivia sit up a little straighter, worry pulsing through her. "Oh, no—we left Zorro behind!"

"Zorro?" Omar repeated, looking justifiably puzzled. After all, he hadn't interacted with the cat directly, and she didn't think she'd ever mentioned his name.

"My cat," she explained. "He was outside when Khalim showed up, but we can't leave him there. And then there are the goats—"

Omar interrupted her, one hand held up to stop the flow of words. "We are not going back there."

His tone was flat, allowing no argument. And while Olivia had learned over the years that the best way to get along was to keep her head down and not make waves, she wasn't about to let this one go, not when they were talking about the animals who had been her only companions for the past four years.

"We have to," she insisted. "Zorro's a tough cat, but he's still used to having someone feed him and let him in at night. And the goats can forage for a while, but without me there to get them water and decent food, they're going to be in trouble."

"They will not," Omar said, still in that flat tone. Not angry at all, but more as though he was in possession of knowledge she somehow lacked and didn't see the need for any further discussion on the subject.

Olivia picked up her water and drank again, wishing it was doing more to get rid of her dry mouth.

Or maybe that was just exhaustion, with a fun little touch of anxiety.

"What are you talking about?"

At last, Omar smiled. Or rather, his mouth turned up just a bit at the corners, as though he was amused by her concern.

"In the very beginning, when my people were planning to release the disease humans called the Heat, we were concerned about all the pets and livestock that would be left behind. That is why we all put our concerted energy into letting the animals know where to find food and shelter, and how to live quite happily without human intervention. Your cat and your goats are perfectly safe."

Should she be startled by the way djinn apparently had plenty of compassion for animals, and none at all for human beings?

Probably not. But still—

"Zorro has been with me for the past four years," she protested. "Are you saying he's going to walk off into the sunset and not miss me at all?"

"Not knowing the inner workings of a cat's mind," Omar responded, still looking singularly unconcerned, "I cannot say for sure. All I can tell you is that this Zorro of yours—and your goats and your chickens—will fare perfectly well without you there. It is foolish to waste so much mental energy on such a thing, especially when we have far graver matters to worry about."

"Like Khalim," Olivia said, her tone reluctant. Although she didn't believe that Omar had ever outright lied to her, she also couldn't know for sure whether he was telling her the complete truth. Maybe Zorro would stumble across a cache of cat food in an abandoned house and be fed and warm, but there was more to life than a full belly. He surely would miss her just as much as she would miss him.

"Khalim," Omar responded, "and also this oddity of my powers disappearing and then returning. I cannot think what could have caused such a thing to happen."

She had to agree that the situation seemed a little strange. Asking a djinn whether his powers had a habit of coming and going felt a little like questioning whether a prospective romantic partner suffered from erectile dysfunction, but she still ventured, "And you're absolutely sure you've never dealt with anything like this before?"

"Never," he replied, his tone so firm that she

knew he was being absolutely honest with her. "That is why at first I thought it must be one of those devices from Los Alamos, even if I couldn't think of how you might have laid hands on one. Nothing else on this earth can block a djinn's powers."

He paused there, something in his expression almost faltering, as though he had thought of something but wasn't sure whether he should say it out loud.

"What is it?" Olivia asked. Maybe it was presuming too much to request that he lay his thoughts bare to her—they'd only known each other for a scant twenty-four hours, and she couldn't say their relationship was exactly cordial— and yet she thought the best way of getting to the bottom of the puzzle was to talk things out.

"Nothing on this earth can have such an effect on a djinn," Omar said slowly. "Nothing except Miles Odekirk's devices. However, in the other-world—the plane we occupied until we were free once more to live upon the Earth—there is a substance called *ni-khar* that suppresses the powers of all fire elementals." He frowned there, a faint line appearing between his brows, as though he'd just realized that the explanation he'd found only raised more questions.

"So...your power is fire?" she said.

He shook his head. "No, that power belongs to

my older brother Aamir, but my other brother Jamal and I both harness the power of the earth." Once again, his brows drew together, and Olivia could see how confounded he was. "Even if by some odd chance *ni-khar* existed on the property where you were living in Cedar Crest, it should not have affected me at all."

"But it obviously did," she responded.

"Yes," he said, his voice heavier than ever. "So it seems we have a mystery on our hands."

Chapter 8

ALTHOUGH OLIVIA APPEARED CONCERNED, it seemed clear enough to Omar that she did not completely understand the conundrum that had presented itself. If *ni-khar* affected all djinn equally, then he would consider the matter closed—or at least, he would be forced to admit that the strange, rare element was buried somewhere on the farm that had been her home ever since the Dying, even if no one had ever encountered it on this world before. Its presence would have explained why he hadn't realized his powers were gone until he attempted to use them, for the grayish metal did not create the same weakness and lethargy as one of Miles Odekirk's devices, but only created a very efficient block of a djinn's otherworldly abilities.

But *ni-khar* should not have affected him at all. He did not control fire, as Aamir did.

Did this world hide a different element, one that touched all djinns' powers equally? Omar would not have thought such a thing possible, but he'd experienced its effects for himself...and had seen how they had also prevented Khalim from using his abilities.

Good thing, too, or that fight in the farmhouse's kitchen might have turned out quite differently.

"Whatever it is, it's obviously something in or around the property itself," Olivia said. Her tone was musing, and Omar could tell she was doing her best to analyze the situation based on the few facts they had at hand. "That must be why you were able to use your powers to leave and then come back—you were outside the field of effect by then."

"That does seem to be what must have happened," he agreed. "For I definitely didn't sense when they were blocked, or when they were available to me once more. It is very odd."

She reached for her glass of water and drank from it again. Her full lips pursed, and he guessed she was doing her best to try to remember if she'd ever seen or experienced anything strange at the farm, some small clue that might have pointed to whatever it was that had affected both his and Khalim's powers.

After Olivia set her glass back down, she sent a glance at Omar that was almost annoyed. "I keep wracking my brain trying to think of anything that stood out on the farm, something that seemed out of place, but I can't think of a single thing. Not," she added, her expression now almost rueful, "that I would have been able to pick up on it if I had. It's not like I had a lot of experience with farms or anything on them."

"If we are dealing with something here like *ni-khar*," Omar told her, "then there wouldn't have been anything to see. It is an element that is mined deep within the earth and not something you would see lying on the ground."

"Well, that makes me feel a little better." She rubbed the palms of her hands on the knees of her jeans, although he didn't know whether she'd done so to get rid of excess moisture from her palms, or whether that was just her way of trying to concentrate. "I don't want to think I'm so clueless that I didn't notice some kind of alien element right under my nose."

Although the situation was anything but humorous, Omar still couldn't help letting out a small chuckle. "No, it would not have been that simple...if that's even what we're dealing with here at all."

Once again, her lips pressed together. Their rosy flush seemed to be natural, as he could not detect that she wore any cosmetics. He supposed, looking at her, that it was not so strange Khalim would have looked at her, and desired her.

It was not desire, Omar told himself, even as he forced his gaze away from Olivia's mouth. *It was a need to dominate, and to slake a thirst that he had not been able to quench in years. That is all.*

True, but he also had to admit she was rather comely...for a human.

"We really should tell someone about Khalim," she said then. "It doesn't seem like a very good idea to have him just rampaging around out there."

Omar had thought much the same thing, loath as he was to make any voluntary contact with his brothers. "I will let it be known that he was seen in Cedar Crest," he replied. "Although I very much doubt he would have remained in the neighborhood. If he came to inspect the area where we disappeared, then he would discover soon enough that his powers had returned, and he would then be able to go wherever he liked."

She didn't look very cheered by that notion. "What if he goes after some other survivor somewhere?"

"I doubt there are many survivors to go after," Omar assured her. "Even if they exist—and I am not sure they do—it is not terribly likely that he would be able to hunt them down if they've been hidden from the world all this time." He paused there, permitting himself a wry smile. "And I have no doubt that if he tried to force his attentions on a woman of our kind, he would find out soon enough that it was a very unwise thing to attempt."

An answering smile, albeit a somewhat reluctant one, tugged at the corners of Olivia's mouth. "Your women have the same powers as the men?"

"Oh, yes," Omar replied. He thought it would be a good idea to point out his race's superiority to hers, so he went on, "We are equals in all things. And because our women do not find pregnancy and childbirth debilitating the way humans do, they recover very quickly and do not experience any moments of undue weakness."

"Must be nice," Olivia remarked with a twist of her full lips. "So, all right. Khalim is out there, but he can only do limited damage because any female djinn he approaches will send him packing, and although human women might be at risk, there aren't any he'd be able to find easily."

"That is the sum of our current circumstances," Omar said, glad she was able to grasp the situation so easily. "Also, the word has gone out that he is loose, and so my people are already on the lookout for him. I do not doubt that he will be captured very soon."

For some reason, Olivia didn't appear quite as reassured by those words as Omar had hoped she would be. Her glance strayed away from his, moving to the tall windows with their views of the river valley. At this time of year, there was not as much to see, for the cottonwoods were bare and the land all around yellow and brown while it waited for winter to do its worst.

"What about me?" she asked at length, and Omar tilted his head at her.

"What about you?"

A small breath escaped her lips, but her tone was measured enough as she said, "It's not safe for me to go back to the farm, so what am I supposed to do now?"

"We will figure out some way for you to go to Los Alamos," he told her, even as he thought she was worrying over nothing. "Djinn cannot go too close, for the people who dwell there have a network of Odekirk's devices protecting the town and the surrounding countryside. But I suppose I can tell my brother that you will need an escort to the human settlement at some point while I am reaching out to inform him that we encountered Khalim al-Usar."

"Okay," she responded, although Omar didn't detect much enthusiasm in her tone.

Not that he cared one way or another. She was only a logistical puzzle to be dealt with, and once she'd been handed over to the Santa Fe djinn or a contingent from Los Alamos, he would no longer have to worry about her well-being.

Rather than say anything else, she once again

reached for her glass of water and drank from it, although he had the impression that she did so only because she needed something to do rather than respond to him.

Irritation flared. Had he angered her somehow? He couldn't think why. It wasn't as though there was any reason for her to stay with him any longer than was strictly necessary.

Several cutting words came to mind, but to his surprise, he pushed them away rather than utter them out loud. No doubt she was still reeling from the shock of Khalim's attack and their precipitous flight from the farm. And besides, he supposed he should be somewhat grateful for the medical assistance she'd provided. True, it was her fault that he'd been injured in the first place, but afterward she'd done everything she could to help the healing process along. He knew deep down that the wound had been a grievous one, even for a djinn, and without her surprisingly expert surgery, he would not have been back on his feet nearly so quickly.

Good thing, too, or he would never have been able to best Khalim.

"I am not sure how long any of this will take," Omar told her. "For now, it is probably best to plan to have you stay here tonight. This house has many spare rooms. I'll take you to one now."

Her lips parted—had she been about to protest?—but then she seemed to think better of whatever she'd been about to say. Instead, she set her glass on its coaster and stood, giving him an expectant look.

"Lead on," she said.

How big was this house, anyway? Five thousand square feet? Six?

Olivia couldn't begin to guess. The biggest house she'd ever lived in had been a little over a thousand square feet, and she'd shared it with two roommates to be able to afford the rent. They would have been on top of each other all the time, except Becky and Taylor were going to school and working two jobs as well, and neither of them had been home very much, either.

Thinking of her two former roommates only saddened her, though. She somehow doubted they had survived the Heat, not when it had killed such a sweeping majority of the population.

As best she could, she pushed those thoughts aside. She'd mourned the people she'd known, as well as the world she'd lost, but enough years had passed that the tragedy no longer overwhelmed her, wasn't the sharp, knifing pain of a newly broken bone but rather the dull ache of an old fracture that acted up in damp weather.

Omar had left her as soon as he opened the

door to the suite, saying he'd be in the living room and that she could meet him there once she was settled in.

Not that she had much to settle, considering the way she'd fled the farmhouse with only the clothes on her back and nothing more.

But the room was large and comfortable, with a big king-size bed and simple, rustic furniture that she thought might have come from Mexico. The windows here looked out on a courtyard rather than the river view she'd glimpsed from the living room, but a fountain splashed on the tile-covered ground, and lots of plants in brightly painted Talavera pots livened up the space, even though they weren't blooming now.

And when she looked in the bathroom, which was equally spacious and well-appointed, she found everything she'd need—a toothbrush and toothpaste, various toiletries, big fluffy towels and the kind of fancy shampoo and conditioner she'd never been able to afford.

Omar's doing, she assumed. Now that he was in possession of his powers again, he could summon pretty much anything she wanted or needed.

A quick glance in the closet told her that he'd also produced a few changes of clothes for her, nothing fancy, just some more jeans and a couple of sweaters in the dark jewel tones she preferred, but still, at least she wouldn't have to climb into dirty clothing after she showered tomorrow morning. It felt odd to be sharing a house with him in a way it hadn't when he'd been convalescing at the farmhouse, although she thought that had more to do with being on his home turf here rather than in a place that was familiar to her.

She still had no idea what was going on with his powers, why they'd been somehow suppressed at the farm but had returned to him once he was far enough away from whatever had been affecting him. Judging by the half-annoyed, half-puzzled expression he'd worn during that part of their conversation, he didn't have any idea, either.

Well, they were safe now. For some reason, the notion of being fobbed off on the people in Los Alamos annoyed her a little, as though she didn't have any true say in the matter. Then again, what else was she supposed to do? It wasn't safe to stay at the farm, and the mountain town that was the birthplace of the atom bomb sounded as though it was the only human community that remained. She had nowhere else to go.

That thought didn't appeal to her very much, even as she made herself acknowledge that it would be good to be in a place where she wouldn't have to worry about djinn popping up out of nowhere. Los Alamos was protected by Miles Odekirk's devices, whatever the hell those were.

But if djinn couldn't go there, then that meant she'd never see Omar again after he handed her over. Part of her thought that would be good riddance—he wasn't the friendliest person in the world, and he'd made it abundantly clear he was only tolerating her human presence because he felt some strange obligation to keep her safe—and yet....

She thought of the way his dark eyes had met hers as they sat at dinner the night before. Nothing there except a desire to make pleasant conversation, she supposed, but at the same time, she couldn't ignore how casually gorgeous he was, how she'd never met a man with eyes so dark and deep, with such thick lashes that on anyone else, she would have thought they couldn't possibly be real.

Oh, stop it, she told herself. *You don't like him very much, and it's clear he doesn't like you, either. Who cares how good-looking he is? Just get through tonight and hope he'll be able to get you to the Los Alamos crew tomorrow.*

Good advice. She'd have to see whether she'd be able to follow it.

As soon as Omar returned to the living room, he sat down on the couch and closed his eyes so he could reach out to Aamir. He supposed he could have also contacted Jamal this way, but because their relationship was even more fraught than the one shared with his oldest brother—and because Aamir was the one who'd contacted him in the first place—he thought it better to keep their lines of communication open.

Aamir, I have news.

The response came back almost immediately. *What has happened?*

Khalim has been seen in a place called Cedar Crest. It is off Highway 14, south of Madrid. He attacked me and the woman who had given me shelter, but we fought, and I bought us enough time to escape.

Escape by the skin of their teeth, but Omar saw no reason to pass along that particular piece of information.

He couldn't see his brother, but he had to believe that Aamir frowned upon hearing this news.

Where is Khalim now?

I have no idea, Omar replied. *I only know that we were able to give him the slip. Perhaps he has already left the area, but I thought it better to let you know where he was last seen.*

I am glad you are safe, Aamir said. *And I will tell Zahrias what you have told me.* A pause, and then he added, *But who is this woman who is with you?*

His mental voice had sharpened subtly with interest—an interest that Omar knew he needed to squelch immediately.

She is no one, he said. *A survivor living alone on a farm in Cedar Crest. But she attracted Khalim's interest, and I had no choice but to defend her.*

That was noble of you.

Omar paused a moment to attempt to determine whether his brother was being sarcastic, then decided to let it go. Much more important to focus on the request he needed to make.

She has been driven from her home, so I told her we would make arrangements to have her go to the people in Los Alamos, he said. *I suppose that is possible?*

It is. I will pass that information along to Zahrias, and he will make the necessary arrangements. We may not be able to do so until tomorrow, however.

Since Omar had already resigned himself to having Olivia under his roof at least for tonight, if not longer, his brother's response didn't trouble him too much. *That works well enough,* he said. *There is one other matter, though.*

Aamir's mental tone sharpened again, although for an entirely different reason. *What is it?*

I experienced something very strange at Olivia's farm, he replied. *While I was there, I had no use of my powers.*

As though she had one of the devices?

That was my first thought, but she claimed igno-rance of the things, and I believed her. Also, whatever was happening, it did not make me feel ill or weary the way one of the devices would have. Then I thought it might be ni-khar, *but that made no sense, either, as that element should not have been able to affect me.*

Aamir was silent for a moment, clearly taking his time to absorb this troubling information. *Was Khalim similarly affected?*

He was. It was not until I was some distance from the farm that my powers returned to me. I have no idea whether Khalim's abilities returned as well, for that is when Olivia and I were able to make our escape. We are now at my home in Placitas.

Another long pause. Was Aamir wondering if he should warn his youngest brother about keeping a human woman at his house? Such things were forbidden, of course, but this situation was entirely different from the time when Aamir took the human woman Isla Dunbar to his home in Telluride. They had fallen in love there and tried to keep their relationship secret from the world, while Omar had absolutely no feelings at all for Olivia Raskin—well, besides being very relieved that she would be taken from his charge within the next day.

Apparently, Aamir had decided that such

warnings were not required in this situation, for he only said, *I will also pass this information along to Zahrias. It is a strange circumstance, and nothing I have heard of before. I have a feeling that Miles Odekirk will want to investigate.*

Omar allowed himself a small sneer since no one was around to see it. He cared very little for what that dangerous human might or might not do...although he was also forced to admit that if anyone could figure out what exactly was occurring on the farm where Olivia had been living, it would be Los Alamos' resident mad scientist.

Let me know when you want me to bring Olivia to Santa Fe, was all Omar said. *I assume someone from Los Alamos will be able to meet her there and take her back with them.*

Yes, I am sure that is what will happen. I will reach out when I have more information.

Aamir's voice faded from his mind just then. Good timing, because Olivia returned to the living room the very next moment, her expression diffident.

"Am I interrupting you?" she asked, and Omar shook his head.

"No, I ended the conversation with my brother a moment before you arrived. He will contact me again when he knows for sure that someone from Los Alamos will be able to take you there." He got up from the couch, sending her a piercing look. "Is something wrong? Did you not like the room I provided for you?"

"It's fine," she said hastily. "Beautiful, actually. This seems like an amazing house."

His shoulders lifted. "It suffices, I suppose. I would have preferred a different location, but this is the one the elders seemed content to give me."

Her head tilted to one side, her expression puzzled. "'The elders'?"

Omar reminded himself that she had been isolated for a very long time. Unlike the humans in Los Alamos, she would never have heard of the elders, would know nothing about the community of djinn and humans in Santa Fe, or the others like it scattered across the globe.

She would have no idea what a Chosen was.

Good thing, too, for he had no particular desire to discuss that subject with her. Better she should think that only monsters like Khalim had any interest in bedding mortal women, even though the truth was much more complicated.

"It is a fine day," he said abruptly. "Let me show you the grounds, since it appears you will be here for a little while."

And although her lovely face seemed even more confused after that pronouncement, Olivia didn't argue, but only allowed him to guide her outside.

Which was how it should be.

Chapter 9

Olivia had to admit that the property was gorgeous—it included not just the courtyard she'd spied from the guest suite, but also a large walled backyard with a swimming pool, pergola, and a covered patio larger than the rented house she'd left behind in Albuquerque—and she allowed Omar to show it off to her, mostly because she didn't know what else they were supposed to do with their time. Sit down and watch TV?

Hardly. After they were done with their tour, he showed her to the home's library, suggested that she might while away the rest of the afternoon by reading, and then told her dinner would be at seven and he would see her then.

The world's most gracious host, he was not. Then again, while he seemed bent on making sure she was safe until she was out of his hands, it wasn't his responsibility to keep her amused.

If it had been warmer outside, she might have taken one of the books to the patio and sat there, but although the day was sunny and bright, it was still chilly enough that she knew she wouldn't be able to brave the outdoor temperatures for very long.

Instead, she took the Janet Evanovich mystery she'd selected and headed back to her room, which had a nice sitting area in front of the window, including a comfy armchair and matching ottoman. She figured that there she'd be safely out of Omar's way, and she could just read until it was time to go to dinner.

That sounded so fancy. More like, meet the djinn in his dining room and see what he had planned for the evening meal. Olivia found herself hoping it would be something exotic, something she'd never tasted before. Growing up, she'd been fed a steady diet of frozen dinners, pizza, and mac and cheese, and once she was out on her own, she'd deliberately made herself try as many different cuisines as she possibly could, just for the experience. Some she loved, some she didn't much care for after closer acquaintance, but at least no one could ever accuse her of not being adventurous with her food.

She had to admit that it felt strange to sit here

and read and not do much of anything. At the farmhouse, she had a few books, volumes she'd pilfered from neighboring houses—the Millers didn't seem to have been big on reading unless you counted the Farmer's Almanac—but there had never seemed to be a lot of time to just sit down with a book, not with all the chores she had to do just to keep the place going. And when she did have some free time, she used it for crocheting or sewing, since with those hobbies, she'd have a useful item when she was done. Reading had seemed like an extravagant indulgence.

Now, though...now she had the luxury of time, if only for a few hours.

In fact, she found herself so lost in the book— even while acknowledging that she was allowing herself to be lost so she wouldn't have to think about the nightmare image of Khalim catching up to her and Omar in that scrubby juniper forest— that she almost jumped when she heard a knock against the doorframe to her room.

"Ready for dinner?" Omar asked.

She set down the book. Yes, she'd paused to turn on a light and close the curtains as dusk fell, but still, she found it hard to believe that so many hours had passed. "Sure," she said easily, even as she hoped he hadn't been able to tell that he'd startled her.

If he had, he showed no sign of it. He only said,

"Follow me," and led her out of the wing where the bedrooms were located and over to the other side of the house, where a vast darkness showed outside windows that were tall and narrow, a match to the ones in the living room, although this space was dominated by a long walnut table and matching chairs. In one corner, a kiva-style fireplace sent some welcome warmth into the room, although overall, the temperature in the house had been comfortable enough even though Olivia hadn't been able to detect a furnace pulsing on and off.

Maybe djinn didn't need such things. Maybe they decided how warm they wanted their house to be and it just...was.

"Any preferences for dinner?" Omar asked as she seated herself. He hadn't pulled out a chair for her—not that she'd expected him to.

"Surprise me," she said, and couldn't help grinning as she spoke. After all, a lot of people probably would have told her that wasn't a very smart thing to say to a djinn.

He didn't smile in return, though. No, instead he looked thoughtful, as though doing his best to decide what would be a suitable response to such an invitation.

Then he spread his hands, and a veritable feast of Indian food appeared on the table—tandoori chicken and lamb korma and naan and cucumber salad and rice, the sort of thing she'd only had a few times in her life and never believed she'd ever be able to eat again.

"Does this suit you?" Omar asked as he sat down at the head of the table.

"It smells wonderful," she replied, which was only the truth. It had been a long, long time since such a delectable combination of aromas had met her nose, even though she'd worked very hard to make the food she prepared at the farm at least a little interesting.

He seemed content with that reply, because he nodded, then placed a napkin in his lap. A moment later, a bottle of what she thought was Beaujolais appeared in his hand.

No protests from her. She'd never had Beaujolais before, but after that harrowing escape from Cedar Crest, wine sounded like a great idea.

Wine glasses already waited at each of their place settings—stoneware with a rustic biscuit-colored glaze that matched the furnishings perfectly—so Olivia handed hers over when Omar inclined his head toward her, then waited as he filled it. A pause while he did the same for himself, and then she lifted her glass to her lips.

"I thought perhaps we could toast our escape," he said, and she stopped so abruptly that she almost slopped some wine on her hand.

Right. She supposed that was worthy of a toast, even as she recalled that he hadn't been so inclined when they'd been drinking wine the night before in the farmhouse.

But they'd thought they were perfectly safe then, and his leg had been bothering him. Maybe he hadn't deemed the occasion worthy of a toast.

He seemed ready to share a toast now, so she dutifully clinked her glass against his, then took a small sip of the wine. It was lighter than most red wines she'd drunk, fruity and pleasant, and probably chosen so it wouldn't overpower all the delicate flavors in the Indian feast that stretched across the table before her. There was enough food here for at least five or six people, but she wouldn't argue over the bounty, not when she had a good idea that Omar could magically make it go away just as he'd made it appear in the first place.

They filled their plates with korma and salad and rice, and in between mouthfuls of the various dishes, each one more delectable than the last, Olivia had bites of naan to clear her palate so she could move on to the next thing. Had she ever been treated to this sort of feast before?

Not really. The closest she could come was one time when she'd gone with a bunch of other nursing students to an Indian buffet not too far from the university. That had been good, but this was divine...and something she wouldn't have to worry about paying for when the meal was over.

"Where does all the food come from?" she

asked as Omar ladled more chicken curry onto her plate. "I mean, I'm no physicist, but I'm pretty sure you can't make something out of nothing."

"We can't," he said calmly. "However, all we need to do is gather the necessary elements to create what we're visualizing. It still looks like magic, I suppose, but creating food like this has its basis in science...if you look deeply enough."

She supposed that made some sense. Matter was matter, whether you used it to create a bowl of rice or a set of new clothes.

Or a couple of brand-new bottles of Bumble and Bumble shampoo and conditioner like the ones she'd found in the bathroom earlier.

"It must be fun, being able to conjure whatever you're in the mood for," she said. "I suppose djinn don't have to worry about calories?"

She ended the question on an upward inflection, mostly because she honestly didn't know. Omar was lean and fit, with just the slightest suggestion of some decent muscles under those loose-fitting clothes he wore, and Khalim, while terrifying, had been slim, too.

"Our metabolisms are different from those of humans," Omar responded as he took another piece of naan from its basket. "So no, we don't have to worry about calorie consumption the same way humans do."

That would be nice. Not that she'd ever had to

worry too much about gaining weight—she was always running around like a madwoman, juggling school and jobs, and although her mother had fed her junk when she was a child, there had never been a whole lot of it. But working in the health field, she'd seen far too many people struggle with eating disorders just because they were trying to conform to an impossible set of societal expectations rather than trying to be healthy with the body they'd been given.

It would be amazing to live in a world where that sort of thing wasn't even an issue...and, she had to admit to herself, where you could conjure yourself a carton of Ben and Jerry's or a whole apple pie if you wanted, and not have to worry about the consequences.

And maybe she should slow down now, but everything was so good that she wanted to taste all of it—and have a second helping of her favorites, just because she could.

"This is all wonderful," she told Omar. "Thank you."

He shrugged, although whether that was because he didn't care if she was grateful for the meal, or whether it had taken no real effort on his part and therefore didn't deserve her thanks, she couldn't say for sure.

"I heard from my brother late this afternoon," he said. "He told me that a group from Los Alamos was already planning to visit Santa Fe tomorrow morning, so I will arrange to take you there at that time so you can go with them when they leave."

Although Olivia had already told herself this was the best outcome for everyone involved, the wonderful food she'd just eaten now felt like a heavy lump in her stomach. It was one thing to calmly consider a future in the mountain town and quite another to be confronted by that reality with less than twenty-four hours to get used to the idea.

However, she knew any protests she made would sound foolish, so she nodded and replied, "Thanks for arranging that."

"It was not a problem," he replied, then reached for his glass of wine and drank.

The question had been bouncing around in her head for a while, and since it didn't sound as though she'd have another opportunity to ask it, she went ahead and inquired, "So...what is it about Santa Fe? Is that a djinn community the way Los Alamos is a community of humans?"

His brows drew together, and she got the distinct impression he wasn't too thrilled that she'd broached the subject. However, he sounded measured enough as he said, "It is not exactly the same. The people in Los Alamos live there because that is where Miles Odekirk was living and where he was able to create a sanctuary of sorts, due to the devices that protect them. In Santa Fe, those djinn are there because that is the place in New Mexico they determined would be best to live with their Chosen."

Something in the way Omar pronounced the word gave it a definite capital letter, even though Olivia had never heard it used that way before. Also, even though she could tell he was taking care to deliver his answer in an almost too-neutral tone, it sure felt to her as if something about the situation didn't meet his approval.

It probably would have been better to leave it alone, but she still found herself asking, "'Chosen'?"

A pause while he swallowed some more Beaujolais. "I would prefer not to explain ancient history."

The glitter in those dark eyes under their heavy lashes would have been enough to put off a lot of people. And maybe under other circumstances, she would have backed down, since a good majority of her life had been spent trying not to make waves.

Knowing how much effort he'd expended earlier that day to keep her safe gave her a measure of courage, though.

Or maybe it was just the glass and a half of Beaujolais she'd consumed so far that allowed her to return, "Fine. If you don't want to tell me, that's your choice. I'm sure I'll find out from the Los Alamos people soon enough."

For a long moment, he only gazed back at her,

unmoving. Then he set down his glass and said, "You are a stubborn woman."

She'd never thought of herself that way, had always thought she was far too accommodating of other people's needs rather than her own. But it was possible that living on her own these past four years had allowed her to develop some character strengths she'd otherwise been lacking.

Meeting his eyes stare for stare, she replied, "I don't think wanting to know about something is an indication of stubbornness."

To her surprise, he was the one who looked away first, an uneven smile tugging at his lips. "Very well. If you must know, among the djinn is a group we call the One Thousand—our conscientious objectors, to borrow a phrase from your world's past. They did not support the eradication of the human race, so each of them was allowed to choose a mortal partner who was immune to the fever. Those humans are Chosen. They are given long life and infinite health due to their connection with their djinn partners, and those who were from New Mexico live in Santa Fe. There are similar communities elsewhere in the world." He stopped there, one brow lifting slightly. "Is there anything else you would like to know?"

Was there anything else? She'd sat there quietly while he gave his speech, but inside, her mind was going a mile a minute. So, there were djinn who'd taken humans as romantic partners— lifelong partners, according to what Omar had just said? The whole thing sounded crazy to her, but from the way he'd spoken, it appeared to be just another fact of life to the people involved.

"The humans who were chosen," she began, then paused, trying to gather her thoughts. "Did they have any say in the matter?"

Omar's lip curled, but he kept his gaze steady on her as he said, "No. Not precisely, anyway. It's my understanding that most of them were happy— grateful, even—to have someone as their protector in a world that had gone mad. But not having been among them back when all that was happening— or ever since—I cannot say more than that."

No, of course he hadn't been among those djinn who'd wanted to save humans. Just the opposite, in fact.

At least he'd been honest about his role in all this, though. Olivia still didn't know exactly how she wanted to view him, but one thing was for sure.

He wasn't a liar. And that meant that what he'd told her about the Chosen and their djinn was the truth.

Mind-boggling. However, it made her understand a little bit more why she'd been the object of Khalim's lust. He certainly hadn't been among the One Thousand, but he also wasn't above using a human woman to satisfy his horrible needs.

A whole lot of other things began to click into place as well. "And you're mad at your brothers because they took human partners."

At once, Omar's eyes glinted in anger. "That is not anything I need to discuss with you."

By that point in the meal, she'd eaten enough that she had no desire for anything more...or maybe the shift in his tone had killed her appetite.

Either way, she was fine with settling against the back of her chair, wine glass still in hand, as she said, "And here I thought we were getting along so well. Are you afraid of sharing your deep, dark secrets?"

His gaze narrowed. "There is nothing secret about the Chosen," he said curtly, "or about the unfortunate fact that my brothers decided to lower themselves by taking human partners. And my reaction to their decision is no business of yours."

Fine. It seemed clear enough to Olivia that, while Omar might have been willing to share a few details she probably would have learned anyway after relocating to Los Alamos, he had absolutely no desire to tell her anything of true importance to him. Right then, she wasn't even sure why she'd pressed him, except that it had seemed as if they were beginning to have some sort of rapport—an impression that had obviously been very, very wrong.

"I suppose it isn't," she said coolly, then put her

wine glass next to her plate. "Thank you for dinner. It's been kind of a day, so I think I'll go to bed now."

His gaze didn't flicker for even a second. "I hope you have a good night's rest," he said, his tone all politeness.

Somehow, she doubted it, but she'd never let him know that. "You, too," she responded as she got up from her chair. "I'll see you in the morning."

And she walked away, leaving him sitting there in his lonely seat at the head of the table.

For a second or two, Omar experienced a moment of doubt. Perhaps he shouldn't have been so harsh with Olivia...but on the other hand, she'd been probing where she did not need to. Even if he'd been inclined to share confidences with a human—which he wasn't—he saw no reason to deepen their acquaintance, not when she would be going off to Los Alamos the next day and he very likely would never see her again.

Instead, he drained the rest of the Beaujolais in his wine glass and then poured what remained in the bottle into the glass as well. No point in letting it go to waste, and besides, it was not as if such an amount of wine could affect a djinn. It would take two or three times that much to make him even the slightest bit drunk, although he had no intention of drinking that much.

He got up from his chair and tilted his head at the litter of bowls and plates and half-eaten food on the tabletop. At once, it all vanished, the dinnerware cleaned and returned to its proper place in the kitchen cabinets, the partially consumed food either stored in the refrigerator or made to vanish completely, depending on how much of it had been left over.

With that task managed, he went to stare out the windows as he slowly consumed the wine in his glass. There was not much to see, for the moon had not yet risen and the landscape below was utterly dark. Still, it felt better to stand here and allow his eyes to become accustomed to the darkness, to see the blurred contours of hillsides and junipers and the faint, faint glint of the Rio Grande as it moved through the dim countryside some five miles from where he stood.

Not even a hint of sound from the wing of the house where the bedrooms were located...not that he expected there to be. Olivia might have been annoyed with him, but she did not seem the kind of woman to stomp her feet or bang objects to show her anger. No, she was a quieter, subtler sort, someone whose temperament might have suited him if she had been a djinn. Some people thrived on high drama, but he certainly did not. He'd had enough of that to deal with in his long, long lifetime.

He finished the wine a few minutes later and sent the glass to join its newly scrubbed comrade in the kitchen cupboards. Although he could have blinked himself into his bedroom, it seemed better to walk there quietly, to pause ever so briefly to make sure all was still in the guest room where Olivia was staying.

Just in case.

But she didn't make a sound, which made him think she was already safely in bed. The hour wasn't late, and yet Omar knew he was weary as well, tired after that tussle with Khalim, and also carrying with him the weariness of his healing wound. His leg was almost back to normal, and he knew another good night's sleep would finish the work Olivia had started.

So, a quick, hot shower to wash away the dust of the day, and then he climbed into bed, glad of a few hours of oblivion. Tomorrow she would be gone, and he could allow his life to return to normal...

...whatever that was.

Sleep came quickly, so fast and so deep that when the blow rocked through the house, he had to sit up in bed and blink a few times before he could determine what was happening.

Another blow, one that felt like an earthquake and yet not at the same time, even as the night turned orange outside.

What the hell?

He'd left his door partly ajar, and Olivia came hurrying in, her long, dark hair loose around her shoulders rather than pulled back in the ponytail she'd worn all day. Among the items he'd left for her use had been a flowing white nightgown, and even through his shock, he had to admit to himself she had never looked more beautiful than at that moment.

"Someone's attacking the house," she gasped. "I think it must be Khalim."

Sure enough, the house shook again, and flames roared outside the window, licking higher, hungry.

Omar flung back the covers. He'd only been sleeping in a pair of briefs, but at least he wasn't completely naked. Another of those explosions hit the structure, followed by the sound of collapsing walls. Not too near, most likely in the section of the house where the kitchen and great room lay. The place was made of stucco, and therefore should not have burned so easily, but he knew ordinary physics mattered little when a djinn's powers were involved.

"We must go," Omar said urgently. While part of him wanted to stay and fight, his senses told him that part of the house had fallen already, and the flames were spreading fast. Better to get out of there and decide what to do next after he and Olivia were both safe.

"Go where?" she asked. In the dim light, her eyes were wide and frightened and dark, but she wasn't panicking, was obviously doing her best to keep calm.

"A safe place," he said. "Come here—we must travel in the djinn manner."

He could see the way she swallowed, but she didn't argue, only came closer so she could put her arms around his waist. Although they'd traveled in this manner before, that other time they'd both been fully clothed. Now he could feel her breasts pressing against his bare torso, separated from his flesh only by a thin layer of cotton, and despite everything, despite the roar of the flames and something that sounded like distant, wicked laughter, he could sense the way his body wanted to respond to hers.

No time for that, though. No time for anything except to hold on to her as tightly as he could while he took them away from the ruin of his home.

Chapter 10

THEY CAME TO REST IN A ROOM THAT WAS utterly unfamiliar to her, with a huge river rock fireplace that dominated one wall and wood paneling on all sides. It was freezing in there, but Omar lifted a hand, and immediately a fire burst to life within the hearth.

"Are you all right?" he asked, and Olivia did her best to nod.

"I-I'm fine," she replied, her teeth chattering despite her best efforts.

"It will warm in here soon enough," he told her. "But this should also help."

Immediately, she was cocooned inside a thick fleece robe, and warm slipper socks covered her bare feet and calves. And—probably more out of concern for the nearly naked figure he presented than because he was suffering from the chill—

Omar was covered up in the same instant, although in more of the black Middle Eastern–inspired garb he typically wore rather than a bathrobe.

"Where are we?" she asked.

"A safe place."

"You said your house was safe."

At once, his mouth twisted. "It should have been." He looked away from her and toward the set of brown leather couches that faced each other across a live-edge oak coffee table. "Go ahead and sit down. Some mulled wine, perhaps?"

Although a drink sounded really good right then, Olivia thought it better to do what she could to keep her wits about her. "Some green tea would be fine."

She'd barely finished speaking before a cup appeared on the coffee table, steam wisping up gently from the pale liquid inside. That seemed like as good a reason as any to make her way over to the couch and sit down, while Omar followed so he could seat himself opposite her. A mug appeared in his hand, but the fruity, spicy aroma that drifted toward her seemed to indicate it was something a little higher octane than green tea.

A sip or two helped to calm her shivery nerves, although Olivia knew she'd have a hard time trying to sleep after what had just happened. She supposed it had been a lucky thing that she'd had some difficulty sliding into dreamland back at

Omar's house, and instead had been lying there with her eyes open and fixed on the ceiling. Because of that, she'd been wide awake when the first fireball hit the place.

At least, she thought it was a fireball. All she knew was that something had shaken the house to its foundations, and outside her window, the black sky had lit up with angry hues of orange and yellow.

And she'd remembered that Khalim was a fire elemental.

No conscious thought after that, just sheer action as she jumped out of bed and ran down the hall to Omar's bedroom. Luckily, he'd been awake, too, and apparently had guessed that the house was already a loss, since he hadn't hesitated for a second and had only done what he needed to, which was to get the two of them the hell out of there.

He drank as well, his expression almost too calm, considering how he'd just lost his gorgeous home. "You asked what this place is. It is a house in Red River, a hideaway my brothers and I have used in the past. However, very few people know I have any connection to this location, so I think it should be safe."

For now, Olivia thought, although she didn't say the words out loud and only took another sip of tea. "How did Khalim know to find us at your home in Placitas?"

Omar's brows pulled together, and his expression turned to one of mingled anger and confusion. "That, I cannot say. It is not as though the djinn have their own version of the internet, or even a phone book. And Khalim was banished to the outer circles months before the elders granted me the house in Placitas, so it is not as if that was information he would have carried with himself into exile. No, someone must have told him, although I cannot think who. He should have been in hiding, unwilling to approach anyone lest he give away his current location."

If that was really what had happened—if another djinn had told Khalim where Omar lived, whether out of malice or simple stupidity—then Olivia wasn't sure how safe she could feel here. "How many people know about this house?"

To her annoyance, he only smiled at her obvious worry. "As I said, very few. My brothers, of course, and then Zahrias al-Harith, leader of the Santa Fe djinn, and Qadim al-Syan, another member of that community. Oh, and a few from Los Alamos, but I do not think they are in any position to be speaking to one of the rogue djinn."

No, probably not, especially if the mountain town was as protected by Miles Odekirk's devices as Omar claimed it was. Still....

"And you're sure Zahrias and Qadim can be trusted?"

That too-indulgent smile didn't slip even an inch. "If they are members of the Santa Fe settlement, that means they have no love lost for someone such as Khalim al-Usar, who was banished specifically because of the crimes he committed against their Chosen. I will admit that Qadim has not always kept the best company, but he seems to be a reformed character these days, and surely would do nothing to jeopardize his place in that community."

Under most circumstances, those bona fides would have been enough to satisfy her. However, she didn't know Zahrias al-Harith or Qadim al-Syan from a hole in the wall, so she wasn't sure she liked having Omar's word as the final comment on the subject.

"If Santa Fe is so safe, why didn't we go there?"

She thought it a logical enough question, but clearly, Omar didn't care for it too much, based on the way his frown deepened.

"Because I am not a member of that community. It is for djinn and their Chosen only. As I said, this house is safe. We can shelter here for the night, and then tomorrow I will take you to Santa Fe so you can meet up with the people from Los Alamos."

Which again made her wonder why they couldn't have gone there directly and skipped the middleman, but maybe it was one thing to hang there for an hour or so and something else entirely to stay the night.

"What about your house?" Olivia asked. He seemed remarkably calm for someone who'd just lost everything he owned, but she supposed that sort of thing was different for a djinn. It wasn't as though he had to live in a Residence Inn or something while he fought with an insurance company over the replacement cost of his new eighty-inch TV. No, he probably just had to snap his fingers and have it all go back exactly the way it used to be.

His answering shrug told her everything she needed to know. "It will be replaced eventually. The important thing is that we were able to get away without suffering any physical harm. That was Khalim's intent, after all—he wanted to hurt either one or both of us, for he knows that losing material items is not the sort of thing to trouble a djinn."

Apparently not, based on Omar's non-reaction to the whole situation. Olivia sipped some more tea, hoping it would help her feel a little calmer without injecting too much caffeine into an already roiling bloodstream.

"Also," he continued, "I will contact Aamir and let him know what has happened. He and Zahrias may well want to start making their own inquiries, just to ensure that no one in their community provided the information Khalim acted upon."

This comment made Olivia look up from her mug in some surprise. "Do you really think someone in Santa Fe would betray you like that?"

"I doubt it," Omar replied at once. "For while I have no reason to believe I am a favorite of theirs, they would be even less inclined to provide any assistance to Khalim, not after he killed several of their Chosen, wounded another, and kept one of their women as his particular toy for some time. And certainly, he would not be so foolish as to go anywhere near that community. No, whatever the answer is, I am certain we will have to seek it elsewhere."

His explanation, delivered in the same calm, almost dry tone, helped to soothe her rattled nerves somewhat. If he'd been truly worried that Khalim would locate them again, then she thought he surely would have gone straight to Santa Fe despite any rules saying that only djinn who had Chosen could live there.

Before she could respond, Omar added, "It is getting late. You should drink your tea and go to sleep—the guest bedrooms are upstairs."

Meaning, she supposed that the main suite was located on the ground floor—and that he thought he was the one who should have it, not her.

Which was fine. Even though she didn't know whether she'd be able to sleep a wink after what had happened, the thought of being able to at least lay her head somewhere comfortable sounded awfully good to her.

The green tea had cooled a good bit during their conversation, so it was easy enough to finish it off in a couple of swallows and then place the empty mug on a coaster. When she stood, she pulled the thick robe a little closer around her. Yes, it was now plenty warm in the living room, thanks to the blazing fire a few feet away and whatever Omar might have done to activate the home's central heating system, but she couldn't quite forget that she'd gone running to him in a skimpy cotton nightgown and nothing else.

How she'd put her arms around him and felt his flesh hot against hers, blazing against her body as though she'd been wearing nothing at all.

Heat flooded her cheeks, and she prayed that the dimness in the room would be enough to prevent him from seeing the way she'd blushed out of nowhere.

"I'll go check out the upstairs," she said hastily.

"I'm sure everything is in order," Omar replied.

Of course he would say something like that, as if she was accusing him or his brothers of leaving the place in disarray. From what she could see, it looked like a lovely house, a little too lodge-y for her taste—a joke, considering her budget had never allowed much room for "taste"—but certainly better than any of the places she'd lived.

Not including the farmhouse. It had been hard to be alone, and yet she knew her lonely existence would have been much more difficult if she hadn't had the great good luck to find someplace so quiet and yet so welcoming.

She probably shouldn't have been thinking about the farmhouse, though, because her thoughts went immediately to Zorro and the goats. Omar had assured her they would be fine...but would they?

However, she guessed if she brought up the subject of the animals again, he would only tell her that they had far more pressing matters to worry about, and she sort of had to agree he would be right about that one, as much as she hated to admit it.

"Okay," she said lightly, and decided to leave things there. "I'll see you in the morning, I guess."

He nodded. "Sleep well."

Somehow she doubted that would be the case, but she only replied, "You, too," before turning away so she could mount the steps to the second floor. All the bedrooms up there were decent-sized and had their own *en suite* bathrooms, so she chose the one closest to the stairs—just in case they had to make another hasty escape—and went inside and shut the door. It was warm up here, so she knew she wouldn't have to worry about shivering her way to sleep.

And sometime while they were talking, Omar had thoughtfully supplied all the toiletries and other odds and ends that had been lost in the fire, although she'd already washed her face and brushed her teeth.

But she'd drunk that tea, so another quick brush seemed in order, after which she made her way over to the bed and turned off the light, then slid under the covers.

It felt very dark in here, somehow darker than the house in Placitas. Maybe that impression came from the pine forest she'd just barely glimpsed outside the window before she closed the curtains, although she couldn't tell whether the trees crowded the property on all sides or just the rear.

Or maybe it was simply because she now knew for a fact that Khamil was out there somewhere, hunting them. Omar seemed confident the rogue djinn would never be able to find this place, but....

She clutched the covers and made herself breathe in, then breathe out. Again and again, until at last her eyes closed on their own accord, and the sleep she'd been chasing so hard finally rose up to take her.

Omar paused at the foot of the steps and listened, but he heard nothing. Or rather, he could tell

Olivia had been moving around in her room earlier because the wooden floor had creaked every once in a while, and it sounded as though she'd left the bedroom door open at least a crack. All seemed still now, which meant she must be in bed and, with any luck, fast asleep.

Which meant it was time for him to retire as well.

First, though, he went out the back door and onto the patio so he could listen to the wind. It was much colder here than in Placitas, with unmelted patches of snow in the shadowy spots and an icy breeze blowing from the northeast, but he paid it no mind. Much more important to hold himself still and wait for the wind to tell him what he needed to know.

It sighed softly in his ears, bringing only the haunting whisper of the breeze soughing in the pines and far, far away, the hooting of an owl. Nothing else here that he could sense, as though even the coyotes and the foxes knew better than to roam on such a cold December night.

True, the current stillness in Red River didn't necessarily mean that Khamil might not be plotting to appear unexpectedly, but Omar did not believe that was a true possibility. Somehow he'd managed to locate the house in Placitas, and yet only four or five people in the world knew the al-Qadir brothers had used this place as a hideout, which meant it was very unlikely that Khamil even knew it existed.

He went back inside, glad of the flames that leaped in the hearth, of the way his powers had awakened the furnace so it might send warm air into every room. Yes, they would sleep here, and then tomorrow morning he would make sure Olivia was sent away with the contingent from Los Alamos to a place where he knew she would have nothing to fear from Khamil al-Usar.

Another of those annoying little pangs went through him at the thought, one Omar knew he would do his best to ignore. He had to admit that she'd shown an impressive command of herself, hadn't screamed or panicked or done anything except keep her head and inform him of the situation, then allow him to take her away. Would most human women have been able to maintain that kind of aplomb in such a frightening situation?

Somehow, he doubted it.

The downstairs suite was very large, with an oversized king bed and a walk-in closet that probably would have served as a separate bedroom in many human homes. Not that he had much to fill it; this was a way station and no more, a temporary refuge so they might gather their wits and get some much-needed rest.

He attended to his face and teeth, then removed his outer robe and hung it from one of the hooks in the closet, ignoring the hangers. This would do well enough for now—if the garment wrinkled, then he would simply summon himself another one.

No sooner had he let go of the robe and turned to exit the closet than an ear-curdling scream shrieked its way down the staircase. Omar didn't even pause to consider what might be happening upstairs and instead blinked himself directly into Olivia's bedroom, thinking he would surely encounter Khalim assaulting her there.

But she was alone, although she writhed in sleep, breath coming in quick pants, eyes wide and staring. Still, he guessed she could see nothing of her surroundings. That one scream was the only one she appeared prepared to utter, although now she moaned, frightened little noises that sounded almost like the mewling of a newborn rather than the sounds a grown woman might make.

"Olivia!" he said in an urgent whisper, but she seemed as unhearing as she was unseeing, caught in some nightmare trap she could not escape on her own.

Unsure what to do, he stepped closer to the bed.

"Olivia," he said again, now a little louder, hoping his urgent tone would be enough to penetrate whatever dark visions haunted her sleep.

Her eyes flared wide, so wide that he could see

the whites around the deep green irises, almost black in the darkness. Then she gave a hiccupy little gasp and said, "Oh, thank God," just before she reached out and threw her arms around him.

For a second, he stiffened, and then he reminded himself that she had just awoken from a nightmare and clearly wasn't herself. "I am here," he said, then, as gently as he could, removed her arms from around him.

At once, she folded her hands in her lap, head drooping as though she didn't dare meet his eyes. "Sorry about that," she said. "It was kind of a doozy of a nightmare."

He'd already surmised as much. "Do you want to tell me about it?" he asked, surprising himself. It had been in his mind to inform her that he was glad she was awake and he was now going back downstairs, but something in the strained pallor in her face prevented him from being quite so brusque.

Her fingers knotted themselves together, almost as pale as the nightgown she wore. "Not really," she replied, and now she looked up at him, lips twisting into a half-smile. "Just the standard kind of crap. Khalim...you know."

Unfortunately, Omar did know. "We are safe here," he reminded her, and she only shook her head.

"My brain understands that, but I guess the

rest of me hasn't gotten the memo." Her gaze moved away from him to the clock on the nightstand. Not quite eleven o'clock, which meant this long, dreadful day still wasn't entirely behind them. She pulled in a breath, then added, "I think I'll go downstairs and see if there's any chamomile tea."

A good idea. She could have something to calm her nerves, and then they would both have a chance to get some sleep. "I can always summon some if there isn't any in the pantry," he offered as he rose from the bed.

Once again, her full lips moved into something that was almost a smile. "I might take you up on that. But first, let me see if I can do this the old-fashioned way."

A little mystified by the request, he waited off to one side as she shrugged on the robe he'd provided earlier, although he noticed that she didn't bother to pull on the slipper socks. Both of them barefoot, they descended the stairs and headed into the kitchen, while Omar directed some of his energy to the hearth so the fire he'd banked down earlier might leap up again.

Somehow, he guessed this might take a little while.

The pantry did in fact have an unopened box of chamomile tea, along with a cinnamon variety. Olivia filled the kettle, obviously determined to do all this under her own power without any djinn help.

Omar thought he understood. Ritual was a powerful thing, and right now, she wanted to focus on something familiar and routine, actions she'd probably performed hundreds if not thousands of times before.

All the same, once the pot was on the stovetop and little blue flames were licking at it from underneath, he directed a bit of extra energy to the water so it might boil much faster than it usually would.

When the kettle began to whistle only a moment later, Olivia sent him a semi-suspicious glance, albeit one overlaid with amusement.

"You did that, didn't you."

It wasn't a question, but he thought he should answer her anyway.

"Yes, I did. Standing around and waiting for the kettle to boil did not seem like a very good use of our time."

She actually chuckled, although she didn't comment as she lifted the bright red enamel kettle from the stovetop and filled their waiting mugs.

"There," she said. "Now we can go sit in front of the fire while we drink our tea."

Omar had to admit it was cozy in the living room, with flames bright in the hearth, sending dancing light and shadow against the wood-paneled walls. He'd left on the sconces in the stairwell, but otherwise, the only illumination in the house was from the fireplace itself, warm and mysterious at the same time.

"I used to have the worst nightmares," Olivia confessed, then blew on the surface of her tea to cool it down. "Night terrors, the whole thing. But I grew out of it after I hit junior high. Most of the time, I don't even remember dreaming at all, which is why I never expected to have a nightmare like this one."

"It has been a very trying day," Omar said with a curl of his lip, and she let out another chuckle.

"You could say that." She went quiet then so she could blow on her tea once again before allowing herself a cautious first sip. "Still, I didn't even have nightmares right after...well, right after everything happened. Or maybe I did, but I never remembered any of them."

Probably a good thing. Omar had never spared a thought for what it must have been like to survive the Heat, only to realize most of the world was dead.

And that didn't even take into account having to dodge someone like him or any of the other reavers.

Looking at Olivia's pale, lovely face, he experienced a twinge of emotion that took him several seconds to recognize.

Was that guilt?

No, it couldn't be. He'd never allowed himself to waste time on such a useless concept.

And yet....

Right then, he couldn't help feeling just the slightest bit guilty for what she'd suffered during the Heat and during the long months and years that followed. Destroying humankind had seemed utterly logical to him, the only way to protect a fragile world that was collapsing under the weight of mortal technology and overpopulation.

But he found himself wishing Olivia had not been forced to endure all the pain and hardship that had come as a result of the Dying.

She deserved something better than that.

"You're very quiet," she said.

He gave what he hoped was a careless-looking shrug, although he had his doubts as to whether it appeared that way to Olivia. "I suppose I am thinking," he said, then sipped some of his cinnamon tea.

"About...?"

It would have been easy to lie and say that the destruction of his house—and their pursuit by Khalim—was what occupied his thoughts. However, he did not want to hand her false words, not when they were alone here and there was no one else around to hear what he was saying.

"About everything," he said simply, which

perhaps was still something of a dodge if not an outright lie.

However, Olivia didn't challenge his reply, only sat there and drank from her mug of tea, her expression now thoughtful. "Why do you hate humans so much?"

Of all the questions she might have asked, that was the one he truly did not wish to answer. But again, he had no wish to sidestep and prevaricate.

For a second, their eyes met. He could not precisely describe what he felt as he looked into her lovely face, only that he knew he wanted to keep on gazing at her while he still could.

Voice barely a murmur, he said, "I don't hate all humans."

She didn't try to pass his comment off as a joke, to chuckle awkwardly and do her best to change the subject. "I'm glad to hear that," she said. "I know you've taken very good care of me when you didn't have to. But still...."

The words trailed off, although Omar thought he knew what she was trying to say.

I am only one person, but you have killed hundreds, maybe more.

Truly, he didn't know how many. He had lost count years earlier. His brothers had liked to notch their belts or keep track of their kills some other way, but he had never seen the point in doing so. This wasn't a game.

No, it was a necessary extermination.

Any attempt to change the subject would be seen for the obvious ploy that it was. And he knew he possessed the true answer to her question, even if he didn't want to confront it...even if a human was the last being to whom he should confess such a secret.

Paradoxically, though, Olivia might be the one person who understood.

A sip of cinnamon tea—he found himself regretting that it wasn't brandy or cognac—and then he said, "My people have something called the draught of the dark sleep. It is a drug that brings calm, peaceful death. There are some djinn who grow weary of their long lives and wish to move on to the next place, and they drink the draught when they can think of no other reason to remain alive."

Olivia nodded but didn't speak, as though she could tell if she interrupted him, he might not continue with his tale.

"My family is somewhat unusual among my people," he continued. "Very rarely do djinn women have three offspring, and rarer still that they would only be separated by a few years the way my brothers and I are. Most of the time, a djinn woman might have a child with one partner, then decide hundreds of years later that she wants another child with a different man. But because of the way we were raised, my brothers and I were very close, and we stayed much more connected to our parents than most djinn."

"No wonder," Olivia murmured, and Omar tilted his head at her. She looked reluctant to speak, as though she feared if she said anything else, he might not go on with his narrative. But as he continued to wait, she seemed to realize that he wanted to hear what she had to say. "No wonder that you're so angry with your brothers," she added. "If you weren't close, it would be one thing if they went off and got human partners, but with the way you were raised...."

She paused there, and he nodded. "Precisely. Yes, they are beings with free will and can do as they please, but still, it has been difficult to accept their willingness to abandon everything we believe in. You see, our parents did not agree with the destruction of humankind. Voices like theirs were in the minority, however, and because they had already been committed partners for centuries, it was not as though either of them had any desire to break apart and take a Chosen. Instead, they decided they did not want to live in a world built on so much destruction and death, and so they took the draught of the dark sleep and left this existence for one they hoped would be better."

Olivia's eyes practically glowed with concern... or perhaps that was only a reflection of the dancing flames in the hearth. "I am so sorry."

He wanted to shrug again but knew that would appear like a flippant response to the obvious sympathy in her expression. "It is a thing that happened," he replied. "My brothers and I have learned to live with it."

"Maybe," Olivia allowed. "But...that's why you hate humanity, right? In your mind, if the djinn hadn't been forced to get rid of humans, then your parents would have had no reason to take their own lives."

This was close enough to what he had intended to tell her, although the words sounded terrible when stated so simply. But Omar was forced to admit that grief and rage at his loss had fueled his need to make sure not a single hated human lived and breathed on this earth.

Looking at Olivia, though, he knew he did not hate her.

Not at all.

Precisely what he felt, though, he had no clear idea.

"I suppose it is something like that," he allowed, and now she smiled, although the expression had little humor in it.

Instead, she pulled in a breath, then said, "Well, if we're sharing secrets, I've got one of my own."

Omar raised an eyebrow. Somehow he doubted that anyone so kind, so quietly strong, could be harboring any truly deep, dark secrets.

"What?"

She gazed down into the mug she held, almost as though she wanted to read her fortune in the leaves there—well, except that they'd used teabags, and therefore there weren't any leaves to read.

"After it happened," she said, then paused. Another silence before she went on, "After I realized that almost everyone was dead, this horrible part of me was relieved. Not because I wanted all those people to die," she added hastily, eyes not meeting his. "But because my mother was one of them, and I knew I wouldn't have to worry about her wrecking my life anymore."

Her expression was so distraught that Omar found himself setting his mug of tea down on the coffee table so he could reach out and take her hand. Almost immediately, her fingers wrapped around his, cold despite the warmth of the room.

"What did she do to you?"

Olivia's grip on his hand tightened. "She was a drug addict, and she drank, too, when she couldn't get her hands on some pills. I lost count of how many times she was in and out of rehab. She never married my father—he was just some guy she hooked up with when she was high, and she went through with the pregnancy because she was too far gone to have an abortion once she realized what was going on. He tried to stick around for a while, but he bailed out when I was only three."

A pause while she pressed her lips together. To keep herself from saying anything else?

Apparently not, because after a moment or two passed, she seemed to find the strength to continue her story.

"Mine wasn't what you could call a stable childhood," she said. "We moved all the time, kept getting evicted when the latest job fell apart. Even after I graduated from high school and moved out so I could go to college and do something with my life, she was always calling me and asking for money. And if it wasn't her, then it was some halfway house or rehab place or the hospital trying to get hold of me, since she still had me as her emergency contact even though I'd told her I was done and couldn't deal with her drama anymore."

"That must have been very difficult for you," Omar murmured, struck by the sort of pity he'd never expected to feel for a human. While the pain of his parents' intentional passing would stay with him forever, at least he had enjoyed a happy childhood, had always been certain of the love of his family. What must it have been like for Olivia to know she'd never been wanted, while at the same time being forced into playing the parental role for her self-destructive mother?

She was so strong, so beautiful, that he couldn't imagine a mother not wanting to have such a daughter.

"It was a living hell," Olivia said frankly. "But I survived. Just like I survived the Heat...and was happy to know I was finally free."

Omar continued to hold her hand, partly because he found he liked the sensation of her strong, slender fingers twined around his, and partly because he knew that to let go now would send a signal that he disapproved of her feelings regarding her mother.

Nothing could have been further from the truth.

"Am I a terrible person?" she asked at length.

"No," he said quietly. "No, not at all."

Chapter 11

THERE HADN'T BEEN MUCH TO SAY AFTER that. Olivia had pulled her hand away from Omar's, but gently, so he'd know it was only that she thought it might be awkward to keep holding hands like a couple of frightened kids.

But at bottom, maybe that was what they both were. It didn't matter that he was a djinn whose lifetime was infinitely longer than hers, or that she'd been a functioning adult on her own for years when the Heat came along.

What mattered was the hurt they carried within.

She went upstairs to her borrowed bedroom, while Omar headed down the hall to the ground-floor main suite. The whole time they'd been talking, she'd kept one ear cocked for any sign that Khalim might have discovered their hideaway, but all had remained quiet, telling her that it seemed as if they'd really given him the slip this go-'round.

Unless he was just biding his time, waiting for the right moment to strike.

As best she could, she pushed that unwelcome thought aside and brushed her teeth again before climbing into bed. For some reason, she could still feel the pressure of Omar's fingers on hers, a firm, quiet reminder that, improbable as it might seem, he'd stepped into the role of protector for her.

She'd never had a protector before. Not once. Everything had always begun and ended with Olivia Raskin. Sure, she'd had a few friends from work and school—the only ones who hadn't been driven off by the continuing drama in her life—but she still couldn't have named any of them as people who would stick around when the going got really rough. That might have been partly her fault, since it was her natural tendency to put up walls around herself to avoid getting hurt, and yet she still had never experienced a situation where someone had literally gone to bat for her.

Or at least, literally gone to frying pan.

Just as well that she hadn't been present for that particular altercation, but she couldn't help thinking she would have really liked to be there when Omar hit Khamil al-Usar upside the head with a cast-iron skillet.

A smile tugged at her lips as she did her best to

visualize the scene, a smile that faded when she realized she would have to say goodbye to Omar tomorrow. Sharing confidences was well and good, but in the end, it didn't matter. He was still all too willing to hand her off to the Los Alamos community and allow her to find her destiny with them.

Well, of course he was. What did she think was going to happen? She'd practically blown his leg apart; she was lucky he hadn't killed her after that, despite his vow not to harm women and children. Now she knew she was nothing more than an unpleasant duty for him, a burden he'd be all too happy to pass along to the humans in Los Alamos.

Maybe that was being too harsh, though. If he thought her that unpleasant, she doubted he would have confided in her, or held her hand to give her the strength she needed to tell him the truth about her mother, about that heretical sensation of freedom she'd experienced after realizing she'd never have to deal with the whirling tornado of chaos that was Maryanne Raskin ever again.

She'd told him the worst about her, and he'd looked at her with sympathy, not revulsion.

That had to mean something, right?

Not enough, though.

Not enough.

She pulled the covers tight and forced herself to close her eyes. Tomorrow morning was going to come way too soon, and there wasn't a damn thing she could do about it.

Except face the worst, just like she'd always done.

———

Before retiring the night before, Omar had communicated with Aamir, telling him what had happened to the house in Placitas. His older brother had been properly horrified, although also relieved that it didn't seem as if Khalim had been able to follow them to Red River.

And tomorrow you can bring Olivia to us, Aamir added. *The group from Los Alamos plans to arrive at eleven o'clock in the customary spot at the north end of town.*

Omar knew it, if not well. The highway came into Santa Fe near a military cemetery, and it was in that location that the "official" sway of the djinn community began. For obvious reasons, it was a place he had always avoided, but now he must go there directly so Olivia could be with her own kind.

That thought did not please him as much as he'd thought it would.

However, he did his best to push his disquiet aside, saying, *We will be there. I know it will be a relief for both of us to know she is someplace safe. My house can be rebuilt, but Los Alamos will provide the true shelter Olivia needs.*

Something of a mental chuckle, and Aamir said, *You are quite protective of her, little brother.*

I would be protective of anyone who was preyed upon by Khamil al-Usar, Omar retorted.

True enough. Very soon, she will no longer be your responsibility. Sleep well—I will see you tomorrow.

Their contact ended, and Omar went to bed soon afterward, although he did not sleep as well as he would have liked. Instead, he tossed this way and that, never able to find a truly comfortable position. He blamed his restless state on the bed, but he knew the problem was most likely much more than a mattress not to his liking.

However, he did his best to seem brisk and matter-of-fact that morning, putting away the fireside confidences he and Olivia had shared the night before. He might have told her secrets he had never before uttered to another living being, and yet she would soon be gone from his life, so he saw no reason to continue with such sharing.

She seemed subdued, although she told him she'd slept well and was looking forward to meeting the people from Los Alamos. Whether this assertion was entirely true, Omar couldn't say for sure, but he wasn't about to challenge her on that topic, not when he was so close to making sure she was no longer around to trouble his thoughts.

To give them both strength, he summoned a hearty breakfast of omelets and bacon and blueberry muffins, accompanied by strong coffee and all the cream and sugar she could want. As before, she seemed cheered by the bounty before her, and if she was harboring any misgivings about having to start over in a new community, her worries certainly weren't reflected in her appetite, which seemed more than healthy. In fact, she helped herself to a fourth and fifth piece of bacon, although she demurred when he offered her another muffin.

"No, I don't think I could fit another thing in my stomach," she told him with a grin. "But this was an amazing meal. Thank you."

Last meal? he wondered, although he only said, "You're more than welcome. I thought it would be good to feed you something you hadn't eaten in a while."

"It was wonderful," she assured him. "I really thought I'd never have bacon again. And even though I made muffins, blueberries were in kind of short supply in Cedar Crest. I don't think they even grow in New Mexico."

Not wild, certainly, for Omar knew he had never seen them during his wanderings through the state. However, it was easy enough for him to summon those sorts of muffins, which he had to admit he had a certain fondness for. Human food could be quite enticing.

After breakfast, they both went to shower and get dressed, with Olivia descending the stairs a while later, dark hair still damp on her shoulders, gleaming against the forest green sweater she wore. In one hand she carried a large duffle bag he'd summoned for her, thinking she would probably like to pack some of the wardrobe he'd placed in the guest bedroom upstairs.

"Are we late?" she asked, sending a worried glance at the clock that sat on the mantel.

"Not at all," he told her. "After all, it is not as though we have to get in a car and drive to our destination. We will be there soon enough, so a matter of a minute here or there will not make any difference."

Olivia appeared reassured by his comment, although he saw her expression take on a diffident cast as she approached him, as though she knew exactly what was about to come next and wasn't sure how she should act.

Probably to cover up her awkwardness, she said, "You'll be able to manage me and the duffle bag?"

"Of course," he replied. "In fact, I'll take it. That should make things a little easier."

He extended an arm, and she looped the duffle

bag's handles over it. With that out of the way, she came closer so they could hold on to each other, ensuring that she would not get lost during the brief but dangerous trip from Red River to Santa Fe.

Well, dangerous for her. Djinn traveled in this manner all the time, but if a human let go while mid-flight, so to speak, they would be lost in that space- and time-bending plane between worlds for all eternity.

This close, the soft coconut and amber smell of her shampoo drifted up to him from her damp hair, and Omar had to stop himself from bending closer so he could breathe it in even more deeply. He should not act so foolish, not when he would be saying goodbye to her in just a few short minutes.

Why did that thought hurt so much?

He could not shake his head, not when Olivia might notice the gesture and comment on it. No, he only told himself this was the way things must be. He might admit, somewhere in the deeper recesses of his heart, that he had enjoyed her company these past two days far more than he ever would have thought, and yet it was time for her to be with her own people.

Now he needed to fix in his mind the image of the empty highway as it stretched north of Santa Fe, of the rows of white headstones in the cemetery to one side and a wide, empty field on the other. He thought something else might have occupied that space once upon a time, but apparently, the djinn in the former capital city had decided to remove it, for whatever reason.

They materialized in that very spot, where Omar saw right away that the Santa Fe djinn were already there to await their visitors from Los Alamos. Or rather, Zahrias stood in the middle of the roadway, his younger brother Dani next to him, although there didn't seem to be any of the human members of the community present.

"Good morning," Zahrias said gravely.

"Good morning," Omar replied, knowing he needed to be polite, no matter what he might think of the Santa Fe djinn and the choices they had made. "This is Olivia Raskin."

"Thank you for arranging this," Olivia said. Whatever her inner feelings might have been regarding the situation, she looked calm enough, even slightly eager.

Or was that only a façade she'd put on to hide what she was truly thinking?

Omar couldn't say, and of course he couldn't ask her, not with Zahrias and Dani al-Harith standing there and watching everything they said.

"It is nothing," Zahrias said. "I am glad we have a place that will give you shelter." His gaze moved to Omar as he added, "That was a grievous tale

Aamir told me about your house. It seems Khamil al-Usar is more of a mad dog than ever."

No use arguing with that statement, not when Omar had thought much the same thing. "At least it seems we thwarted him by fleeing to Red River. And the house can be easily rebuilt."

Zahrias nodded. "I suppose so, but still, I cannot believe the elders will be inclined toward leniency when they recapture him, not when they learn he has indulged in a little casual destruction along the way. But there—I see the group from Los Alamos approaching."

Sure enough, a trio of vehicles had begun to drive down the incline that led to the spot where everyone stood. Although Omar was certainly not an expert on human vehicles and would never have been able to call out their makes and models, he at least could tell that a big yellow SUV had the lead position, while the other spots were occupied by equally large pickup trucks, one white, one black. He had heard that in town, most of Los Alamos' residents drove much smaller electric vehicles, but it seemed they still wanted to rely on more intimidating transport when they ventured outside the safety of the zone provided by Miles Odekirk's devices.

One of which they always brought with them to be safe so they'd have a traveling circle of protection no matter where they went. Omar still was not entirely sure how it all worked, but he and his brothers had surmised that they must shut their device off as soon as they were within Santa Fe's borders and therefore safe from attack by any reaver djinn who might be interested in seeking revenge.

If those sorts of djinn even existed anymore. As far as he knew, he and his brothers were the only ones still interested in carrying out that particular vendetta, in which case the residents of Los Alamos might have been taking precautions that no longer mattered.

The trio of vehicles slowed and came to a stop. One of the doors began to open...

...and out of nowhere, a wall of fire rose from the ground to block the yellow SUV, just as a fireball exploded on the ground only a few feet away from where Omar stood next to Olivia.

"Khamil!" he cried out, even though he saw no sign of the rogue djinn.

Not that it mattered. Only one man would be mad enough to attack here in the heart of the Santa Fe djinns' territory.

But it is not the heart, he thought. *It is the very border of their lands, and only Zahrias and Dani are here. Khamil must have decided this was the best place to attack.*

How Khamil had known exactly where they would all be at that particular time was a question that must be answered at some point, but for the moment, Omar could think of only one thing.

He had to get Olivia out of there.

No point in wasting any further breath; he knew Zahrias and Dani would do what they must. Also, a single second of hesitation might cost him his chance to escape, for he guessed that the humans were about to hurry back inside their vehicle and switch on the device, even though doing so was forbidden in djinn territory.

His arm went around Olivia's waist, and although she gasped, when her eyes met his, he saw the sudden comprehension in them, the realization that they had to get out of this place...and they had to get out now.

They blinked away, leaving Santa Fe behind them.

It had all happened so fast—the rain of fire, the frightened shouts of the people who'd just emerged from the vehicles. Omar's dark eyes meeting hers, urgent, and his arm around her middle as they disappeared into that swirling darkness and reemerged somewhere else.

Someplace *very* somewhere else, as the air was at least ten degrees warmer here. They stood on a wide loggia that overlooked empty fields and gardens that had once probably been carefully tended but had now run wild, with vines everywhere.

Despite its air of general neglect, something about the place seemed oddly familiar, as though she should know where they were even though she didn't think she'd ever been here before.

"Where are we?"

Omar looked down at her, unsmiling. Yes, they had escaped, but it had been another narrow one, and she could see why he might not be in the best of moods.

"It is a place that was once called Los Poblanos. A resort, I believe."

Right. Even drinks and an appetizer here would have been way out of her budget, but she knew about the resort, just like almost every other person who'd spent some time in Albuquerque would. She looked up from the fields and saw the familiar bulk of the Sandia Mountains off to the east.

If it had been nighttime and the world the way it used to be, she probably could have seen the light of the restaurant where she once worked resting on the peak like a fallen star.

She sent a curious glance up at Omar. "Why here?"

"Because it is a place I found while exploring the area, but I have no reason to believe Khalim even knows it exists. Also, I never spoke of it to a single soul, so there is no way anyone could possibly know we are here."

That made sense. Also, since this had been a resort once upon a time, that meant there would be plenty of places for her and Omar to crash while they tried to figure out what to do next.

"Follow me," he went on. "I know where we can go."

They made their way inside the building, which seemed like a maze to Olivia but which Omar appeared to know well enough. Past a room that she thought had once been the bar, clubby and lined with bookcases, past spaces she thought might have been used for meetings or even small weddings, down a hallway and then into a large, luxurious suite with a huge kiva fireplace in one corner and a kitchen that displayed gorgeous hand-painted tile on the backsplash. Wide windows overlooked a rose garden that was still lovely despite years of neglect and the dormancy of winter.

"This will be yours," Omar said as he went to the window. "And I will stay in the one just across the way."

He pointed to another space attached to the main building, not quite facing the suite he'd said should be hers.

Olivia experienced a moment of relief as she

realized he didn't intend for them to share the same room...quickly followed by a twinge of concern.

"Do you think it's safe for us to be separated like that?"

A moment as he contemplated the empty rose garden, and then he turned back toward her.

"As I told you, no one can possibly know we are here. The world is large and holds many hiding places, and we could have gone anywhere. A djinn has no way of determining where another djinn has traveled, so Khalim could not have followed us."

That was good to know, but still—the rogue djinn had managed to track them down in Placitas, even though it seemed as if they'd escaped his notice in Red River.

And then there was the way he'd attacked the caravan from Los Alamos, as if he'd somehow known they were going to be there at that exact hour. How in the world had he managed that?

Maybe it was a stupid question, but Olivia figured she should go ahead and ask it anyway.

"Are some djinn psychic or something? Because otherwise, how did Khalim know the group from Los Alamos was going to be there at that particular time?"

Omar didn't quite frown, but she could tell from the shift in his expression that he'd pondered the same conundrum and hadn't been able to come up with any satisfactory answers, either.

"No, we are not psychic," he said. "Family members who are close, like I am with my brothers, can communicate nonverbally, and I have heard that djinn can do much the same thing with their Chosen. However, that is not the same as being able to read another person's thoughts. And while we can sense when a human is nearby, that sixth sense cannot be the reason why Khalim was able to find us. No, there is something else going on here, something I can't quite put my finger on."

None of that was at all reassuring, although Olivia thought it interesting that djinn and their Chosen could speak to one another without saying anything aloud.

"But," Omar went on, "it also seems clear enough to me that he had no idea we were in Red River, or I'm sure he would have attacked us there when it was just the two of us, rather than risk such a thing when a much larger group was involved."

True, although she had a feeling that Khalim hadn't bothered to count the humans present at the meeting as much of a threat. He'd made sure a wall of flame separated the Los Alamos group from the Santa Fe djinn, but otherwise, it looked as though he'd planned to concentrate his attack in such a way that he would be able to get close to her, presumably so he could snatch her up and disappear.

Merely contemplating such a possibility was

enough to make her stomach clench in worry, even as she told herself that Omar was probably right and that Khalim surely would have attacked them in Red River if he'd had the chance.

And that meant they were probably safe here, too.

Still....

"Are there any other djinn in the area?" she asked then. "I mean, even if Khalim doesn't have any idea where we went, all it would take would be some other djinn spotting us and then passing that information on to him."

Omar came back over to her and, to her surprise, laid a hand on her arm for just a moment, as though he'd guessed she needed more than verbal reassurances. "As far as I know, there is no one at all in the greater Albuquerque area. Qadim al-Syan was granted land here, but he relinquished it when he took a human woman as his Chosen and moved to Santa Fe. Otherwise, I was the only djinn around for miles and miles, and obviously, you know where I am."

He smiled a little as he spoke those words, a genuine smile, not one that was forced or indulgent or a little too far into smirk territory. It made him look different, almost approachable. Still handsome in a way that was clearly not human because he was far too perfect, but for the first time, Olivia thought she could see why a human might not be utterly intimidated by one of the immortal elementals.

"Yes, I do," she said lightly, hoping that nothing of what she'd just been thinking had revealed itself in her expression. "And it's good to know there isn't anyone else around who could give away our location."

"This situation is not permanent," he replied. "I need to communicate with my brother and let him know we are all right. Then, perhaps, we can come up with a plan to neutralize Khalim so we are not always looking over our shoulders."

Yes, it was definitely no fun to feel like a hunted animal. Then again, she reflected as she glanced around her surroundings, at the room that certainly wasn't ostentatious but still possessed the quiet sort of luxury that indicated it must have been very, very expensive back in the day, not that many hunted animals got to live in five-star hotels.

"This place once had a fine restaurant," Omar went on. "Let us meet there for an early dinner. In the meantime, you can familiarize yourself with your suite and some of the grounds—as long as you do not wander too far—and I can discuss the situation with Aamir and see what he has to say."

Even an early dinner felt a long way off, but Olivia got the feeling he was trying to let her know that he didn't intend to babysit her every single minute while they were stuck at Los Poblanos.

Which was fine—she'd never expected that of him. She could explore a little, maybe go into the library-style bar and find something to read among all the volumes that crowded the shelves there.

"Six-thirty?" she suggested, and he nodded.

"I will see you then."

She almost said, *It's a date,* but she knew it wasn't. No, it was just the two of them sitting down to share a meal because eating by themselves didn't make a lot of sense.

Instead, she managed a smile as he told her goodbye and left the suite through the door that opened on the courtyard so he could make his way to the other room around the corner. As he walked through the overgrown garden, it seemed to Olivia that the plants appeared to grow pruned and tidy, the long yellow grass trimmed to a more manageable length.

Earth elemental, she thought. Even though he'd told her that very thing just the day before yesterday, it was only now as she watched this subtle display of his abilities that she realized there was a lot more to controlling an element than simply using it as a weapon.

No, it could be something beautiful, just like he was.

She let out a breath and closed the door.

Chapter 12

OMAR OPENED THE DOOR TO THE SUITE HE intended to use during the time they would be here at Los Poblanos and gave an approving nod. Perhaps it was not quite as large as the one he'd given Olivia, but it was still beautifully appointed, with a king-size bed in a black iron frame and a large window that overlooked the garden, now a bit tidier than it had been when they'd first arrived. And while it appeared somewhat dusty—normal dust, not the kind left behind when the Heat consumed a human body—that was a bit of housekeeping he could take care of with a single thought.

Too bad it was December, and therefore the trees were bare and the flowers dormant for the winter. And while djinn did not have to worry about the temperature unless it was utterly freezing or boiling hot, he knew it was chilly enough outside that Olivia would not want to sit out there for any great length of time.

Which was just as well. He might have left her to her own devices for the rest of the afternoon, but he knew he had much to do.

So he sat down on the small leather couch in the sitting area and shut his eyes. Perhaps it would have been easier to go to Santa Fe and speak to his brother in person, but Omar knew he could not risk such a thing, not when he had no idea how Khalim had been able to track them down. He would not even tell Aamir exactly where he and Olivia were, only that they were safe.

Aamir.

His brother's response was so immediate that Omar guessed he had been waiting for this contact.

You are safe?

We are, Omar assured him. *I did not stop to think, only took Olivia to a place where Khalim could not reach us.*

And where is that?

It is better not to say, Omar replied.

A small silence. Was Aamir offended at this apparent lack of trust, or had he only paused to consider his brother's words, realizing there was no such thing as being over-cautious in such a situation?

It seemed the latter, for he said, *I am glad you were able to find refuge somewhere. As for us, no one suffered any true injuries, although it was close for Brent Sutherland, the man driving the SUV. They have all gone back to Los Alamos, and I am not sure they have any appetite for venturing forth any time soon.*

Odekirk's devices should protect them, Omar pointed out.

True, but if they are coming to Santa Fe, they have to shut the things off when they enter the town. Since Khalim knew to attack them at that moment of weakness, one can see why they would feel safer remaining in Los Alamos for the time being.

Making it that much more difficult to get Olivia to them, although Omar decided to set that worry aside for now. He did not think it would be much of a hardship to shelter here at Los Poblanos for a few days while they all regrouped and came up with a plan for what they should do next.

Zahrias did get a request from Miles Odekirk, however, Aamir went on, and Omar could feel his brows lifting in surprise.

What does he want?

Something that sounded like a chuckle in his brother's inner voice, and Aamir replied, *It seems that your description of the way both you and Khalim lost access to your powers at the farm where Olivia Raskin was living has piqued the scientist's interest. I have heard that he has been working for a long time to discover a way to have his devices block a djinn's power without causing any weakness or other debilitating side effects. Whatever is happening at the farm, he is hopeful it might aid him in finally discovering an answer to the problem.*

Omar was not quite so sure about that, but because he knew almost nothing about how the devices actually worked, he didn't see the harm in allowing Miles Odekirk to investigate the situation.

What does he need from me?

Only the location of the farm where Olivia was living. It sounds as though he plans to go there to investigate for himself.

On the surface, this did not sound like the wisest of plans, not with Khalim out there, waiting to strike. But of course the scientist would have one of his devices with him, thus ensuring that the rogue djinn would stay far away...or would soon regret coming close if he abandoned caution in favor of revenge.

Also, even though Omar did not much like to admit such a thing to himself, he knew deep down that Khalim had attacked this morning precisely because he had known Olivia would be there. He wanted to take her so he might prove his dominance.

And that was never going to happen.

At any rate, Khalim would not risk giving his location away by going after Miles Odekirk and anyone else he might have brought along with him on his scientific expedition. The rogue djinn had to know that word had gone out among their people to pass along any information they might have regarding his current whereabouts, which meant he would only emerge from wherever he was hiding when his target was within reach.

Well, the location is simple enough, Omar told his brother, even as he fixed in his mind an image of the farm with the juniper-covered hills to either side, the white-painted territorial-style house with its tin roof and the words "Miller Farm" spelled out in heavy wrought iron above the gate.

I see it, Aamir said. *I am sure that is enough information for Odekirk to find the place. Whether or not he will actually discover any useful information, I cannot say, although I will admit that I am somewhat curious to learn exactly what is happening there.* A pause, and then he added, *I cannot help thinking you would be safer here in Santa Fe.*

Perhaps he and Olivia would be. On the other hand, being surrounded by other djinn was no guarantee of safety. And besides....

It is a place for djinn and their Chosen, he said, knowing how curt his mental voice sounded. *It would not be suitable for us to be there. As I said, we are in a safe place now. We will not leave our current sanctuary unless it is proven somehow that it is not as safe as I had thought.*

Aamir did not answer right away, most likely

because he was trying to think of another argument that might make his brother change his mind. Omar was set on this, however. If it had been at all possible, he would have taken Olivia to Los Alamos himself. Circumstances being what they were, however, it seemed the best thing to do was to remain in a neutral location.

He also had the impression that Aamir considered these conversations on the logistics of keeping Olivia Raskin safe to be some kind of reconciliation, and Omar was definitely not ready to acknowledge such a thing. They were speaking because they had a common problem that needed to be solved. It certainly did not mean he had forgiven Aamir—or Jamal—for the way they had so casually abandoned their beliefs.

At length, though, Aamir said, *I can see your mind is set on this, so I will not press you. But thank you for providing the information about the farm in Cedar Crest. I can only hope it might lead to a development that may be beneficial for all involved.*

I hope so as well, he said, knowing he sounded far too formal.

At least his brother seemed to realize there was no way he could convince Omar to come to Santa Fe, and for the time being, they had no further need to communicate with one another.

The inner dialogue concluded, he got up from

the sofa and went to gaze out into the garden. Yes, it did look much happier, although even a djinn could not speed the seasons along so it might be glorious spring rather than the beginning of winter.

But he had helped a little, which he supposed was the important thing.

He wondered where Olivia was. Not out in the courtyard garden, or he would have spied her right away. Perhaps she was exploring the historic building where their suites were located, or perhaps she had gone to look at the other outdoor areas. A twinge of worry went through him at that thought, although he knew she was smart and careful enough not to venture too far.

When he stepped out of his suite, though, he immediately sensed her presence in the bar-cum-library that occupied the northeast corner of the building, and so he knew she was perfectly safe.

Or at least as safe as she could be when neither of them knew exactly where Khalim was...or what he might be plotting next.

As best he could, Omar brushed that thought aside. Rather than stand here and brood, he would go to the separate building that had once housed the resort's restaurant and see what he might do with it.

He wanted their first meal here at Los Poblanos to be a memorable one.

To Olivia's surprise, the afternoon passed more quickly than she'd thought it would. Maybe it was just that it was almost impossible not to feel safe in the dark, clubby environment in the hotel's bar, with its eclectic collection of antique and modern pieces and the friendly scent of old books all around...or maybe it was more that she was all too glad to lose herself in a book and not have to worry about the dangers that lurked outside Los Poblanos' serene grounds.

In fact, the transition from daylight to dark was so subtle that she barely noticed it, although she did see how Omar had made sure to have strategic lights turned on both inside the building and outside on the grounds so she wouldn't have any trouble finding her way. Those lights weren't very bright—she guessed that no one would even be able to tell people were here at the resort at all, thanks to the way the property was ringed with tall pines—but at least she wouldn't have to stumble her way in the dark.

The thought had crossed her mind that maybe she should change for dinner, but she pushed it aside. The last thing she wanted was to make it seem as though she thought this meal would be anything special. Besides, it wasn't as if she had anything even moderately dressy to change into.

Yes, Omar had provided some new jeans and sweaters that were nicer than the ones she'd been wearing at the farm, but they were still simple, basic pieces that normally wouldn't have been suitable for dinner here.

However, she did go to her room so she could brush her hair and put on some tinted lip balm, just so she'd look a little more put together than she had after they'd first arrived here. So far, she hadn't seen anything of her djinn companion and didn't know what he'd been up to, although she knew he wouldn't have gone far, not when he'd been taking such care to keep her safe from Khalim al-Usar.

If the situation hadn't been so deadly serious, she might have thought it was funny. Omar, the avowed hater of all humankind, playing babysitter to one lone human woman whom no one seemed to know what to do with.

"Babysitter" didn't seem like the right term to use, though. She might have made some mistakes in her life, but she'd been taking care of herself with no one else's help for a very long time now.

Bodyguard, then. That seemed about right for someone whose attitude toward her seemed fiercely protective and impersonal at the same time.

The clock in her room said it was about twenty minutes after six. She had no idea whether it was at all accurate, but the time corresponded more or less to the level of darkness outside and the time of year, so she figured she'd go with it. The ticking clock must have been Omar's doing, the same with the lights and the impressively unobtrusive heating system, and she thought that must have been his way of trying to make her feel more comfortable here. After all, a nearly immortal being certainly didn't need to worry about the time the way a human would.

Out through the courtyard and along a walkway illuminated by low-slung landscape lighting. Again, it wasn't anything that could be seen from a distance, but the subtle lighting allowed her to find her way from the main building to the one several hundred yards distant that housed what had been Campo, the resort's restaurant. Some of her fellow employees at 10-3 on top of Sandia Peak had viewed Campo as a sort of rival, since both restaurants offered fine dining in an unforgettable setting, and yet Olivia had never thought of the two places as being equivalent. People went to them for entirely different reasons—10-3 for the breathtaking views and extensive wine list, Campo for its unique farm-to-table cuisine and historic location.

She'd never eaten at Campo, of course. Like so many other things in her former life, it had been way outside her budget.

Soft lights gleamed from inside, beckoning her into the interior of the restaurant. The place had a sort of farmhouse industrial vibe, clean and under-stated, and Omar had eschewed most of the over-head lighting and instead placed simple white pillar candles everywhere, each of them centered on an equally simple black iron plate. One table in a corner had been set with plain white dishes and a centerpiece of another candle encircled by a wreath of what she thought were bay leaves.

It was the exact opposite of fussy, and she gave an approving nod as she walked toward the table. Apparently sensing she was there, Omar emerged from a back room she guessed must be the kitchen.

"I trust it was not too difficult to find your way here."

"Not at all," she replied. "The landscape lights helped." She paused there to glance around the room. It had been designed to accommodate some thirty or forty diners, but it still didn't feel glaringly empty to have only the two of them there, and in fact had an airiness she might not have been able to experience on a crowded Saturday night. "This looks lovely."

His expression was almost approving. "I thought it wiser not to have the place too brightly lit, just in case. The trees block a great deal of the light, and I can use my powers to dim it even further, but still, no reason to tempt fate."

"None at all," she agreed.

"Then go ahead and sit," he said. "I trust you are hungry."

Considering she hadn't eaten since breakfast, she was. True, it had been a very big breakfast, the kind she hadn't enjoyed since well before the Heat changed the world, but still, even the heartiest omelet in the world could only hold off hunger pangs for so long.

"I could eat," she said with a grin, and headed to the closer of the chairs with a place setting in front of it. Since she knew better than to wait for Omar to pull out the seat for her, she went ahead and sat down.

Immediately afterward, he followed suit. As always, he wore his dark djinn robes, and it certainly didn't seem as though he'd expended any extra effort on his appearance.

Then again, why would he need to? He always looked model-perfect no matter what might be going on.

"I am glad you are hungry," he said politely. "And although I know we could have anything we liked, I thought it might be interesting to have something of what they once served here in the restaurant. While I never ate here, I have studied the menu, and I feel confident that I can re-create the same dishes."

Just as he finished speaking, a plate appeared in front of Olivia, one filled with probably the most delectable-looking salad she'd ever seen, with field greens topped with roasted apple slices and pistachios and crumbles of bleu cheese. At the same time, her wine glass was filled with a light white wine.

"Chardonnay," Omar explained. "All the wines were still here in the cellar, so I did not even have to go looking for them."

"Handy," she said with a smile. As she'd been reading this afternoon, the thought had crossed her mind that she could get up and make herself a cocktail if she liked, since all the necessary spirits still occupied the bar in the far corner of the room. However, she'd decided against doing so in the end, partly because she had never been a huge fan of mixed drinks in the first place, and partly because she'd decided it wasn't a good idea to make herself tipsy when she knew they'd probably be having wine with dinner.

But, as Omar had pointed out, all those bottles of wine were still here. No refrigeration, of course, but if they'd been stored in a real cellar, then they should still have been in pretty decent shape. And Los Poblanos seemed like the kind of place that would have an actual wine cellar and not a bunch of refrigeration units.

She reached for her glass, and Omar lifted his as well.

"To finding a safe haven," she said, and he

inclined his head toward her, a gleam of what looked like approval in his dark eyes.

"A good toast."

They clinked glasses, and she took a small sip. Yes, light and not oaky at all, with a flavor redolent of the apples that had been mixed into her salad. No wonder it had been the suggested pairing when the restaurant was still operating.

When she helped herself to her first bite of her salad, it was just as good as it looked. Not that she was too surprised, since Omar had already proved to her that he could conjure some damn tasty food.

"This is wonderful," she said.

"Yes, it turned out quite well," he agreed. "And it is not anything I have had before, which is always pleasant."

Olivia could see that. When you lived as long as a djinn did, it would be hard to avoid repeating meals, and something new might be exactly what he wanted.

She was glad the menu at Los Poblanos had been able to provide a little novelty.

They ate in silence for a moment, and then Omar said, "It seems that Miles Odekirk is interested in investigating your farm."

"He is?" she responded, startled. "What for?"

"Because he wants to know what caused both Khalim and me to lose the use of our powers while we were there. Aamir says it sounds as though he hopes it might be something he could use in his research."

All this was delivered in a dispassionate, almost dry tone, but Olivia was still able to pick up the hint of disapproval underneath. If it hadn't been for Miles Odekirk and his devices, Omar and his two older brothers would have been much more successful in following their goal of eradicating any human survivors.

She didn't want to think about that, though, not when she was sitting in such lovely surroundings, not when her djinn companion was being pleasant and almost non-threatening.

True, he had never posed a threat to her, thanks to her sex. At the same time, she couldn't quite allow herself to forget how much blood must have stained the shapely hand that was even now reaching for his wine glass so he might have another sip.

Why did that thought not bother her nearly as much as it probably should?

"That sounds like kind of a long shot to me," she said, and also drank some of her wine.

"Perhaps it is," Omar allowed. "Because I know very little about how the devices work, I cannot comment on whether Dr. Odekirk is going on a wild-goose chase or not. Still, the phenomenon seems quite unprecedented, so I can see why some research might be in order. I suppose if he finds anything, Aamir will let me know."

It sure seemed as though the nonverbal communication Omar shared with his brother was a helpful way of getting up-to-date information without having to let anyone know where they were hunkered down. At the same time, Olivia couldn't quite ignore the frisson of unease that went through her.

Exactly how long was Omar planning on staying here?

As long as it took, she guessed. Djinn didn't have the same time sense as humans, probably didn't get impatient as often just because they could afford to play the long game. While she thought she could understand that outlook—and even respect it somewhat as a welcome change from the constant hustle of human life—she also didn't know if she wanted to stay in hiding here for weeks or months...or years.

Then again, what else did she have to do with herself? Did it really matter whether she was living a quiet life here at Los Poblanos or back at the farm?

Deep down, she knew there was a huge difference. In Cedar Crest, she'd been alone except for the animals. Here, she had Omar with her, and the mathematics of the situation had changed greatly. Under other circumstances, she could have done her best to ignore those odd little twinges when she noticed again how breathtakingly handsome he was, or found herself unexpectedly warmed by something he had said.

But faced with the realization that they might be here for quite a long time, she found herself wondering how long she could maintain her façade of indifference.

For as long as it takes, she told herself. *Compared to some of the other stuff you've been through, this will be a walk in the park.*

And although the thought crossed her mind that if they were going to be here for some time, she should have Omar go find Zorro at least, if not the goats, she realized right away that wouldn't be feasible. He would never leave her alone, for one thing, and for another, he simply couldn't risk returning to the farm, not when they didn't know where Khalim might be skulking around.

"It will be interesting to know for sure what was going on with your powers," she said, doing her best to sound casual and engaged at the same time. "I wonder if it had anything to do with the earthquake."

At once, Omar's brows drew together. "You felt it, too?"

"Yes," she said. "The night before you showed up at the farm. A decent shake, but I don't know how strong it actually was. I suppose someone from California would have thought it wasn't that big a deal, but I know I've never felt anything like it."

He didn't respond right away, his brows still drawn together in thought. The moment seemed to pass, however, and his tone was neutral enough as he responded, "I would say it was something around a five on the Richter scale, perhaps a little more."

Olivia stared at him in astonishment, forgetting to maintain her neutral act. "You know about the Richter scale?"

"Of course," he said imperturbably, then helped himself to a bite of roasted apple and bleu cheese. "I am an earth elemental, after all, and I thought it amusing to acquaint myself with the ways you mortals attempted to measure the movements of that element."

She supposed she could see why he might have wanted to divert himself with a study of the way humans approached geology. "Do djinn ever cause earthquakes?" she asked.

"Sometimes," he said. "When we settle disputes, we use our elemental powers against our opponents. However, the great majority of earthquakes are exactly what they appear to be—movements of the earth as its plates attempt to slide past or under one another." A pause there as an amused light flickered in his obsidian eyes. "I certainly did not cause this latest earthquake. They are not common in this part of the world, but neither are they completely unprecedented. Some might have said this region was due for one."

No, she supposed not. When she was a really little girl, maybe around five or six, Albuquerque had a small earthquake that was about a 4.1, and she remembered how shaken—no pun intended—everyone had been by that one. To have something now that was more than a 5 was definitely not the norm.

Then again, the whole world had been pretty much not normal for the past four years, so she knew they'd have to roll with this one just like they had everything else.

"As to your question about whether the earthquake might somehow be connected to the loss of powers that both Khalim and I experienced, I have no idea," Omar went on. He paused there, brows drawing together to signal his displeasure with the situation. Olivia got the feeling that he hadn't had many times in his life when he'd had to admit to ignorance and wasn't too happy to be doing so now, especially to a mere human.

"Well, I suppose we'll just have to see what Miles Odekirk digs up," she said, figuring it was probably better to be diplomatic and not press the issue.

Omar didn't look exactly relieved, although he

said, "Are you done with your salad? We may as well move on to the next course."

As a matter of fact, she was, although she wasn't sure she appreciated his tone. He made their dinner sound as if it was something he needed to get over with rather than a meal they both had plenty of time to sit with and savor.

But she'd had lots of training in holding her tongue rather than sparking a confrontation, so she only said, "Yes, I'm done. It was delicious."

He gave a perfunctory nod, and the dishes that had once held their salads vanished, to be replaced by the most gorgeous ribeye she'd ever seen, accompanied by grilled vegetables and roasted potatoes. At the same time, her wine glass also disappeared, and another one, this time filled with red wine, appeared at her place setting.

"Perhaps I should have inquired as to your preferences," Omar said, possibly noting the way she stared down at the steak rather than picking up her knife and fork. "Do you not eat red meat?"

"Oh, no, I do," she replied quickly. "Or at least, I used to. I suppose I was just staring because I haven't had a steak in years."

Years and years. Olivia tried to remember the last time she'd allowed herself such an indulgence and honestly couldn't recall. Maybe on her birthday the year before the Dying? Her friends from school had taken her out, trying to cheer her up after a nasty breakup, but no, they didn't have steak, but instead went for a big Mediterranean feast at a kabob place nearby that had an affordable buffet.

It was probably on one of her dates with Ron, although she didn't want to think about him, or the havoc he'd caused in her life before she found the courage to end things.

"No, I suppose you wouldn't," Omar remarked. "I don't recall seeing any cattle on your farm."

Olivia shook her head. "No cows. And even if I'd had them, I would've used them for milk and butter. I've gotten pretty good at skinning rabbits the past four years, but I don't think I would've been up to slaughtering a cow."

Definitely not. Even catching rabbits and quail had been hard for her at first, but the one time she'd tried to go without any kind of meat had only left her feeling sick and dizzy, and realizing she couldn't sustain herself on that kind of diet without the sort of supplements and complex grains she definitely didn't have on hand.

Something that looked like the beginning of a smile touched Omar's mouth. Even that hint of one utterly changed his features, made him look far more approachable, and Olivia found herself smiling in return.

When he wasn't being an utter asshole, he was kind of charming.

"That would certainly be a lot to expect of anyone," he said. "But I'm sure it was good for you to have the goats. That goat milk butter you gave me at the farm was surprisingly tasty."

"I'm glad you liked it," she said. "Although it wasn't nearly as good as this steak. What's in the sauce, anyway?"

He explained that it was a demi-glace made with chile and lavender from the farm here at the resort, and after that, the discussion moved to the other items he'd found on the menu at Los Poblanos, and what they might like to try for dinner the next evening. An innocuous topic, she supposed, but at the same time, she found herself wondering yet again what she would do if they had to stay here for an extended period.

Well, she'd do what she always did—figure out a way to make it work. No one could say she hadn't had plenty of practice.

Dinner concluded with tiny ramekins of rich custard topped with fruit that shouldn't have been in season for months. Olivia hadn't thought anything could be better than the steak she'd just consumed, but after tasting those luscious raspberries and blackberries, she wasn't sure. She'd tried to grow strawberries at the farm but hadn't had much luck, and although she hadn't been completely without fruit thanks to the apple and apricot trees in the area, it had been years and years since she'd tasted anything close to this.

After dinner, they walked back to the main building where their suites were located. Omar waited until she had opened the door to her room, then said briefly, "Goodnight," before heading to his own quarters around the corner.

And that, Olivia thought, was that. She closed the door and wanted to shake her head at herself. Exactly what had she expected? For him to lean in and kiss her goodnight?

There was a joke. He hadn't said a single thing at dinner, hadn't sent a single glance her way, that would have indicated he had any romantic interest in her at all.

Because he didn't, and she didn't want there to be. Yes, he was the best-looking man she'd ever seen, and he'd showed an odd protective streak that she definitely hadn't been expecting, but it was a long way from there to romance. They were stuck here together, and that was the end of it.

With those no-nonsense thoughts to buoy her up, she went to wash her face and get ready for bed.

Problem was, she didn't know for sure whether she believed them.

Chapter 13

THERE HAD BEEN THE BRIEFEST INSTANT just as he'd told Olivia goodnight that he'd found his gaze straying to her mouth, to those full lips that always seemed to possess their own luscious color and had no need of cosmetics. It was a beautiful mouth, one that most men would have said begged to be kissed. And in that instant, he'd had the sudden urge to bend down and kiss her, to feel their lushness for himself.

Reason had prevailed, of course, and nothing had happened. Now that he was back in his room, he could safely berate himself for such a ridiculous moment of weakness. What in the world had he been thinking?

The logical response to such a question was that he hadn't been thinking at all. He'd allowed instinct to rear its ugly head, if only for a second or two, but that was enough. Olivia Raskin was a human and therefore could hold no possible interest for him.

And yet, she had looked very lovely tonight, in that dark purple sweater that seemed to enhance the greenish hues of her eyes and show off the interesting highlights in her deep brown hair.

Which mattered not one whit. He could acknowledge that for a human, she was quite beautiful. She still could not begin to compare to the women of his people.

Not that he'd had much to do with them of late, either. Once the plan had been set to eradicate humankind—and once his parents had taken the draught of the dark sleep, leaving their three sons behind—he had had very little time to think of anything else other than the coming reckoning. He had been with a woman, Ayanna, who had pleaded with him not to let his heart harden beyond repair. They had argued, and she had left, for women of the djinn were powerful beings in their own right and certainly had no need of male companionship to make them whole and fulfilled. Even his brothers had told him that he should attempt to reconcile with her, for they seemed to think she had been a good influence, but he would hear nothing of it.

In fact, Olivia reminded him somewhat of Ayanna—not in looks so much, for his djinn lover had been very fair for one of their people, with honey-colored hair and sea-blue eyes—but more in her quiet diplomacy, her way of trying to make the way smooth no matter what else might be transpiring in her life.

Well, that must have been the reason for that troubling flash of need. A little too much wine, a realization somewhere inside that Olivia's personality bore a passing resemblance to that of a woman he'd once cared for. Those circumstances had been enough to make some part of him think it might be desirable to kiss her. And now that he'd made his way through the puzzle, he would have to take care to avoid such feelings in the future. He still had no idea how long they might be trapped here together, but that mattered little.

His will and his heart were hardened, and he would never allow himself such a moment of weakness again.

Olivia slept much better than she'd thought she would, although she supposed it would be hard to have a bad night's sleep on such a comfortable mattress, on such silky-smooth sheets. The morning sun shining down on the courtyard was what finally woke her, since the draperies at the window had been placed there more for privacy than to make any real attempt at blocking the light.

She sat up and glanced around, reacquainting herself with the suite, then got out of bed and went to the window so she could pull the semi-sheer curtains aside and take a look at the day. As she'd thought, it was bright and sunny, with just a few clouds floating by, the sort of day she had always looked forward to, shining with possibilities.

Not that she was expecting a lot of possibilities today. It seemed they truly were safe here, that Khalim hadn't figured out where they were hiding, but she and Omar were still stuck at Los Poblanos until the djinn in Santa Fe were able to track down the escaped prisoner.

Then again, there were far worse places to be trapped, especially since Omar was keeping the heat and the lights on—as well as the apparently endless hot water she used to wash away some of her worry and fear. The solar water heater at the farm had done a pretty decent job, but it was nothing like this.

After that hugely indulgent shower, she got dressed and used the blow dryer supplied in the bathroom to dry her hair, another luxury she hadn't allowed herself very often during the past few years. By the time she was done, it was nearly nine o'clock, according to the clock in her suite, and she wondered if her djinn companion was going to give her grief over how long it had taken her to get ready that morning. He didn't seem like the type to have much patience for dawdling.

But when she emerged from her suite and headed off to find him, she didn't have too far to go. The rich scent of coffee drew her to the bar, and that was where she found Omar, drinking a large cup of Italian roast and reading a leatherbound book he must have found on the shelves there.

"Coffee?" he inquired, and she nodded.

"That would be great."

In the next instant, an off-white ceramic mug that was a match to the one he held appeared in her hand. "Cream or sugar?"

"Cream, please." That was how she'd drunk it on the farm; sugar was too precious a resource to waste on daily cups of coffee, but the goats had provided plenty of milk, so she'd gotten used to taking it that way.

At once, the liquid in her mug shifted from deep brown-black to a warm cocoa color, just the way she liked it. She wouldn't inquire as to how Omar had known the exact amount of cream to add to her coffee. More djinn magic, probably.

He set down his book. "I found no sign of

anyone coming near last night, so I do think we've successfully given Khalim the slip. Wherever he is, I am sure he's not pleased."

Probably not. There had been an amused smugness in Omar's voice that told her he was all too happy to have caused their adversary some additional frustration, and she was just fine with the situation as well.

Except for the part where she didn't know when they'd be able to get away from here…or what might happen between them if they remained at Los Poblanos for any real length of time.

"So, what's on the agenda for today?" she asked, seating herself on the same large leather couch he occupied. Not right next to him, of course, but still, she could see the way his mouth tightened and guessed he wasn't too thrilled by her proximity.

Well, she'd just gotten out of the shower and had used the excellent in-house soap and shampoo and conditioner, so it wasn't as though she smelled bad. Omar would just have to suck it up.

"There is no agenda," he said coolly. "Or rather, you may do what you wish to amuse yourself. I thought we could have breakfast in here, though. You need only tell me what you would like to have."

God, so many things. Eggs benedict, or huevos rancheros, or an omelet she'd had once that had been rich with brie and caramelized onions. Pancakes...French toast...Belgian waffles.

Actually, a waffle sounded great. One with whipped cream and strawberries, and bacon on the side.

She relayed her request to Omar, whose expression grew sour. However, he didn't tell her it was impossible—she guessed not too many things were impossible for a djinn—and a moment later, the breakfast she'd asked for appeared on the coffee table before them. Right afterward, a second plate, this one laden with eggs and ham and a biscuit, popped into existence next to her Belgian waffle.

At least she knew she wouldn't starve here— the exact opposite, actually, which meant that whatever else she planned to do with her time, she needed to take a brisk walk around the grounds to work off some of those calories.

They both picked up the forks that had appeared alongside the plates and got to work on their breakfasts. Neither of them said a word, but Olivia was fine with that. She'd always been a naturally quiet person, and people who felt like they had to constantly chatter about anything and everything drove her up the wall after a while.

Then again, some might have remarked that Omar's silence bordered on taciturnity, but she wasn't going to force it. She could already tell he was less than thrilled to be stuck keeping watch on her for the foreseeable future, so the best thing for her to do was to be as unobjectionable as possible.

Once they were done eating, though, and their plates had vanished back to wherever they'd come from, Omar said, "I am going to take a walk around the grounds. I have no reason to believe anyone has come near here, but still, I want to check to make sure."

"Do you mind if I tag along?" Olivia responded, a little surprised by her boldness. Then again, she'd already planned to roam around a bit to work off some of her breakfast. It didn't seem like that strange a request to her.

For just a moment, Omar's brow furrowed, but then he gave a shrug that felt a bit forced. "I suppose not. It will be good for you to get some exercise."

He got up from the couch, and although Olivia experienced a brief surge of irritation, she couldn't help being amused by his comment. Was he also worried that she might start to gain weight if she didn't stay active?

To be honest, there wasn't much chance of that. She'd been thin her entire life, although maybe that was more because she never got all that much to eat than because she had a naturally fast metabolism.

Rather than respond directly to the remark, she got up from the couch as well and followed him outside. The day felt especially bright after the purposely dim spaces in the hotel's bar, and she found herself blinking.

"Some sunglasses?" Omar asked, his tone a little too solicitous, as if he was secretly glad to see this further evidence of human weakness.

"That would be great," she replied.

At once, a pair of dark glasses settled on her nose. She couldn't see exactly what they were, but, judging by their weight and distortion-free lenses, she guessed they weren't some cheap gas station knockoffs. But she had to admit they helped a lot to block the glare, making the walk much more pleasant.

It was chilly out, although with the sun shining down on them, she thought she should manage all right in just her sweater. Much better to be here than up in Santa Fe, where she knew she'd never be able to take a walk at this time of year without putting on some kind of outer layer.

Or Los Alamos, she thought. She'd never been there, but she knew it was about as far north as Santa Fe, and even higher in elevation. Most likely, its climate wasn't too friendly, either.

Nothing she needed to worry about right now, since it didn't look as though she would be moving there anytime soon.

They walked across the former parking lot, which had a few cars abandoned there, not as many as one might have expected, considering the way vehicles were left in place wherever people expired from the deadly fever. But then, this wasn't the local Target or grocery store. People had come here for rest and relaxation, and as soon as news of the terrible plague began to spread, whoever had been staying at the resort had probably fled for home. These cars very well might have belonged to La Posada's employees.

That thought saddened Olivia. The Dying was such a huge and overwhelming tragedy that even now, her mind didn't quite want to absorb the enormity of it, but she hated the thought of these people perishing far away from their homes and loved ones.

"It's very quiet," she said, mostly to distract herself from thoughts of a tragedy no one could have possibly predicted.

"It is," Omar agreed. He obviously didn't need sunglasses, because his head was lifted toward the sun as he gazed around them, taking in the landscape. Painted in sunlight, his profile appeared particularly fine this morning. "And I honestly do not think Khalim has come anywhere near here. I see no sign that anything larger than a coyote has come onto the grounds since we arrived."

Olivia didn't know for sure whether she liked the idea of packs of coyotes roaming around Los Poblanos, but even if there had been more than one of the wild animals, they didn't seem to have come near the buildings. Most likely, they'd only been passing through on the way to the river, since the Rio Grande was located less than a mile away from the spot where she and Omar now stood.

"That's a relief," she replied. "Still, it's too bad that you can't set up some sort of djinn alarm system to warn us of any trespassers."

A corner of his mouth curved upward. "No need for anything so clumsy. I have made it so I will know if a djinn comes here unannounced."

That comment made Olivia slant a glance up at him. "What...like a magic spell or something?"

"'Or something,'" Omar agreed. "Not magic in the way humans think of it. More that I have allowed my senses to become focused on the perimeter of this place. As I said, if anyone else tries to come here, I will know."

Well, that was handy. It seemed as if every day she learned something new about the djinn—not that hard, she supposed, since before she met Omar, she'd known they existed and that was about it. But now she knew for sure that they bled like humans and could be hurt, even if they healed a hundred times faster than any human being could hope to.

And she knew their smiles could be just as brilliant and blinding as the sun overhead.

Oh, stop it, she scolded herself. *Just stop it.*

Maybe her brain and her will had gotten soft during those four years of isolation, but she was still damned if she was going to make a fool of herself.

"That's good," she said lightly. "Then I'll stop worrying."

"I did not tell you to do that," Omar replied. "Some worry is good. Too much will make you sloppy."

Olivia sent another sideways look up at him, although she couldn't tell for sure whether he was joking or not. But she supposed he was right in a way. If you spent all your time and energy fretting over every disaster that might possibly occur, you were a lot less likely to see it when it finally did arrive.

"I'll keep that in mind," she said.

They walked in silence after that, moving along the borders of the property, but not so close that anyone standing outside would have been able to detect their progress. Eventually, though, Omar turned back toward the main building, and Olivia couldn't help being a little relieved. As much as she'd wanted to get out there and get her legs moving, they'd probably covered a couple of miles when all was said and done, and she thought that was enough exercise for the morning.

"We did not have lunch yesterday," Omar said once they were back inside. "That was an oversight.

We can meet at twelve-thirty for our midday meal, and then at six-thirty for dinner."

It seemed a sensible enough plan, so Olivia only nodded. It left them both to their own devices for quite some time, though, and she wondered how many days might pass before she got tired of reading for hours on end. She supposed she could ask Omar for some crochet supplies so she could work on a project while she was here, but some part of her wasn't all right with that idea, as though doing so would feel like surrendering to the notion that they might be spending days or even weeks at Los Poblanos.

"At Campo?" was all she asked.

"Yes," Omar replied. "That is the best place for us to eat. I will see you there at twelve-thirty."

And then he was gone, walking with purposeful strides in the direction of his suite. Exactly what he planned to do there, she didn't know, but she supposed that was his problem.

For herself, it looked like it was time for her to go back to the library/bar.

As she went, she did her best to hold back a sigh.

That had gone quite well. Their conversation had been utterly unremarkable, and he had seen nothing in Olivia's expression nor heard anything in her voice to make him think she was harboring some sort of unrequited feelings for him. At another time, he might have been slightly annoyed to realize that a human did not find him attractive, but for now, it was better to know they would not face any true complications during their time here.

Well, emotional ones, at any rate.

It was true that he had seen absolutely no sign of Khalim—or anyone else—coming anywhere near the resort, but Omar still could not allow himself to relax completely. The rogue djinn had caught him unaware at his home, and he did not want a repeat of that unfortunate event. At some point, he supposed he would have to go back and rebuild, or perhaps he might make a case to the elders that the site was tainted and he would prefer that they provide him with a different house. However, those actions would have to wait until the more immediate mystery was solved.

He had just sat down on the easy chair in his suite, thinking perhaps he would rest for a while before going over to Campo and perusing the old menus there to see what might be a good option for his and Olivia's noontime meal, when he heard Aamir's voice in his mind.

Omar, I have news.

At once, he pushed himself against the seat

back so he sat a bit more upright. *Already? What did Miles Odekirk find?*

This is not about Dr. Odekirk, Aamir replied.

Then what is it about?

We have found the traitor who betrayed you to Khalim al-Usar. Zahrias wants you and Olivia to come to Santa Fe right away.

Chapter 14

THEY GATHERED IN A MEETING ROOM AT the La Fonda Hotel, in a space outfitted with a large conference table and some oversized chairs upholstered in red. It was the kind of place that Olivia doubted had ever seen a gathering like this.

The introductions had been hurried and brief —Julia Innes, the gorgeous blonde woman who was Zahrias' wife, and Aamir, Omar's older brother. Olivia still hadn't quite gotten her brain to wrap itself around the obvious reality of a human woman being a djinn's wife, but she knew that was something she needed to put aside for now.

Two other people stood in the conference room, an oversized djinn named Murrah, who seemed utterly bewildered about the whole situation...and a beautiful human woman, Martine, her striking, model-exotic features pinched with worry and shame, her dark eyes haunted.

"Tell them, Martine," Zahrias said, and although his voice was calm, almost quiet, an edge of steel underlaid it as well.

It was the voice of someone you ignored at your peril.

"I told Khalim where to find you in Placitas," she said simply, and Olivia stared at the other woman in shock.

"Why would you do that?" she burst out. "You don't even know us!"

Martine pressed her pale lips together. Although Olivia got the impression the woman was partnered with Murrah, just as Julia and Zahrias were obviously together, she could tell that relations between the woman and her djinn partner were somewhat strained.

Omar crossed his arms and stared at Martine, black eyes glittering with fury. "Yes, Martine," he said, his tone soft, menacing. "You do not know me, or Olivia Raskin. So why would you think it a good idea to betray us to Khalim al-Usar?"

The woman's fingers knotted themselves in the hem of the black tunic-style sweater she wore. "I had no choice," she said, her voice not much more than a desperate whisper. "Khalim came to me when I was alone. I—I like to go riding," she added, her tone now almost defensive. "The stables are in Santa Fe, but on the outskirts. It should have been safe, but it wasn't. He told me he'd take me away with him again if I didn't tell him what he needed to know."

Zahrias' and Julia's eyes met for a moment. There was a whole world of personal history here that Olivia knew next to nothing about, but in that moment, she thought she understood at least a little of what was happening here.

Back at the farmhouse, Omar had called Khalim a rapist and hinted that he liked to prey on human women. That single eloquent, despairing "again" in Martine's words seemed to make it abundantly clear that she had been one of Khalim's victims.

"And what, precisely, did Khalim need to know?" Zahrias' voice was still cool, but beneath it was a note of compassion, as if he knew all too well what Martine had endured.

"He had fought Omar al-Qadir and had a grudge against him," Martine replied. "But he did not know much about him otherwise. He told me if I didn't let him know where Omar lived, he would definitely take me away. I didn't know, of course—it's not like I'd even heard of Omar before all this—but I was chatting with Isla, Aamir's partner, and I got her to say something about Omar living in Placitas."

Aamir's eyes narrowed. He was a little taller

than his brother, features a little harder, but the family resemblance was still strong. Through all of this, he'd remained silent, but now that his partner's name had been mentioned, he clearly thought it was time to say something.

"I apologize for my partner's indiscretion," he said, and although his tone was even enough, Olivia could tell he was not happy about Isla's loose lips. "I am sure she was merely trying to make conversation and could have had no idea that Martine had been suborned by Khalim al-Usar."

"You don't have to apologize for her," Martine cut in. Although she was still pale, it seemed obvious she wasn't about to let Isla take the fall for something that had been an innocent slip-up. "I made sure to guide the conversation so she'd give me the information I needed. It was wrong, but I figured that since Omar was another djinn, he should be able to handle himself."

"And I would have," Omar said crisply. Like his brother, he held himself straight and tall, and although Olivia guessed he was angry, not much of that emotion seeped into his words. "But Khalim came in the night like a coward and set my house ablaze. Fortunately, Olivia and I were able to escape, but it was close."

It didn't seem as though Martine had known about that, because she grew even paler, almost sickly under skin that seemed to have a natural warm tone, the kind of complexion that easily tanned. "I am so sorry," she said. "I was desperate to keep him away from me. I suppose I thought he was going to fight you the way djinn usually do, power against power."

"But there is more, is there not?" Zahrias prompted, and once again, Martine pressed her pale lips together.

"He found me again and wanted to know about Omar's movements, and where he could be found. I overheard Julia and you talking about meeting with the people from Los Alamos the day before yesterday, so I passed that information along to Khalim."

Standing next to Olivia, Omar let out a hiss of a breath, and anger knotted her stomach as well. They had been attacked because Khalim had known exactly where they were going to be, thanks to the information Martine had provided. Bad enough that she and Omar had almost been hurt, but the group from Los Alamos—innocent bystanders if there ever were some—had nearly suffered their own injuries.

"And he used that information to attack us on the outskirts of town," Omar said, voice hard. "As it is, while some part of this mystery has been cleared up, we still have not answered the central question, which is where Khalim is currently hiding. Did he say anything to you about that?"

At once, Martine shook her head. "No, he didn't say a lot, other than threaten me. And as soon as I promised to get him the information he needed, he disappeared."

"Which means he could be anywhere in the world," Zahrias said, disapproval clear in the way his brows drew together.

Something Olivia knew was only the truth. She still wasn't entirely clear about all the powers djinn possessed and the ways they were able to use those powers, but it was obvious to her that they could blink themselves from place to place as they wished. Khalim could be hiding somewhere in the ruins of Albuquerque...or in an abandoned villa in Tuscany.

Or in a deserted science outpost in the Antarctic, although she kind of got the impression he wouldn't want to stay anywhere that would cause him too much physical discomfort.

It also seemed as if the djinn didn't have any kind of central authority other than the "elders" Omar had mentioned on several occasions, so it wasn't like they could send the elemental equivalent of the FBI after Khalim to hunt him down.

Then again....

"Do the elders know what he's been up to?"

she asked, a question that elicited a few uncomfortable glances exchanged between the djinn present.

"It is always difficult to say for sure what the elders do or do not know," Zahrias said after a pause. "They are a power unto themselves. They are not omniscient, however, even though they have a far greater ability to discern what is happening in our world than an ordinary djinn."

"Maybe it's time to reach out to them for help," Julia suggested. She'd remained quiet during Martine's questioning, but she seemed to think it was time to jump in now. "I know they prefer the djinn to handle their problems themselves whenever possible, but this is kind of an extraordinary situation. If nothing else, they need to know the outer circles aren't quite the impenetrable fortress they thought they were."

Omar nodded, although something about the way his eyes narrowed told Olivia he wasn't too thrilled to be openly agreeing with a human. "This is true. I had thought—and I have no doubt many of you thought as well—that they would be able to detect such a breach. But while Khalim is the most dangerous of those exiled there, I do not much like the thought of the others also being able to make their escape."

"Surely we would have seen or heard of them if such a thing had happened," Aamir said. "For

Khalim had almost a dozen in his crew, and if that many people returned to this plane after exile, it would be much more obvious."

"One would think," Zahrias replied. "And yet this is not the only place where they could hide. We have grown accustomed to the comforts of living on this plane, but the otherworld still remains, and would still be something they might see as desirable after the privations of existence in the outer circles."

Olivia had no real idea of what this "otherworld" was—the place where the djinn had lived before they conquered Earth?—but all the elementals present in the room gave reluctant nods, as though they knew this was a possibility they needed to confront.

"Then perhaps it is time to reach out to the elders," Murrah put in. He had also been quiet during most of the discussion, obviously embarrassed by the role his partner had played in the attacks on Olivia and Omar, not to mention the group from Los Alamos. "For I cannot see what we can do on our own, not with no way of knowing where Khalim even is. I will make sure that Martine stays close to home so there is little chance of him approaching her, but I fear much of the damage has already been done."

That was for sure, with Omar's house burned to cinders and the people from Los Alamos afraid to even set foot in Santa Fe until the threat from Khalim was dealt with.

Martine didn't look too pleased with this development—although Olivia didn't know the woman, she had a feeling that Murrah's partner used horseback riding as a way of dealing with the trauma from her assault by Khalim—but she remained silent, full lips clamped shut as if to prevent herself from saying something that might cause further argument.

"We will think about it," Zahrias replied.

Was he reluctant to allow the elders to see what he thought was a weakness on his part? Olivia honestly didn't know what else Zahrias could have done...it seemed pretty major to her that they'd even been able to discover the source of the information leak...but then, she didn't know him at all, didn't know if he was overly proud or too invested in his role as leader of the community here to reach out to the elders for help.

And she didn't think she could ask Omar once she was alone with him, simply because he wasn't a part of the Santa Fe group, either, and therefore probably didn't know much more than she did.

"In the meantime," Zahrias went on, "we must all be on our guard. Murrah, you may take Martine home. Aamir and Omar, I would like to speak to you in private." He paused there, his gaze moving to Olivia, and he added, "And you as well, Olivia Raskin."

Should she be glad to be included in that group? Honestly, even though it had been good to learn that Khalim wasn't somehow magically pulling the information about her location out of thin air, she found herself wishing that she and Omar could go back to Los Poblanos. She still wasn't sure what to think about having to stay there indefinitely, but at the same time, the place was quiet and peaceful, not filled with undercurrents of shared history she knew nothing about.

About all she could do was nod.

"But let's go back to the house," Julia suggested. "It'll be a more comfortable place to sit and talk."

Zahrias didn't appear inclined to argue with her, even though he frowned slightly before saying, "That is fine. Omar, Aamir will show you where to go."

Through the odd connection they shared, Olivia supposed, although she only saw Aamir nod before Omar came over to her.

"We could walk," he said, "but the djinn way is faster."

That was for sure, even though she couldn't quite stop herself from flushing as he placed his arms around her waist so they could blink away from the La Fonda hotel's conference room. A fraction of a second later, they appeared in a gracious space decorated in neutral tones to high-light what she guessed must be extremely expensive art on the walls. Niches set into the diamond plaster showcased small sculptures and pieces of Native American pottery, and if it hadn't been for the large cream-colored leather sofas in the center of the room, Olivia might have thought they'd landed in a high-end art gallery rather than some-one's home.

"Go ahead and sit down," Julia said. It seemed they'd traveled even more quickly than the rest of their guests, since they were already standing in the living room when Omar and Olivia and Aamir appeared. "Coffee or tea or water?"

Olivia was feeling jangly enough that she thought coffee wouldn't be that great an idea. But because she could tell it was much colder here than in Albuquerque, a cup of hot tea sounded wonder-ful. "Tea, please."

Omar and his brother asked for coffee, and it appeared Zahrias was of a similar mind, because he conjured a cup for himself along with all the other beverages people had requested.

Now that they all had their refreshments, the djinn leader indicated that everyone should take a seat. Olivia sat on the couch nearest her, with Omar settling himself at her side just a moment later. It seemed to her he'd hesitated for a second or two, as if he wasn't sure whether he wanted to sit that close to her, but then decided it was better not to call any notice to his reticence. Luckily, Aamir had been occupied with sitting on his brother's other side, while Zahrias and Julia lowered themselves to the couch opposite theirs.

After taking a sip of his coffee, the djinn leader said, "I did not know whether I could speak frankly in front of Murrah, for although he has vowed to keep an eye on Martine, I cannot say for sure whether there is still a chance that Khalim might approach her."

Olivia flicked a worried glance at Omar, but he seemed unmoved by this comment, still staring straight ahead at Zahrias as though waiting to hear more.

Aamir only nodded without replying. Clearly, it seemed that both brothers were waiting for the other djinn to continue.

"I have been in contact with the elders," Zahrias went on. "Again, I did not wish to say anything in front of Murrah, for I saw no reason to tip my hand, not with his wife presenting such a weak link in the community here. They have told me that they know of the breach in the outer circles, but it seems Khalim was the only one who escaped. The rest of the circles have been secured, so there is no risk of any of his compatriots reaching this world."

Well, that was something. Olivia couldn't allow herself to relax completely, not with the rogue djinn still out there somewhere, but at least she wouldn't have to worry about a whole horde of similarly nasty types showing up on their doorstep.

"But they do not know where Khalim is?" Omar asked then, and Zahrias shook his head.

"Unfortunately, no. They will get a sense of him somewhere, but then he will disappear before they can track him down. It seems that when he doesn't settle anywhere for very long, even the elders cannot catch him—which I am sure is the reason why he keeps moving." The djinn leader stopped there, mouth tightening, before he added, "It is clear that Khalim believes such an unsettled existence is still preferable to being caught and returned to the outer circles."

It sure sounded that way. But if even the elders couldn't catch up with the escaped djinn, then Olivia had no idea what the rest of them were supposed to do.

Neither Omar nor Aamir appeared too thrilled by the situation, either. "He is a crafty one, I'll grant him that," Aamir remarked. "And it seems we are at an impasse."

"Sooner or later, he will make a mistake," Omar replied. He still looked impassive enough, although the tension in his fine jaw told Olivia he had been hoping for a better way out of all this. "In the meantime, though, it seems the best thing I can do is take Olivia back to where we are staying. The odds of Khalim finding us there are very low... unless we should have the very bad luck to have him appear at that same location while he was on the run from the elders."

God, she hoped not. That would be one of the worst coincidences of all time, even though she tried to reassure herself that with all the millions of hiding places available to the escapee, the chances he would land at Los Poblanos must be practically nil.

"I still think you would be better off here," Aamir responded. "Perhaps it is more visible, but at least you would have other djinn around you. In your current location—wherever it is—you would be alone."

That comment made Olivia realize that Omar truly hadn't revealed their hiding place to anyone, not even his brother. True, he'd said as much, but she still hadn't known for sure whether she could really believe him.

Then again, he and his brother hadn't been on the best of terms lately, so maybe it wasn't so strange that Omar would want to keep his secrets to himself.

His eyes narrowed. "We have already discussed this," he told Aamir. "Santa Fe is not a place where I feel comfortable dwelling, if even for a short time.

Olivia and I have stayed in our hiding place for more than a day with no one finding us there, which tells me that Khalim has no idea where we are. As far as I am concerned, the situation is stable, and will suit us well enough until a more permanent solution to our problem presents itself."

His tone was firm, making it clear he didn't want any further arguments on the issue. And although Julia glanced over at her partner, as if to gauge his reaction, Zahrias remained impassive, while the slight frown Aamir now wore told Olivia that he knew better than to keep pushing the matter.

A high-pitched beep pierced the silence that had ensued after Omar's comment, and Julia startled.

"That's the two-way radio with Los Alamos," she said as she rose from the couch. "I'd better check to see what they want."

"I hope Khalim isn't causing more trouble," Olivia remarked, and Zahrias immediately shook his head.

"No, he is a criminal...but he also possesses enough intelligence to know that Los Alamos is the one place he dare not go. Whatever has happened, I doubt it has anything to do with our escaped prisoner."

They weren't left to ponder the situation for too much longer, because a minute or so later, Julia returned to the living room, her expression now one of shock.

"That was Miles," she said. "He figured out what blocked your powers, Omar." A pause, and then she added, "He wants us to come to Los Alamos so we can talk."

Chapter 15

HOW HE'D GOTTEN TALKED INTO THIS, Omar had no idea. And yet a remarkably short amount of time had passed before he squeezed into the back seat of the large vehicle—something called a Chevy Suburban—that Julia was now piloting expertly down the empty highway that stretched between Santa Fe and Los Alamos.

Zahrias sat in the front passenger seat, while Olivia, quiet and tense, was seated less than a foot away from Omar. Her proximity only underscored the ridiculousness of the situation.

He, Omar al-Qadir, riding along like a mortal in the back seat of an SUV?

However, it seemed Miles Odekirk had been insistent that they come to Los Alamos, rather than have him drive to see them in Santa Fe. They'd left Aamir behind, since it seemed his presence was not needed for this particular errand, but Miles had also wanted to make sure that Omar and Olivia would be there.

He did his best to focus on the strange sights and sounds around him, the oddly chemical scent of the vehicle's interior, as though everything in it had been made of plastic, from the door panels to the short-cropped carpet beneath his feet, and even the seats as well. It made him feel vaguely ill…or perhaps that was merely the uncomfortable sensation of being forced to sit back here while the Suburban bounced over every available pothole and crack in the roadway.

It was certainly better to believe it was their progress making him feel queasy, rather than the unwelcome nearness of the woman who sat next to him. Olivia had been quiet the whole time, her entire aura that of someone who knew they had to undertake an unpleasant duty and was determined to see it through to the end, no matter what.

Could it be she was worried that she might be left there, and that now she had come to Los Alamos, there was no reason for them to be forced to go to Santa Fe to fetch her?

Omar supposed such fears weren't implausible, although there had certainly been no discussion on that particular subject. No, this errand seemed to be focused entirely on Miles Odekirk's discovery… whatever that might turn out to be.

Zahrias also did not appear to be too pleased by their method of locomotion. He'd even argued with Julia that they could simply blink themselves to the outer limit of the devices that protected Los Alamos and have Miles and his team pick them up there, but she'd shot down that idea.

"Too many things could go wrong," she'd argued. "We've already seen how Khalim pounced the second the people from Los Alamos weren't protected by their devices. It's better for me to drive you there. No, it won't be pleasant for you, although Miles is having me come in the back way to the labs, where there aren't as many overlapping fields."

Small comfort. Unlike his older brother, Omar had never purposely subjected himself to the effects of the field the devices projected. However, everything he'd heard had told him it was going to be far from pleasant.

And it wasn't. He could feel the exact second when they crossed over into the protected area, could sense his powers ebbing even as his limbs turned weak and useless.

How that had shown in his face, he didn't know, but something must have changed, for Olivia turned toward him and said, "Omar? Are you okay?"

"Not particularly," he replied.

"We've crossed over into the area where the

devices are operating," Julia said from the front seat. "It'll probably take a little getting used to."

There was an understatement. Omar did not think he would ever become accustomed to the sensation of his very life force being drained from him, or to the way he knew in the depths of his soul that if he reached out to use any of his powers, he would find nothing there.

Olivia's expression was all sympathy. "I'm sorry," she murmured. "Hopefully, this won't take very long."

He hoped so as well, but since they had very little to go on other than Miles Odekirk's cryptic claim that he'd found the explanation for the loss of Omar and Khalim's powers at the farm, he could not be very sanguine.

Soon enough, though, Julia turned off the highway and onto a narrow two-lane road that bumped along through a rough, hilly landscape dotted with junipers, snow still gleaming in the shadows beneath the trees. None of it looked terribly hospitable, and Omar wondered exactly where they were going.

That inner question was answered soon enough, though, as she paused to pull the Suburban onto an even narrower lane, one that passed a set of abandoned guard shacks and a chain-link fence. Here, all was paved, although the asphalt had begun to buckle with constant exposure to the weather, and the small outbuildings he spied appeared similarly shabby.

"This is the former Los Alamos National Labs property," Julia explained from the driver's seat. It seemed she was ready to play the part of tour guide, for she went on, "Miles still works in the main building here, but the rest of it has been pretty much abandoned, as you can see."

The place did seem somewhat forlorn. Or perhaps that was only Omar's reaction to the constant drain from the device that guarded the laboratory grounds. As far as he and his brothers had been able to determine, each of the devilish little boxes could protect around a square quarter-mile, perhaps a bit more. One would probably be enough to cover most of the grounds here.

He leaned his head against the back of the seat, thinking that if what he was experiencing was the effect of just a single device, he hated to imagine what several of them working in concert must feel like. Olivia still watched him with concerned eyes, but she remained silent and refrained from reaching out to provide some other form of reassurance.

Not that he needed it. This was all thoroughly unpleasant, true, and yet he tried to remind himself that it was also temporary, and as soon as they were done with their meeting with Miles Odekirk, they could go back whence they had come. Or rather, he would ride along with Julia and Zahrias until they reached the edge of the effective range of the devices, and then he would take Olivia and go back to Los Poblanos. No point in suffering for a single second longer than he absolutely had to.

Besides, something of the beauty and tranquility of the spot seemed to linger in his soul. It would be good to return there and look on the winter-dormant gardens, and ponder what they might be like when spring came around again.

And it would also be good to peruse the old menus from the restaurant and decide what might be best to tempt Olivia's appetite that evening.

Julia pulled up to a tall, ugly building made of some sort of pale concrete or other manmade material, then turned off the Suburban's engine. "Here we are," she said, quite unnecessarily. "Miles's lab is on the third floor, unfortunately, but last I heard, they've got enough solar to run the elevators."

After opening her door, she went around to the passenger side so she could help Zahrias out. From the way the djinn leader gritted his teeth, he was none too happy to be assisted in such a way, although he did not protest, but only laid his hand on his partner's arm as he climbed down from the oversized vehicle.

At once, Olivia's worried green gaze met his. "Do you—?"

"I am fine," he said, cutting her off. There was

no way in the world he would allow himself to show such weakness as to accept her assistance. Perhaps he would have to maneuver himself out of the ungainly vehicle inch by inch, but better that than have to hold Olivia's arm the whole way.

Her lips parted—perhaps to protest?—but then she seemed to think better of it and instead opened the door on the passenger side so she could get out.

Omar pushed down on the door handle, gritting his teeth as he swung his legs over the edge of the seat. For just a moment, he thought his knees were going to buckle beneath him, but he held on to the door as he regained his balance, then made himself breathe in and out for a moment to make sure he had enough strength to take a step.

Zahrias' eyes met his for a moment, his mouth halfway curled in a grimly amused smile. However, he did not comment on Omar's foolish attempt at independence and instead turned toward his partner.

"Lead on, my love," he said. "You know this place, and we do not."

She nodded, then walked slowly over to the front door, taking care not to leave the debilitated djinn too far behind her. Olivia took up the rear of their little party, as if knowing she should stay a few steps back in case one of them stumbled or flagged.

Luckily, that precaution was not necessary, and

soon enough, they entered the lobby and made their way over to the set of elevators placed against the far wall. Omar guessed the space had never been beautiful, with its beige linoleum floor and equally beige walls, with some uncomfortable-looking furniture set near a receptionist's desk off to one side, but the past four years had only served to make it look even shabbier. Clean, as far as he could tell, with no noticeable dust and a floor that did its best to shine despite the multiple scratches and scuffs on its surface, and yet it still was not the sort of place where he had any desire to linger.

Loitering here was clearly not Julia's intention, however. She pressed a button set into the wall next to the elevator, and soon enough, the button flashed green and the doors opened to reveal a rectangular box even less inviting than the lobby had been.

They all squeezed in. Olivia stood very close to Omar, so close that he thought he could detect the lavender scent clinging to her hair, probably left there by the hotel-supplied shampoo she'd used. The faint perfume reminded him of springs long gone, of times happier than this, even though back then his hours on this earth had been stolen ones, precious fragments of time he could use to take with him back to his palace in the otherworld.

And he was all too conscious of the heat of Olivia's body, of how oddly elegant she was, even in that plain plum-colored sweater and jeans and boots. Because her hair was newly washed, it fell loose on her shoulders, dark and rich like newly turned soil.

Despite the weakness in his limbs, he could not quite hold back the rush of need in his body, the way he knew he desired her, even if his brain and will did not want to acknowledge such a thing. Yes, she was beautiful...too beautiful.

The elevator doors opened then, and to his infinite relief, they all exited the cramped little box. Reason returned to him now that Olivia did not stand so close...or at least, he had an easier time convincing himself that she was not quite so lovely after all. She certainly could not compare to a djinn woman, not in those plain, shabby clothes, garments that seemed designed to subtract from the wearer's beauty rather than enhance it.

Julia led them down the hall to a room at the far end, a room whose double doors stood open to the corridor. As they went inside, Omar saw the space was filled with long tables whose surfaces were crowded with bits and pieces of various electronics, wires and screens and odd little objects he could not begin to identify.

Standing at one of the tables was a tall, thin human man with wire-framed glasses and gray-streaked short brown hair. Next to him was a woman who appeared much younger, lovely and lush with her long, honey-colored locks, warm-toned skin, and striking green eyes.

"Hi, Julia," the man said, sounding utterly casual, as though he had djinn stroll into his laboratory every day. "Thanks for coming so quickly."

"Well, Miles, it sounded like you had something pretty important to tell us," she replied, then glanced over at the woman who stood next to the scientist. "And hi, Lindsay."

"Hey," the woman said before turning her gaze on Omar. "I'm Lindsay Odekirk, and this is my husband Miles."

"Omar al-Qadir," he returned. "And this is Olivia Raskin," he added, as she put on a small smile for their hosts. Perhaps these introductions were necessary, but all he wanted to do was get on with this so he could escape the omnipresent dulling sensation caused by those terrible devices.

In fact, one of them was sitting on the table in front of Miles Odekirk. It looked innocuous enough, a simple cube perhaps some four inches square, covered on all sides by a glassy substance that he knew was actually a touchscreen, but Omar could not help staring balefully at it nonetheless.

As he watched, Odekirk picked up the device and did something to it, moving his long-fingered hands over its surface.

At once, that terrible drained sensation vanished. But—

He still could not use his magic. It was blocked somehow, although not by Miles Odekirk's device.

What the—

Zahrias' face was a study in consternation. "What is happening here?"

In answer, Odekirk reached beneath his worktable and brought out a grayish lump of crystal, its various planes and angles reminding him of a pyrite cube, although it was not nearly as shiny. "This is what we found when we went to the Miller farm in Cedar Crest. A hundred yards or so past the barn, a fissure had opened in the ground, most likely as a result of the earthquake from two days ago. I'd never seen anything like it before, although I will admit that geology and crystallography are not my fields of expertise. And when I began testing it with a spectrograph, I realized it possessed properties similar to the output created by my devices, although it wasn't exactly the same. That's why I needed you to come here—I had to see what its effect on a djinn would be."

Zahrias studied the lump of rock for a moment, then nodded slowly. "It must be related to *ni-khar* somehow."

"That's an element from your plane?" Odekirk asked.

"Yes," Zahrias replied. "It blocks the power of fire elementals but causes no other debilitating side effects."

Odekirk's blue-gray eyes narrowed behind his spectacles, and then he glanced over at Omar. "Are you a fire elemental?"

"No," Omar said shortly. He did not care to discuss such things with the man who had caused so much misery for the djinn, yet he also realized that they needed to determine exactly what had happened at the Miller farm. "My element is the earth. Khalim al-Usar, on the other hand, is a fire elemental."

A pause as Odekirk picked up the grayish crystal and turned it over in his hand. "So, this thing affects both earth and fire." He glanced over at Zahrias as he added, "I don't suppose you could have an air elemental and a water elemental come over here so we could see if their powers are similarly neutralized."

"I doubt I would have many volunteers," Zahrias observed dryly. "But if you procured more than one specimen, I could take it with me."

Julia raised an eyebrow. "I don't know if that's such a good idea," she said. "If this stuff really does block your powers, then I doubt most of the djinn in Santa Fe would be too thrilled to have it anywhere near them."

"Point taken," Zahrias replied. "But this is still a positive development, is it not?"

"It is," Odekirk said. "Lindsay and I have been working for years to modify the devices so their effects aren't so debilitating. If we can shift to using crystals such as these, it means that we can at the very least set up safe zones where our people can meet and the djinn won't have to worry about feeling as if they're going to faint. What I'd like to know now is how far the range extends."

Omar thought it was time for him to step into the conversation. "Well, that should be easy enough to discover. Are there any other devices operating nearby?"

"No," Lindsay said. "We wanted to make sure there wasn't any overlap when we turned this one off. You'd need to walk to the front gate before you started to be affected by the one located at City Hall."

Clearly, Odekirk and his partner trusted Zahrias, or they would never have made themselves so vulnerable by turning off their device with several djinn standing right there. It crossed Omar's mind that he could simply reach out and snap Miles Odekirk's neck, for while he did not possess his djinn powers, he certainly felt strong and hearty enough, and more than a match for the skinny human who stood so casually only a few paces away.

As soon as the notion had come, however, he thrust it out of his thoughts. While he considered Odekirk responsible for a great deal of pain and suffering, Omar would never betray Zahrias' trust by doing such a thing.

Also, Olivia was standing only a few paces away. He could only imagine the anguish and horror—yes, and disgust—in her expression if he committed such a cold-blooded murder right in front of her.

There would be no more quiet suppers at Los Poblanos if he gave in to his basest impulses.

Irritation stirred deep within. Why should he care what Olivia Raskin thought, or whether they would be able to share any more time together? She was a burden, an unwelcome charge, and nothing more.

Except he knew, even deeper in his heart, that she was much more than nothing.

He cleared his throat. "Then I will go that way and see how long it takes before I cannot feel the effects of this rock you found."

"And I will go the other," Zahrias added. "That should provide the data you need, even if perhaps this experiment would be even more effective if there were more of us."

"Actually, no," Miles said, not looking at all worried about directly contradicting a djinn. But then, despite the scant few minutes Omar had spent in the scientist's presence, he had already formed the impression that the man cared little for what others thought of him. "I'm almost certain the field of effect is a circle, just as it is with the devices. So having two of you test that hypothesis should be enough. Lindsay?"

Looking somewhat resigned, the human woman—obviously used to her husband's quirks —produced two cans of fluorescent spray paint, the stuff Omar knew the mortals used to mark the boundary of the safe zone surrounding Los Alamos and Española. He recognized it because it was the same paint his older brother had utilized to create a false boundary at the northern end of the zone, thus allowing him to trap Isla.

Of course, none of them could have foreseen the consequences of that particular gambit.

But Omar took one of the cans and Zahrias the other, and together, the two of them headed out of the lab and over to the elevator so they could descend to the ground floor. As they went, the djinn leader wore an ironic smile.

"I had not expected you to be so cooperative with Dr. Odekirk," he remarked.

Omar's lip curled at the honorific. Yes, it was probably true that the scientist had at least one advanced degree, but in his mind, no one should call themselves a doctor unless they cared for actual patients. In his mind, Olivia was much more of a doctor than Odekirk when one considered the quick first aid she'd administered and the deft way she'd stitched up the wounds the buckshot had left behind.

"I will admit to some curiosity about those rocks he found," Omar said. "It will be interesting to see whether this experiment supports what I experienced in Cedar Crest, where my powers returned once I was a quarter-mile or so away from the farm."

The elevator dinged, indicating that they'd reached the ground floor of the building. "Well," Zahrias said, "I suppose we shall find out soon enough."

After delivering that comment, he strode purposefully toward the rear exit, obviously intending to retrace their steps.

Which meant it was time for Omar to make his own contribution to this little experiment.

He made his way to the front door and stepped outside. There had been no real effort to make the building at all decorative, which meant the entrance opened onto a small parking lot currently occupied by a single vehicle, a sort of SUV that was much smaller than the one Julia had driven here. As he began to walk, following the signs that directed him toward the exit from the complex, it became clear to him that Miles and Lindsay Odekirk were the only people currently working at the former labs, for there was no sign of any other occupation. He imagined it must have been very different back in the world before, when this place had probably hummed with activity and accommodated hundreds if not thousands of workers. Indeed, he guessed the laboratories had been the main reason for the town's existence, and that most other businesses here had survived by supporting the staff at the labs.

As he went, he looked inward from time to time, waiting for the small, subtle twinge that would tell him his powers had returned. Sure enough, after he'd walked several hundred yards, he could tell he was in full possession of his abilities.

Just to be sure, he reached out a hand. A second later, the asphalt near him buckled, revealing a patch of rich earth.

Very good. Although he had not been keeping track of the exact distance when he and Olivia had fled Khalim back in Cedar Crest, it seemed to him that he had just walked roughly the same amount, perhaps a little less than a quarter of a mile. So it seemed that a chunk of rock the size of the one in Odekirk's lab provided just a little less than the same amount of protection that one of his devices would.

How much was there of the stuff, anyway? Miles Odekirk hadn't mentioned such a thing, but perhaps he would provide further illumination once Omar and Zahrias had returned to the lab.

Satisfied with his findings, Omar bent and

sprayed a small pink "X" on the ground to mark the spot, turned around and began walking back to the tall gray building that housed the mad scientist's laboratory. As he went, though, he couldn't help wondering how Odekirk's discovery might change the world...and whether that would be a good thing or not.

Chapter 16

Olivia hadn't contributed much to the conversation about the strange mineral Miles Odekirk had found near the farm, mainly because she felt entirely out of her depth and didn't believe she had much to say on the subject. Even so, she couldn't help thinking that if the grayish substance really did manage to block djinns' powers without making them ill, it could change a whole lot of things.

Also, while she couldn't claim to be an expert on all matters Omar al-Qadir after only a few days spent in his presence, she thought he'd been on his best behavior during the meeting in the lab. Was he doing what he could to avoid embarrassing Zahrias, or was it possible that her unexpected bodyguard was beginning to mellow just the slightest bit?

Hard to say, but she was glad that, except for a couple of pithy remarks, he hadn't exhibited any real hostility toward Dr. Odekirk.

Despite that outbreak of something approaching courtesy, Olivia couldn't quite ignore the creeping fear that maybe Omar wouldn't return to the lab at all. He'd walk far enough away from that innocuous-looking chunk of mineral to be in the safe zone, would sense that his powers had returned...and would also realize that she was now inside Los Alamos' borders, and therefore there was no reason for him to keep protecting her.

As soon as the two djinn were gone, Miles picked up the rock and took it to a complicated-looking piece of machinery on a table a few feet away, effectively ignoring her. Lindsay and Julia, on the other hand, came over at once.

"Were you really living on your own all this time?" Lindsay inquired, and Olivia nodded. "How did you manage?"

"Keeping busy, I suppose," Olivia replied. In a way, it felt good to be engaged by the two other women like this, if only because it helped to take her mind off the fraught topic of whether Omar was going to abandon her here.

"We have a recent addition to the Santa Fe community who did almost the same thing," Julia put in. "Omar's older brother Jamal found her outside Las Vegas."

Meaning the Las Vegas here in New Mexico, Olivia assumed. She still didn't know much about djinn, but it did seem as though they tended to stick close to their home territory.

Omar hadn't talked about Jamal very much. She wasn't sure why, although that could have been because he hadn't been as involved in this whole mess with Khalim, and therefore Omar hadn't seen the point in discussing his other brother.

Still, it cheered Olivia a little to hear that another survivor very much like her had been out there somewhere. Knowing that made her situation feel a little less odd.

"But that's pretty much over with, right?" she said. "It's not as if I can go back to the farm, not with Khamil knowing exactly where the place is located."

Neither of the other two women bothered contradicting that statement. Yes, the mineral deposits that had been exposed by the earthquake might have been able to block his powers, but he still remained very large, very angry. Men like that had been preying on women for millennia.

"No, it's all about gathering in communities with the world the way it is," Lindsay remarked. A pause, and then she said, "You know, you're here in Los Alamos now. Maybe it would be smarter for you to stay with us."

Just about the last thing Olivia had wanted to

hear. Maybe a few days ago, seeking refuge in Los Alamos had seemed like the only logical thing to do. Now, though...now she knew the situation was a lot more complicated, even if she didn't want to admit to the reason why.

Julia's blue gaze flicked to Olivia. Although she didn't say anything, something in that cool, clear-eyed glance seemed to indicate she knew the other woman wasn't quite as keen on seeking refuge in the last human outpost as she might have been.

"Well, maybe," Olivia managed. She didn't want to offend Lindsay, who seemed friendly enough, even if it was still hard to figure out how a gorgeous woman like her had decided to marry a man probably ten years her senior and not exactly what anyone could describe as conventionally handsome.

There was a whole lot more to relationships than looks, though, and she knew it would be incredibly shallow to judge the couple on that one superficial metric.

"I mean," Olivia hurried on as Lindsay's brows began to pull together in a frown, "I think that was always the eventual plan. There's just a whole lot up in the air right now."

"There is," Julia agreed, her tone firm. "And we'll figure all that out at some point. Right now, though, I think the important thing to keep in mind is that Omar has done a really good job of keeping Olivia safe, and with so many unknowns in the equation, it would probably be better to keep things as they are. If that's what you and Omar decide," she added quickly.

Thank God for Julia's perceptiveness. No way in the world would Olivia admit to herself how difficult it would be to step away from Omar now, but it still felt awfully good to know that the move to Los Alamos could be pushed back a bit.

"Yes, I'd want to know what he thinks before I commit to anything," Olivia said. "I mean, he probably has a better idea of what lengths we need to take to make sure Khalim doesn't come sniffing around. I'd hate for him to cause trouble here. After all, look at what happened to Omar's house."

Lindsay had been appearing increasingly mystified during this exchange, and now she planted her hands on her hips and asked, "What happened to Omar's house?"

"Khalim burned it down," Julia said briefly. "He was trying to flush the two of them out. Which is why he's even more dangerous than most djinn."

This explanation appeared to startle the other woman, but still, Lindsay shook her head. "The most dangerous djinn in the world can't get past our defenses. Those devices lay them low every time."

"Most of the time," Julia corrected her,

although her tone was mild enough, and it didn't sound as though she was directly trying to challenge Lindsay. "Remember how a group of them broke into this very lab and kidnapped Miles back in the day?"

Olivia felt her eyes widen a bit. Clearly, there was a lot of history she needed to learn about the interactions between the Santa Fe djinn and the people of Los Alamos, although she didn't know whether now was the correct time.

Rather than take offense, Lindsay only grinned. "Good thing they did, too, or I might never have met Miles...although I kind of doubted that was what Zahrias had in mind when he made me work with him to see if we could figure out a way to alter the devices so they weren't so debilitating." Some of the glow went out of her eyes then, and she shook her head. "But okay, I take your point. I suppose if Khalim was sufficiently motivated, he could still brute-force his way in here, and I have a feeling he could cause a lot of damage before we shut him down."

Olivia didn't doubt that at all. She wasn't sure if she could call the rogue djinn completely mad, but there had been a wild light in his eyes that had frightened her more than she wanted to admit. As far as she was concerned, better to be far, far away in a place he didn't even know existed.

The conversation broke up then, because Omar and Zahrias appeared, looking pretty satisfied with themselves.

"We compared our experiences," Zahrias said as everyone in the lab—even Miles, who'd stepped away from his workbench to hear the news—gathered close. "As far as Omar and I were able to tell, it seems as though the field of effect extends approximately several hundred yards in all directions. Once we were past it, our powers came back to us immediately. So yes, it does seem as if this element you've discovered may be the key to keeping a djinn's power in check without causing any unpleasant side effects."

Miles Odekirk's pale gray eyes gleamed behind his glasses. "That's what I was hoping to hear. Now I just have to determine whether the effect is based on the size of the mineral I'm using, or whether its mass is immaterial to the effect it causes."

"Does that mean you need us to take another walk?" Omar asked. A corner of his mouth had lifted slightly, and Olivia got the impression he was a little amused by the scientist's zeal.

"As you're the only test subjects I currently have, yes, we will need to do that. But first, I'll need to reduce the size of the sample." He went back to the worktable, adding, "I've already bifurcated the stone. Lindsay, would you mind taking one piece over to City Hall? That's far enough away that it won't reach the gates of the lab complex."

"Sure," she replied, then went over to meet him. He placed half of the sample in a small cardboard box and handed it to her.

"You might as well put it in the safe," he said. "No one else knows anything about these stones or their inherent qualities, but it never hurts to take some precautions."

"Will do." Lindsay paused there and looked over at Olivia and Julia. "Want to come along? That way, you'll get a chance to see some of Los Alamos. And Julia, I know it's old hat to you, but you might want to see how we've expanded Pajarito's."

"Love to," Julia said, and then gave Olivia an encouraging smile. "You don't have to look at this as some kind of sales pitch for Los Alamos. On the other hand, it couldn't hurt to explore a bit."

Maybe not, but.... She glanced over at Omar, but his expression was impassive and she couldn't get even a hint of what he might be thinking.

And it wasn't as though she could help with the experiment. While she wasn't that interested in moving to Los Alamos, she also knew her current living situation couldn't last forever. Might as well go take a look.

Just in case.

"Sure," she said clearly. "Sounds like fun."

Miles Odekirk and Zahrias might not have understood the significance of that little exchange among the women, but Omar thought he caught its meaning all too well.

Julia and Lindsay wanted to make sure Olivia got a good look at Los Alamos, no doubt setting her up for an eventual move here. Which, he supposed, was as it should be, but the idea still rankled.

However, he made himself once more take the elevator to the ground floor, only this time, Zahrias headed toward the gate nearest the town while Omar went in the opposite direction, toward the road that had led them to the laboratory complex less than a half hour earlier. He had to admit this was a nicer walk; while everything around him was paved, he could still gaze down into the Rio Grande valley and eastward to the Sangre de Cristo mountains, a blue-gray bulwark topped with snow, a few misty clouds obscuring their peaks.

Unlike last time, he paused after only walking a few dozen yards or so. If the effect of the gray mineral truly was affected by its mass, then the field it generated should be much smaller, meaning he should be able to use his powers now. No little twinge, though, nothing to tell him they had come back.

And when he tried to make the ground shake just the smallest bit, nothing happened.

Interesting.

He walked a little farther, then made the same attempt. Once again, the cracked asphalt remained steady under his feet, telling him the stone must still be blocking his powers.

It wasn't until he'd walked several hundred yards that its effect finally faded and he was able to break apart some of the asphalt and allow rich, dark soil to appear underneath, followed by a single dandelion growing from the exposed dirt. So it seemed that the grayish, blocky mineral functioned the same way regardless of how much was being deployed.

Again, interesting. He could not begin to think precisely how Miles Odekirk's mind worked, but Omar had to believe the scientist would come up with some way to deploy this new find to good effect. No more need to spend hours or perhaps days constructing those clunky devices when a small chunk of rock, perhaps worn as an amulet or attached to a keychain, could have the same effect.

True, the mineral did not weaken a djinn in the same way that one of the devices would, but still, when an elemental could only rely on his muscle and not his inborn gifts, that made the playing field with a human much more level.

When he got back to the laboratory, Zahrias had already returned, but the women were still nowhere to be seen. Again, Omar tried to tell himself that of course it would take much more time to give Olivia a tour of Los Alamos than it would for him to walk several hundred yards or so and then return to the lab, and yet he could not quite hold back a flash of irritation...and worry.

What if she truly did decide to stay here after all?

Then you can wash your hands of the entire situation, he told himself. *For it is not as though you do not have enough to occupy your time. If nothing else, you will need to do something about rebuilding the house, or appealing to the elders for a new one.*

That was an interview he would prefer to avoid. It was not as though he had done anything in particular to run afoul of the elders, but on the other hand, he knew he and his brothers had walked a dangerous line in terms of choosing to pursue the destruction of humankind when the rest of his people had followed the elders' guidance and settled down to a peaceful existence in whatever location they had been granted.

Miles looked over the moment he walked into the lab. "Zahrias told me the effects were the same," he said, not bothering to waste time on a greeting. "Can you confirm this?"

"Yes," Omar replied. "I also had to walk the same distance before my powers returned. So it does seem that the size of the mineral is not a factor."

"Which is good, because we didn't find a lot of it," Odekirk said. "My team and I dug up everything we found, but we're definitely dealing with a finite resource here. Still, knowing that a little goes a long way will be helpful in deploying the stuff."

"What are your plans?" Zahrias asked. His expression was interested but then, Omar supposed he had a vested interest in knowing whether they had finally arrived at a solution for allowing djinn to visit Los Alamos without being adversely affected by all the devices deployed there. How they planned to manage it, Omar did not know for sure, as it didn't sound as though there was enough of the mineral to allow them to abandon the devices altogether.

Miles shrugged. Omar had halfway expected the human scientist to be wearing a lab coat or some other affectation to denote his status, but he was dressed much the same way most other humans seemed to dress these days—jeans, a fleece pullover, work boots. All the same, he did not give the impression of someone who was suited for anything other than indoor pursuits.

"I have a lot more study and analysis to do," he said. "But this is hopeful...very hopeful. We'll have to see how things go with further testing—I'd still like to have a water elemental and an air elemental come here, just to make sure that the mineral is one size fits all when it comes to djinn."

"When Julia and I return, I will ask for volunteers from among my people," Zahrias replied. He didn't sound particularly encouraging, but perhaps that was only him being cautious and not offering the services of one of his people before knowing for sure what they wished to give.

But that careful answer seemed to be enough to satisfy Odekirk, because he nodded, saying, "Once it's established that the mineral works on all four kinds of djinn, then we'll start planning how best to utilize it. One good thing is that its crystalline structure allows it to cleave easily, making it a simple matter to extract pieces as we need them. If we had needed someone who was an experienced gem-cutter to handle the task, it would have been a different story."

Zahrias nodded, but he wasn't able to respond beyond that because the three women returned just then, all of them chuckling at a comment or joke one of them must have made on their way to the lab. Looking at them, Omar thought he had never seen Olivia so animated, her beautiful jade-colored eyes practically glowing, full mouth turned up in a smile.

She looks happy, he thought, and wanted to frown.

Why did she never look that way around him?

"Did you enjoy yourselves?" Zahrias asked, and Julia went over to her partner and squeezed his hand.

"We did," she said. "They expanded Pajarito's into the shop next door, and it's positively huge now. I'm so glad to see everyone doing so well."

"That's because we had a good start," Lindsay said, also looking cheerful. "I think the situation would probably have been a lot different around here if it weren't for the way you set things up in the beginning."

Julia gave a deprecating shrug. "I'm not so sure about that—"

"Well, I am," Lindsay broke in, something in her voice indicating she wasn't going to allow any arguments on the topic. Then she glanced over at her husband, asking, "So, what's the verdict on our mystery crystal?"

"The good news is that the field of effect does not seem to be affected by the size of the sample," he told her. "But we still need to study it much more."

"Which means we have a lot of work ahead of us," she said, then gave a mock sigh clearly intended for her watching audience and not for her husband, who only appeared resigned.

"And that means the rest of us should return to Santa Fe," Zahrias replied. His gaze moved to Omar. "I trust you are ready to return?"

No, he was not. Or rather, now that he knew he need only walk a hundred yards to get to a place where his powers were returned to him, he didn't see the point in climbing back into that uncomfortable SUV and bumping his way along those badly maintained roads until they reached their destination. Much better to go straight back to Los Poblanos.

The question was...would Olivia wish to return there with him?

Better to ask quickly, before he lost his nerve.

Rather than respond to Zahrias' question, Omar looked over at Olivia. "I had thought I would go directly to the place we have been staying. Do you wish to return with me, or would you prefer to stay here in Los Alamos?"

Her eyes widened slightly, as though she was startled by the way he'd asked so boldly in front of so many onlookers. But relief was clear in her expression as she looked right back at him and said, "I think it's better if I go with you. We know we've been safe there, whereas everything else is kind of an unknown."

He would not allow himself to show his own

relief, not with Zahrias and Julia and Miles Odekirk and his wife standing there and watching him. Briefly, he said, "Then let us go."

Olivia turned to Lindsay and Julia. "Thank you for showing me around. It really is a cute town. And maybe—well, maybe soon we'll know whether it's all right for me to come back here permanently."

"I understand," Lindsay said. "You need to stay safe."

While her expression was sober enough, Omar couldn't help thinking that he'd caught a glint in Lindsay's eye as she looked from Olivia over to the spot where he stood, as though she'd begun to guess the two of them might have an ulterior motive for not wanting to go back to Santa Fe.

Such a motive did not exist, however. This was all about keeping Olivia safe and nothing more.

She murmured a goodbye to Julia and Zahrias and Miles Odekirk, and then came closer to Omar.

"Let us go," he said briefly.

They walked out of the lab and over to the elevator. Once it had begun to descend, he said, knowing his tone sounded far too stiff, "You could have stayed, if you thought it best."

"I didn't, though," Olivia returned. Her voice was casual enough, although there was something in the way her gaze wouldn't quite meet his that told him the matter was a bit more complicated than that.

Omar decided it was better to let the topic go for now. "Well, then," he said, as the doors opened onto the building's shabby ground-floor lobby, "we will need to walk a few hundred yards or so. After that, we will be beyond the crystal's field of effect, and I will be able to blink us away to Los Poblanos."

"Sounds good."

A brisk wind met them as he opened the rear exit door that led outside. But the sun remained bright, and Olivia did not seem too bothered by the chill, and didn't even pause to zip up the jacket she wore.

They walked in silence, as though they both understood there wasn't much point in further discussion. Omar wished he could think of something to say to her, something that would express his gratitude that she'd decided to go back to Los Poblanos rather than remain here in Los Alamos, but all those words sounded horribly awkward in his mind, and he pushed them all away.

Perhaps things would be more comfortable once they were away from here.

He recognized the spot where he'd made a dandelion sprout through the cracked asphalt, as no other things were growing there at this time of year, and knew they'd come to the end of the gray crystal's field of effect. "If I may," he said, and moved closer to her so he could put his arms around her in preparation for djinn travel.

This was not the first time he had done such a thing, but he did not know if he'd sensed her presence so acutely on those other occasions—the rustle of the nylon fabric of her jacket against his linen robes, the soft brush of her long hair against his hands as she came to him and had her arms encircle his waist. His breath wanted to catch in his throat, and he told himself not to be so weak.

His body had other ideas, however, and he could feel his groin tighten even as he summoned an image of the bar at Los Poblanos in his mind, so they might appear somewhere that was warm and friendly. Less than an instant later, they were standing in the dark yet cozy space, and he immediately let go of Olivia.

She stepped away, her eyes still not meeting his. But then she looked up, a lopsided smile on her lips. "Maybe someday I'll get used to traveling like that." The smile faded as she added, "You never got to say goodbye to your brother."

No, he did not, because of course Aamir was back in Santa Fe and had not accompanied them on the expedition to Los Alamos. "He will understand," Omar said briefly. "It would have been foolish to return to the capital city merely to bid him farewell."

"Right," Olivia said. A pause, and then she asked, "So...what now?"

"A very good question," Omar replied. "I suppose we will have to wait to hear from my brother to report any developments as Dr. Odekirk continues his investigation of the crystals he found. For now, though"—he paused to glance at the clock that hung on the wall at the far end of the room, although he did not need it to tell him the hour—"I believe it is time for lunch."

Chapter 17

THEY RETURNED TO CAMPO FOR THEIR noon meal, of course, although it looked very different in the bright light of day than it had the evening before. Clearly, Omar hadn't seen the need for candles or pretty greenery, and the place felt almost utilitarian now, with its plain white table linens and simple white plates.

But he conjured more beautiful salads for them, accompanied by a hearty, spicy Mexican wedding soup, which tasted wonderful after that walk through the windy, cold back forty of the laboratory complex. Olivia did her best to keep her attention on the food, and yet she couldn't quite banish from her mind the sensation of Omar's arms around her as they'd traveled back here, the way he felt infinitely comforting in a way she couldn't quite explain.

Which was stupid, of course. The man was a killer, and had shown he had very little care for humanity. The only reason she wasn't dead, too, was because he and his brothers had agreed long ago that women and children were off-limits during their murderous sprees.

"What did you think of Los Alamos?" he asked out of nowhere, and she lifted her gaze from her soup.

"It was cold," she replied, and he smiled in response.

"True. I suppose it would feel cold to someone from Albuquerque. But that was your only impression?"

What was he getting at? Was he trying to make her blurt out that she loved the place and regretted not staying?

That wouldn't be the truth, so she wasn't about to say it. However, she didn't see anything wrong with pointing out the positives of the place.

"Lindsay was nice," she allowed. "And it looks like they've done a lot to make the place feel like a town from before. I mean, I never thought I'd see a functional grocery store or a restaurant again, but there they were. It's pretty impressive when you stop to think about it."

"I suppose so," Omar said, although something in his voice indicated to her that he didn't feel all that impressed.

Well, why would he be? The strivings of humans must seem absolutely puny to a being who could snap his fingers and make pretty much whatever he wanted appear out of thin air.

Besides, Omar and his brothers had worked very hard to continue the eradication of humanity. Hearing about the way Los Alamos was flourishing must be annoying as hell.

That thought made her wonder exactly why she'd decided to come back here. Any rational person would have known that staying among her own kind would have made a hell of a lot more sense.

However, she was beginning to realize that she wasn't exactly rational when it came to Omar al-Qadir.

"Anyway," she went on, deciding it was probably better to brush past his noncommittal response to her previous comment, "I could tell they put a lot of work into the community. I suppose I just wasn't sure whether they'd be able to keep me safe from Khalim, not after hearing how a group of djinn from Santa Fe managed to infiltrate the labs years ago."

"Back then, they were still based in Taos," Omar replied, although something in his tone was almost absent, as though his thoughts were occupied elsewhere.

Olivia decided to ignore that as well. If he was

bored by her, then he could work a little harder to keep up his side of the conversation.

"Okay," she allowed, "but still, it's not like Los Alamos is an impregnable fortress or anything. If Khalim really wanted to get in, he could. And since we've stayed here and haven't seen any sign of him, I have to believe it's probably safer where we are. For now, anyway," she added, since she didn't want to make him think she was ready to stay here indefinitely.

Then again, she didn't have a lot of other options.

"No, you are correct in that," Omar said, and now his gaze met hers, a little more direct than she would have liked.

Their trip back from Los Alamos had told her it was getting harder and harder to act indifferent around him.

Blinking and looking away would give entirely the wrong impression, though, so she did her best to stare back and affect what she hoped was an air of unconcern.

"So I suppose we hang out here and wait to see what happens with Miles Odekirk and those rocks he found," she said. "It seems to me like they could be very useful."

"For humans," Omar said dryly. "Or, I suppose, for djinn who enjoy the company of humans. In Khalim's case, though, I believe that the devices are still much more effective, because you would want him as debilitated as possible."

Okay, he had a point there. For a moment, Olivia wondered if she should give him any grief over that remark about "enjoying the company of humans," and then she decided she'd better let it go. She had the feeling that sometimes Omar didn't realize how offensive his words could be.

Or maybe he just didn't care.

Besides, if she was going to be stuck here with him for God knows how long, the last thing she wanted was to be bickering with him the whole time.

"True," she said, and spooned up some more soup. Maybe she wasn't as hungry as she possibly should be, but it would be foolish not to eat the delicious food Omar had provided for them.

"Also," he went on, picking up the previous thread of their conversation, "if Khalim were to discover you had gone to Los Alamos, he would know there would be no djinn there to protect you. It is not as if anyone living there would be able to immediately take you away, as I or some other djinn would be able to do."

If the devices were operating, no djinn would be able to do much of anything with his powers. Again, though, she didn't feel like poking holes in his argument. If he wanted to think of himself as some sort of invincible protector, then she'd go ahead and let him. After all, he'd rescued her from Khalim not once, but three times, so it wasn't as if he didn't have a decent track record for that sort of thing.

She nodded. "He does seem pretty persistent. Maybe he should get a hobby."

Even as the words left her lips, she wasn't sure how Omar would respond to a comment that had been meant as a joke. From what she'd seen so far, he didn't seem to have much of a sense of humor.

And hadn't she always told herself that she wanted a guy who knew when it was okay to laugh?

To her surprise, though, Omar let out a chuckle as he reached for his glass of water. "Yes, I suppose we would all be in a better situation if he suddenly decided to take up knitting."

"Or ice sculpture," Olivia suggested. "He'd have all winter to keep himself occupied."

Omar smiled and shook his head. Something about the shift in his expression made him seem much more approachable, not the cold, haughty djinn who'd been her companion for the past several days.

No, "cold" wasn't the right word to describe him. Someone who didn't allow emotions to touch him deeply would not have reacted to his parents' deaths the way he had. Olivia would be the first to admit that he could have found much more constructive ways to channel his sorrow and anger, but at the same time, she also couldn't deny that his was a soul that could be easily hurt.

"Alas," he said, "I fear Khalim will not accommodate us in such a way. All we can do is hope that he has withdrawn to weigh his options, and will not trouble us again until we can come up with some means of tracking him down and sending him back to the outer circles."

Like that worked so well the first time, Olivia thought, but she didn't say the words out loud. She knew very little about the djinn elders and what they were and weren't capable of, and yet she had to believe they'd make sure whatever prison they put Khalim in would be twice as secure as the first one.

No, the real problem was figuring out exactly where he was...and what he planned to do next.

"Have you finished?" Omar asked, gaze moving to the empty bowl in front of her, and Olivia nodded.

Apparently, she'd been hungrier than she'd first thought.

"Yes, thanks. It was wonderful."

But of course it was. It seemed djinn were incapable of conjuring anything that was less than perfect.

He looked pleased, though, and after a snap of

his fingers that cleared the table, he got up from his seat.

Olivia rose as well, and the two of them emerged into the bright sunlight outdoors. It would have been too cold to sit outside for any length of time, but she thought the temperature here must be at least ten degrees warmer than it had been in Los Alamos, maybe even a little more.

"Would you like to go back to the library and read?" Omar asked.

Although she'd enjoyed doing that the day before, the thought of spending another quiet afternoon with a book when so much else was going on in the world didn't feel at all appealing. "Would you mind if we took a walk instead? It just feels better to be out in the sunshine."

"Of course," he said, surprising her a little. She'd halfway expected him to demur, to say he had something else he needed to do.

That would have been a lie, though. Neither of them had much to occupy themselves while they were hiding out here at Los Poblanos, waiting for word that Khalim had finally been caught.

"I have been thinking of what I would do with this place if it were mine," he went on as they left the steps in front of Campos and headed toward what had once been the resort's lavender fields. They had all gone dreadfully to seed, but it probably wouldn't take a lot of work to bring them back...especially if an earth elemental was in charge of their restoration.

"Grow lavender?" she suggested, and again he smiled.

"It is a worthy crop, I suppose, but I think it would be better to plant orchards in some of these fields, and in others, to grow the food you humans called 'heirloom'—varieties that were once common and grew scarce as you became more and more industrialized."

That sounded like a great idea to her, but....

"Couldn't you just conjure whatever you needed?" she asked.

His smile didn't exactly disappear, but at the same time, his expression grew more serious. "Yes, of course I could. But there is something to be said for doing it the hard way, for coaxing those plants from the earth and waiting for them to produce fruit and seed. I suppose for a human, it would be the difference between baking your own bread or going to the store to purchase a loaf."

Olivia could understand that. Back in the world before, she'd never had the time to make bread—not that she'd even known how. Teaching herself, though, going through the process until she could produce something that was more than passable, was downright tasty, had been rewarding in a way she honestly hadn't been expecting.

So she could see how a djinn whose element

was the earth would take similar pleasure in watching seeds he'd planted grow and flourish.

"Well, I like the idea of orchards," she said. "And gardens full of heirloom vegetables. One of my roommates back before had parents who were really into growing heirloom tomatoes, and she'd bring some over every once in a while. They were amazing."

"Yes, I have had my share as well," Omar replied. "And I believe they are something that should be preserved."

She nodded, and the two of them walked in silence for a moment, enjoying the fresh breeze and the bright sun. After they crossed a small lane that separated two of the fields, she said, "Why not ask the elders if they can give you this place?"

Omar paused then, gazing down at her in surprise. "We do not make demands of the elders," he said. His tone wasn't quite a rebuke, but Olivia could tell she'd asked a question that was skirting some delicate ground. "They decide who should live where."

"Okay," she responded. "But still, your first house got burned down. It seems to me they should cut you some slack when it comes to giving you the next one."

He chuckled, the sound welcome. At least it didn't appear as though he intended to give her a lecture about not understanding how the djinn world worked.

"Perhaps they will," he said. "And it is a very good piece of land, one that would accommodate a great many different projects."

That it would. Olivia had no idea how many people had once worked here, staffing not just the resort and the restaurant and the spa, but also managing all these fields and making sure everything thrived and remained beautiful. Even a djinn would probably find his hands full keeping track of all that.

It would be nice to stay here and watch him bring Los Poblanos back to life. That wasn't going to happen, though. No, eventually, the djinn in Santa Fe, or the elders—or maybe even Miles Odekirk with his devices and his rocks—would figure out a way to trap Khalim forever, and then it would be time for her to go to Los Alamos and try to carve out some sort of existence for herself there.

She wouldn't allow herself to sigh, not with Omar standing right there.

However, he must have seen some shift in her expression, because he said, "Is something wrong?"

"No, nothing," she managed to reply. "I suppose I just got a little dreamy thinking about what this place would look like with apple and pear and apricot orchards all blooming in the springtime."

"Olivia," he said, and she forced herself to gaze up into his face. He looked very serious, but there was something about the way his eyes met hers that made a rush of heat go through her, even though he hadn't moved, hadn't said anything other than her name.

Was it possible he'd been battling the same sort of feelings she had?

No, that was ridiculous. He was a djinn whose opinion of humanity was painfully obvious.

And yet....

Would he really be staring back at her like that if his interest in her wasn't personal?

Her lips parted. She knew she should say something to diffuse the tension building between them, should make some kind of light-hearted, witty remark that would make this moment go away.

But before the words could come...before she even began to formulate the sort of comment she should make...he bent down and pressed his mouth against hers, arms going around her and pulling her close.

This was so very different from the times they'd traveled in the blink of an eye, carried by his djinn powers. Not just the pressure of his lips against hers, the warm taste of his mouth, but the way her entire body flushed with need and heat as she pressed up against him, sensing as if for the first time how strong he was, how muscular his arms and chest were.

The world seemed to tremble beneath her, but it was no earthquake this time, only the realization that Omar al-Qadir had initiated this kiss, and nothing would ever be quite the same again.

Eventually, he let go, but only so his hands could slide down her arms and his fingers could twine themselves with hers. Dark eyes met her gaze, frank, possibly the slightest bit startled.

"I was wondering if you were going to stop me," he said, mouth quirking.

"Should I have?" she responded, and he shook his head.

"No, of course not." He paused there, his grip on her fingers tightening a little. "But I would have stopped if you had asked."

She knew he would have. He was no Khalim, to force his attentions on women. As startling as that moment had been, however, she had very much wanted it to happen.

Lifting her chin, she said, "I wanted you to kiss me. I've probably been wanting it for a day or so now."

Crinkles showed around his dark eyes as he laughed. "Then I suppose it is a good thing I ignored my better judgment and went ahead and did it."

As wonderful as the kiss had been, that

comment made her eyes narrow as she gazed up at him. "Are you saying it was bad judgment to kiss me?"

"Of course it was," he said easily. "You know my history...my stand on matters such as this. And yet it seems that logic has abandoned me, for I went ahead and kissed you anyway."

"Logic doesn't have much to do with matters of the heart," she told him, even as she resolved not to get angry with him over his perceived view of the situation. He was right, after all—he had regarded humanity as the enemy for a very long time, and expecting him to leave that aside just because he found her attractive was kind of a big ask.

Still, she wasn't sure where all this left them.

"So...now what?" she asked, and he pulled her close so he could place a quick kiss on her lips before responding.

"Now," he said, "we continue our walk. Only I hope you might let me hold your hand as we do so."

How could she turn down a sideways request such as that? It was oddly charming...and that, she thought, was as good a description of Omar al-Qadir as any other she could think of.

It felt good to hold Olivia's hand in his, even if her fingers were a little chilled from exposure to the brisk wind that blew down from the north. And it felt good to look at this land and think of what he might do with it...if only it were his.

As he'd told her earlier, it was completely illogical for him to have kissed her. Once upon a time, he would never have even contemplated doing such a thing with a human woman, had thought his brothers the picture of weakness for giving their hearts to mortal females.

And here he had lost his to Olivia.

Oh, he could do his best to tell himself otherwise, that all he felt for her was a desire that would go away as soon as his need was fully slaked. But he realized now as they made their way along the paths that crisscrossed the property at Los Poblanos that it was simply enough to be with her, to hear the sound of her voice, a sweet, low alto, and to watch the sunlight awaken flickers of copper and gold in her dark hair.

To see the shifting depths in those green eyes, like purest jade.

He could not say he had never loved before. That had been different, though, just as Olivia was different from Ayanna, her own person, someone he could only thank fate or God or the universe for placing in his path.

Yes, even if she'd begun their acquaintance by shooting him in the leg.

"You're smiling," she said, and his shoulders lifted.

"I suppose I am," he replied. "To which I will say that it is easy to smile after sharing a kiss like that one."

She gave a small laugh, low, throaty. Just the sound of it made him want to pull her into his arms again. For now, though, he would do his best to be content with the sensation of her fingers pressed against his, slender and almost delicate, but strong nonetheless.

"I kind of want to be grinning like an idiot, too," she confessed. "Although I'm doing my best to hold it together." A small hesitation, and then she added, her gaze directed toward the resort building that lay ahead rather than at him, "I guess you know now why I didn't want to stay in Los Alamos."

"Yes, that notion had occurred to me," he said. "And I am very glad you did not allow logic to prevail. For I suppose this is a sort of madness, although one I do not want to end."

Olivia went silent for a moment, although he noted how she did not attempt to pull her hand from his. "But it will end, won't it? I mean, I still don't know exactly how all of this works, but it sounds as if a djinn and a human can't be together for any length of time unless...."

She let the words trail off, but he knew what she meant.

They could not be together unless the djinn made a human his Chosen.

But while they were walking, and as he told her of what he could do for this place, he'd realized it then, allowed the truth of the matter to come clear in his heart with the same inevitability as the sun rising in the east.

He loved Olivia Raskin, and if it turned out that she loved him, too, then what they were supposed to do next was simple enough.

"Unless that human is made Chosen," he said, then stopped beneath an arbor whose wisteria vine was probably spectacular in the spring, although it resembled not much more than a series of dry twigs at the moment. He reached over to push a wayward strand of hair away from her forehead and smiled a little at the simple beauty of her face in the clear December sunlight. "Dearest, did you really think I would have kissed you if I hadn't already made such a decision for myself?"

She stared back up at him, expression disbelieving. "You...you want to make me your Chosen?"

"I do," he said firmly. "I realized earlier today that saying goodbye to you would have been one of the most difficult things I've ever done. But when you made it clear you had no wish to remain in Los Alamos, I hoped you felt as I did. That kiss seemed to make your wishes abundantly clear."

To his surprise, she went on her toes so she could press a kiss on his cheek. It was a simple embrace, almost chaste, and yet the sensation of her lips against his skin was enough to send heat rushing through him all over again. "It is what I wished. That is, to be with you…whatever that might entail. But I'll admit that I don't completely understand what all this means."

He bent down to return her kiss, only this time against her mouth, a promise of further things to come. "Then let us go inside, and I will do my best to explain it to you."

Chapter 18

So much to take in—how the conscientious objectors among the djinn formed a group called the One Thousand...how they had each selected an immune human from among the survivors to make their partner.

How those partners were still human but received some of their djinn partners' long life and unending health.

If Omar made her his Chosen, then she would never get ill.

She would never die.

He had summoned them both glasses of wine, and after hearing even a part of what he had to say, Olivia was very glad to take a sip of pinot noir.

"I guess I missed a lot while hiding on that farm," she said, and Omar's mouth quirked.

"You did," he said. "And I certainly don't want

you to think that I am exerting any pressure on you. If you need time to ponder all this, I understand. But I also wanted you to know where I stood, for I am not one to be casual about such things."

No, Omar al-Qadir was probably the least casual man she'd ever met...not that her experience was huge.

Maybe it wasn't really her business, but she couldn't help asking, "Have you ever been in love with anyone else?"

He laughed then—although he also leaned in to press a kiss against her neck, a caress that sent delightful little shivers all down her spine.

"Once, long ago," he replied. "Her name was Ayanna. I had thought to be with her for some time, to even perhaps have a family with her."

Despite knowing that his relationship with Ayanna was buried far back in Omar's past, Olivia couldn't quite contain a spurt of jealousy. "What went wrong?"

His expression sobered immediately. "The decision was made at last to loose a plague upon humankind so that the djinn could reclaim this world as their own. I was glad, as were most of our people, for we could see the destruction mortals had wrought on this fragile earth, and I knew this was the only way to save it. Ayanna, however, wanted nothing to do with the scheme. I told her that I planned to be among those who rid the planet of any surviving humans, and we quarreled. I have not seen her since, although I heard that she had taken a Chosen and is now living somewhere in Italy."

This information startled Olivia somewhat, mostly because, while she understood intellectually that both male and female djinn had probably selected human partners, she had yet to meet a woman of the djinn, let alone one with a mortal significant other.

"Did that upset you?" she asked, and Omar's shoulders lifted a fraction.

"Let us say that it did not make me more disposed to look upon humans kindly."

This confession didn't surprise her too much. While she didn't fear his temper—his unexpected flashes of gentleness showed he was not quite the murderous monster he wanted the rest of the world to see—she couldn't deny that he'd done terrible things in the past.

The real question was, could she look past his crimes? The last thing she wanted was to be one of those women who excused a partner's awful behavior simply because she thought she was in love with him.

"Humans you've killed," she said, her tone flat.

He did not bother to deny it. "Yes, I have killed humans. Men who might have tried to re-create the world, make it the same planet careening into disaster that it once was. We djinn saved it. I suppose the question is whether you wish to weigh the lives of those I removed against all the animals and plants that would have died if I had allowed them to live."

Well, what in the world was she supposed to say to that? As she tried to sort through her chaotic thoughts, she took a sip of wine, and then another. Some people would probably have tried to argue that the life of a palm tree—or even a wild wolf, or a lion, or a giraffe—wasn't nearly the same as the life of a human. But when you weighed millions or even billions of lives...complete ecosystems...against the lives of a group of humans, the math got a whole lot messier.

Omar spoke again, his voice low but urgent. "I am not asking for forgiveness. I am not even asking for understanding, as I know that your frame of reference is completely different from mine. I am only asking whether you are willing to acknowledge what has grown between us, and whether you wish it to continue."

A pause as her fingers tightened on the stem of her glass. Right then, Olivia found herself wishing she could talk to the women who had become Omar's brothers' Chosen, thinking that maybe if she could get their perspective on the matter, then she'd have a better idea of how to respond to his last comment.

But no. This was a decision she needed to make on her own. Those women's situations were theirs, not hers, and while she might have been able to take their experiences into account, this situation with Omar was hers and hers alone.

People could change, though. Not always, and usually at great cost, but they weren't all like her mother, lost in a haze of drugs and alcohol, only able to function enough to make rent and put a little food in the pantry.

Sometimes, during a good month.

No, Olivia had met people in school and in her various jobs who'd lost everything and still managed to put the pieces back together again, people who'd also been addicted and left a trail of pain and suffering in their wake but had somehow managed to find the strength to face what they had done and make a change for the better.

Maybe Omar's crimes were on an entirely different level, but she still had to do her best to forgive him.

"I want it to continue," she said clearly, and he set his wine glass down on the table in front of them, then took her hand in his.

"As do I," he replied. The briefest hesitation, as if he wasn't sure whether he should say anything else, but then he went on, "And was there anyone in your life? Someone you lost?"

The question was such a joke to her that she wanted to laugh. But since she doubted Omar would have understood the flash of grim humor, she only said, "No. I'd been dating a guy for a while, but he was a controlling jerk and we broke up about six months before everything happened. There wasn't anyone after that."

Omar's brows drew together. "If it were not that I am almost certain he perished during the Heat, I would have taken very great pleasure in hunting down this 'controlling jerk.'"

Now Olivia did allow herself to laugh, although it came out more as a brittle chuckle. "He wouldn't be worth the effort. I only mentioned him so you'd know it's not as if I've been pining for someone else these past four years."

"And neither have I," Omar replied. His hand stole into hers, and he said, his tone quieter yet still almost urgent, "Then you wish to do this thing."

A shudder went through her. Although she was still doing her best to absorb what being a djinn's Chosen precisely meant, she understood that life would never be the same afterward. She would never grow ill, would never age.

She would be with Omar forever.

This was crazy, wasn't it? After all, they'd only shared a few kisses—kisses that had made her body come alive in a way she'd never experienced before —but still, it seemed mad to make a promise like this when they'd never even been truly intimate.

"But we haven't—" she began, and then stopped, heat flooding her cheeks. Maybe it was silly to get embarrassed talking about sex, but then, she hadn't been with anyone for a very long time. Even back in the before times, intimacy had been something she struggled with, taking much longer than any of the people she knew to get into bed with someone. Her one and only therapist— someone she could only afford to see for a few months—had told her she had trust issues, which, she'd thought, was the sort of insight she probably hadn't needed to pay a hundred bucks an hour to hear. It was the kind of thing you probably could have seen from space.

"No, we have not made love," Omar said without even a blink. "But I know it will be wonderful with you, Olivia. Either two people have that flame, that passion, between them, or they do not. I can already tell we do. More important to me is how easy the days have seemed with you, even when we were on the run from Khalim. What more could I ask?"

Had it really been that easy? She'd thought there had been plenty of tension between them, but then again, they'd had a lot going on. Even so, she realized they'd been able to talk almost from the beginning, despite the way she'd shot him...and despite the way he'd been intent on finding anything he could dislike about her because of her humanity.

In the end, none of that had mattered. As he'd just said, attraction...love...tended to trump just about anything else.

"Nothing, I suppose," she said, and he smiled, dark eyes lighting up in that way she hoped she would get to see more and more of.

"Besides," he added, expression growing sober once again, "I am not my brothers, to initiate such a relationship with no thought as to what might happen in the end. True, they did decide to be with their human partners permanently, but it was not an easy road to get there."

Olivia couldn't help raising an eyebrow. "And you think ours was easy?"

Now he smiled, a brilliant flash of white teeth in the dimly lit room, making the space seem suddenly bright. Even at the height of day, the space never seemed to get much sun, but it didn't matter when he smiled like that.

"Well, perhaps not easy," he admitted. "And I did not want to acknowledge what I was beginning to feel for you, or perhaps I would have spoken sooner. What I do know is that the thought of you going away hurt more than I'd believed it would...

and that led me to understand that I wanted to ensure you would always be with me."

Coming from someone else, a statement like that might have sounded a bit stalker-y. But Olivia knew he was only trying to impress on her how much it mattered that they would remain together. On the surface, this might have seemed like an about-face, and yet she guessed he had been wrestling with his feelings for some time, just as she had with hers.

The whole thing had felt utterly impossible.

Somehow, though, it wasn't.

"And I want to be with you," she said quietly. "I have a hard time being comfortable with people. But you—for some reason, you were different, even when you should have been the last person on earth I could be easy around."

She'd been holding her wine glass in her hand this whole time, even though she hadn't drunk from it in a while. Omar took it from her and set it on the coffee table in front of them so he could twine his fingers with hers, pull her close, give her another of those kisses that made it feel as if the earth trembled once more beneath her feet.

He tasted so good, of rich wine and something else, something aromatic and delicious. The kiss deepened, and her body ran with fire, even though it wasn't his element. No, she'd never felt like this before, as if his embrace was the only thing in the world that mattered.

When the kiss ended, he pulled away a few inches so he could gaze directly into his eyes. "Are you certain?" he asked, his voice only a little more than a whisper.

"I'm sure," she replied, surprised that she sounded so steady, so certain. "I don't think I've ever been more sure of anything in my life."

Omar smiled at her then, face illuminated with the same inner joy she knew she felt as well. "Then I will say it for you and the universe to hear. Olivia Raskin is my Chosen, and my protection is given to her."

She held herself very still, but as far as she could tell, nothing seemed to have happened. "That's it?" she asked.

He chuckled and pulled her close again so he could press a gentle kiss against her mouth. "Yes, that is 'it.' No grand ceremony—just an announcement to us and all of creation that we are now joined, djinn and Chosen."

Even though she had a feeling she knew exactly what was going to come next, she couldn't help saying, "So...what now?"

"Now," he said as he rose from the couch, helping her up at the same time, "we seal our bond forever."

This was happening. He had made Olivia Raskin his Chosen, and now they were walking down the hall to the wing of the building where both their suites were located. The whole situation had an air of unreality, even though the fingers twined with his felt solid enough, and he knew he was not imagining the brilliant smile she wore as she looked up at him.

But the room they entered was also real—although they had not made a conscious choice, it seemed both of them were intent on going to the suite she'd been using, which was larger and had a luxurious bed hung with the same filmy cotton draperies that framed the tall windows. He pulled her to him and kissed her again, over and over, his body growing hotter and hotter with need.

A welcoming sigh as he pressed his lips against her neck and moved slowly down to the open neckline of the sweater she wore. And certainly, no protest when he hooked his fingers around the bottom edge of the garment so he could pull it up and over her head. The bra she wore was plain white, strictly utilitarian, but the swell of her breasts against it was enough to make his pulse pound a little hotter. He could have simply wished the restrictive piece of underwear away, and yet it was somehow more enticing to reach around and unhook it manually, to let it fall to the floor as he took in the glory of her exposed flesh, full and round and just begging to be suckled.

Although he didn't remember intending to do so, they both sank onto the bed, his mouth on her, licking her exquisite flesh, listening to her moan with pleasure. And if this simple touch was enough to make her react in such a way, he could only imagine what other pleasures were in store.

He undid the button and the zipper of her jeans, then tugged them down. The boots she wore were in the way, and this time he did use his djinn powers to remove them and toss them into a corner, thus freeing him to pull her pants off alto-gether, dropping them to join her bra and sweater on the floor.

Like her bra, her panties were simple white cotton, not the sort of thing that would normally inflame a man's desires. Now, though, he thought he had never seen anything as beautiful as her near-naked body stretched across the light-colored duvet, her loose hair a dark mass against the fabric, rich and beautiful as newly turned earth in the spring.

Soon enough, the panties were gone, and he bent to kiss his way down to her mound, breathing in her exquisite scent. And when he tasted her, she moaned again, body shifting to press against him.

Oh, yes, she was amazing, every inch of her.

The climax came sooner than he'd expected, telling him how receptive she was to his caresses. His body clamored for its own release, and he shifted, pressing against her, feeling how wet she was, how ready for him.

"Yes, Omar," she whispered. "I want to feel you."

Who was he to deny the wishes of the woman he loved?

He slid inside her, feeling her surround him, feeling how the two of them seemed to fit together perfectly. She moaned again, legs wrapping around him, driving him deeper, as though she wanted to make sure this joining was something that would never end.

Perhaps not endless, but he lost himself in the time that passed, feeling the glory of her body beneath him and around him, knowing he was getting close to the edge but also telling himself that he wanted to take care of her first.

Another moan tore itself from her throat, and she tightened on him, driving him to the orgasm he'd been holding back, his own cries blending with hers as a shared climax tore through them both.

He rested on her for an eternity or so more, not wanting to pull away and end such precious, precious contact. But then he finally moved so he could lie next to her, could stare into her lovely face, cheeks flushed, a faint sheen of perspiration showing on the smooth skin of her forehead.

How could a woman who was not a djinn be so perfect?

And yet, she was. Perfect in every detail, perfect in a way he could never have imagined.

"I love you, Olivia Raskin," he said simply, and she reached out to push a lock of hair back from his forehead.

"And I love you, Omar al-Qadir," she replied, the faintest of dimples showing next to her mouth.

And that, it seemed, was that.

———

They went into the bathroom afterward. It had been her suggestion, but Omar seemed fine with stepping into the shower together so they could run soap all over one another's bodies...so she could reach down and take him in her hand, could let him know how much she loved touching him.

Afterward, he bent down to kiss her, dark eyes taking on a glint that told her they'd probably return to bed sooner rather than later. Which was fine. She couldn't think of many better ways to spend their time here than to lose themselves in one another's bodies, learning more and more about each other with every passing hour.

Inside, though, she was a little surprised at

herself. It wasn't that she'd never enjoyed sex, but more that it had been a take-it-or-leave-it activity for her, and she'd never truly understood why people made such a big deal about it.

Well, she understood now. All she could think of was how Omar felt, how he tasted, of how magnificent his body was with all those heavy robes cast aside to reveal the defined muscles underneath. She'd gotten a small glimpse when she dressed his leg, in an incident that felt as though it must have taken place a hundred years ago, but that tiny look still hadn't prepared her for the beauty of his naked form.

As she'd thought, they started kissing as soon as they emerged from the bathroom and had just fallen on the bed, hands moving over bare flesh, when Omar sat up suddenly, expression shocked.

"What is it?" Olivia asked. A second ago, he'd seemed ready to lose another hour or so in lovemaking, but now he looked as if someone had just thrown a bucket of water over him.

"Aamir just reached out to me," he said, brow furrowed with worry.

"Khalim al-Usar just tried to burn his house down."

Chapter 19

Olivia hadn't thought she'd ever return to Zahrias and Julia's elegant home near Santa Fe's plaza—especially not so soon—but she and Omar had rushed there after hearing the news about Khalim's attack, only to find Aamir and his partner Isla at the house as well, looking a little smudged but otherwise not much worse for wear. Also present was another djinn who looked so much like Aamir and Omar that Olivia guessed he must be the middle brother, Jamal. With him was a strikingly pretty red-haired woman who had been introduced as his Chosen, Rowan Aames.

"I am fine," Aamir said in response to Omar's worried question. "Luckily, we were both home, and I was able to stop the blaze before it spread very far. It took out two bedrooms in the wing we use for offices, but it will not take much effort to replace those."

No, probably not. Olivia had a feeling all he'd have to do was snap his fingers to make things go back to normal.

Or at least, it would be easy to fix the house. Getting past this brazen attack on someone in the Santa Fe community might be a little more difficult.

It seemed Zahrias was thinking the same thing, because he was frowning mightily. "What in the world did Khalim think he would achieve with such an attack?"

"He probably wanted to unsettle us," Aamir said. "I believe he was angry because he had no idea where Omar had taken Olivia Raskin, and so he thought he would strike against someone in his family, thinking that might flush my brother out of hiding."

If that had been his goal, then he had succeeded. Then again, Olivia wasn't sure whether it mattered all that much, since they'd come straight to Zahrias and Julia's home, which was located in the heart of town and therefore was probably one of the safest places for them to be.

"He was also probably pissed off that I wasn't in my pottery studio," Isla put in. She looked more irritated than anything, as though the attack was an inconvenience but not much more. "I'd actually been there in the morning, but I finished the pot I was working on and put it on a shelf before heading inside. I have the impression that he'd been watching the house for the past day, trying to get a feel for when I'd be out there alone...and vulnerable."

A little shiver went through Olivia at that mental image. It did seem like the sort of thing Khalim would do—skulking around while he determined his best plan of attack.

And if they couldn't find him...if he kept dropping in to cause some form of mayhem before disappearing again...then she knew they'd never be able to relax completely, would never be able to stop looking over their shoulders. Maybe she and Omar were safe at Los Poblanos, since there hadn't been a single indication that Khalim had ever come near there, but she didn't like the idea of being able to hide in their sanctuary while the rest of the Santa Fe community was at risk.

"He is a wily fox, I will give him that," Aamir said. "But we cannot go on like this. Whose house is next?"

"Ours probably," Jamal replied. He held his partner's hand, and his jaw was set, expression grim.

"No, that would be too predictable," Omar

said. He was standing close to Olivia, but she noticed that he hadn't tried to take her hand or do anything that might reveal the change in their status.

Was he embarrassed by what had happened between them only a short time ago?

No, Omar wasn't the sort of person to hide things about himself. It seemed much more likely that he was trying to downplay the situation because he knew they had more urgent matters to focus on right now.

"My guess is that he will try to attack someone else who lives on the edge of town, someone who might be vulnerable in a way those of you who live closer to the city center might not be," Omar went on. "Who else has a home like that?"

"Qadim al-Syan and Madison, his Chosen, live in Las Campanas, to the west of here," Zahrias replied. His frown hadn't lessened in the slightest. "And then there are Jasreel al-Ankara and his Chosen, Jessica Monroe. Their home is up in the hills, past where Canyon Road ends."

Olivia didn't know Santa Fe very well, but both those houses sounded as though they were ripe for an attack by Khalim. However, her worries were eased somewhat as Jamal said, "I can go and warn them, for I have been to both their homes and can travel there quickly."

"Do so," Zahrias replied at once. "For it is obvious that Khalim relies only on stealth and sneak attacks, and will not be brave enough to approach a place where someone is obviously keeping watch."

Without replying, Jamal disappeared. Olivia wanted to startle—she still wasn't used to the way djinn could blink themselves in and out of existence without batting an eye—but since everyone else was acting as though it wasn't a big deal, she did her best to be just as blasé.

"Now Qadim and Jasreel and their Chosen should be safe," Zahrias said. "And I will send word to the rest of the community here that we must be doubly on our guard against Khalim's depredations. However, this is by no means a permanent solution. We must think of some way to catch him, to make sure he is handed over to the elders and can trouble us no more."

Everyone went silent then, obviously worried. Olivia was quiet as well...even as a terrible idea entered her mind.

Maybe there was a way to catch Khalim al-Usar...if she could be brave enough.

Although she hated to draw attention to herself like this, she knew she needed to speak up.

"We have to lay a trap for him," she said distinctly, while everyone stared at her in surprise.

"And I need to be the bait."

As soon as Olivia spoke, fear and worry coursed through Omar.

How could she volunteer to put her life on the line when they had only just now discovered one another?

"There has to be some other way," he said.

She shook her head, even as she reached out to take his hand. Although he had been doing his best to act as though nothing had changed between them...mostly because he saw no need to bring up the topic when so much more was happening...he clung to her fingers now, hoping that the pressure of flesh against flesh would be enough to tell her what a very bad idea this was.

Watching them, Aamir's eyes narrowed, but he didn't say anything. And although Zahrias and Julia exchanged a weighted look, it also seemed as though they didn't wish to comment on that unexpected touch.

"I'm not exactly thrilled to have thought of it," Olivia said, mouth tugging into a lopsided smile. "But it makes sense. Khalim has always been trying to go after me, and he's causing mayhem because he can't get his way. So it seems to me the best thing to do is to lay a trap for him and grab him when he least expects it."

"And how exactly would we lay this trap?" Zahrias inquired.

"We need to lure him to some kind of neutral location, like maybe another house in Cedar Crest," Olivia replied. Her brows had drawn together, and Omar could tell she was thinking furiously as she spoke. "Make him think that I wanted to go there to be by myself. I would have suggested the farm, but he's got to know there's something odd about it because of the way neither his nor Omar's powers worked when they were there. However, it wouldn't seem too weird that I'd want to go back to a place that felt familiar to me."

"And what is to stop him from disappearing with you the second he discovers where you are?" Omar demanded. He did not like the sound of this, not at all. Too many things could go wrong.

"Because we'll get a piece of that crystal from Miles Odekirk," Olivia said calmly. "The good thing about those rocks is that you don't notice your powers are being blocked until you try to use them, right?"

As much as he hated to acknowledge that point, he made himself reply, "Yes, that does seem to be how they work."

"Then they're the perfect thing to trap Khalim," she said.

Zahrias had been listening to all this intently, but now he said, "The problem is that if Khalim does not have access to his powers, none of the rest of us will, either."

"True," Olivia agreed. She did not seem as much on edge now, as though she'd had a chance to pick at any holes in her plan to make sure it would work. "However, it will be one djinn against a bunch of you. I saw how Omar gave him hell at the farm, so it's not like he's invincible or anything close to it."

"We will be able to take him," Aamir stated, his tone firm. He looked over at Omar as he added, "You know there is no way he will be able to withstand you and I and Jamal working together."

The idea of having his brothers there to lend their aid was unexpected...even as Omar made himself acknowledge that he was the reason for their current rift. Would it not be best for everyone involved to present a united front and eliminate this threat once and for all?

"No," Omar said, "I suppose he would not. But how are we to even get word to Khalim that Olivia has returned to Cedar Crest?"

"That will be easy enough," Zahrias replied. "It is clear that Khalim has been lurking around the area, spying on us. I will ask Murrah to lift his restrictions on Martine and allow her to go riding once again. I do not doubt that Khalim will approach her as soon as he realizes she is easy prey."

Judging by the way the women in the room frowned at that remark, none of them seemed to think this was a very good idea. However, Omar believed it an acceptable risk. Khalim had no morals and no true idea of right and wrong, but even he would not harm Martine when he knew doing so would earn him a much harsher punishment. No, he had only approached her for information and nothing more.

And if he had done it once, he would most likely do so again.

"Very well," Omar said. "You can speak to Murrah and Martine...and then we can see whether that part of our plan is working."

"I don't like the idea of using Martine as bait," Olivia told Omar as soon as they returned to Los Poblanos, but he only shrugged.

"Khalim has already shown that he sees her as a vessel for useful information and nothing more," he replied. "For he has his intention set on a greater prize."

That comment made a little chill run down her spine, even as Olivia was forced to admit to herself that Omar was right. For whatever reason, the rogue djinn had fixated on her, and would much rather pursue a woman he thought was alone in the world, rather than the Chosen of probably the biggest djinn she'd ever seen.

"What if Martine doesn't go along with this little scheme?" she asked next, but Omar didn't look too concerned.

"She will," he said. "She is a member of the Santa Fe community, and from what I can tell, they all do what they must to keep their people safe and happy. No, the only real complication I can think of is that Khalim might not believe what she tells him."

Olivia had already entertained that disturbing possibility. One could say a whole lot of things about Khalim al-Usar, none of them good, but she hadn't seen any evidence to prove he wasn't clever and cunning. Otherwise, he would have already made a mistake that would have led to his capture.

"What do we do if that happens?"

"We proceed anyway," Omar said calmly. They'd come back to the bar at Los Poblanos, and he now led her over to one of the leather couches so they could sit down. "For even if Khalim is not entirely certain of the intelligence Martine provides, it will be easy enough for him to come to Cedar Crest to assess the situation for himself. And once he is there, he will sense your presence, and we will be able to spring the trap after all."

This made some sense. Olivia supposed at some point she'd get used to the ease with which djinn did everything, and would realize that a complication that might be a hindrance to a human was no big deal to one of the elementals. So yes, she could see why popping down to Cedar Crest would be only an eye blink to Khalim.

Omar reached over and took her hand. As always, his fingers were warm, and although she couldn't be completely reassured, she had to admit she felt a whole lot better with him there next to her, offering his own comfort and strength.

Besides, this entire scheme had been her idea. It would be pretty stupid to start throwing out objections when she was the one who'd put herself in this position in the first place.

"All right," she said, and allowed herself a sigh, even as she snuggled against his shoulder. "But I really hope Khalim doesn't approach Martine until tomorrow. I'd like a last meal in this place."

Omar chuckled, then bent to press a kiss against the top of her head. "It will not be your last meal. But yes, I find myself hoping for the same thing."

The rest of the afternoon was quiet, leading Omar to believe that even if Martine had ventured out to the stables after the plan was explained to her, it seemed Khalim had either not noticed that she'd returned to her previous habits...or was watching her carefully to see whether this was a resumption of her old patterns or a one-off occasion.

Whatever was happening in Santa Fe, Omar knew he could not control it. And that was all right, for it allowed him to concentrate on where he was...and who he was with.

A fine dinner at Campo, of course, followed by another night with Olivia in her suite. He would not allow himself to think of it as a "last" meal the way she'd referred to their dinner, but only a means of confirming the bond between them. It seemed fairly obvious to him that his brothers and Zahrias had detected his new connection with her, although, mercifully, none of them had deemed the occasion appropriate for commenting on it. There would be a time and place for that later...a time when, he had no doubt, Aamir and Jamal would delight in making him eat crow over his change of heart...but until then, the focus should be on Olivia.

As before, he told her to meet him at Campo a little after six, only this time his reason was not so he would have some time alone without her distracting presence. No, he wanted to make sure the restaurant was ready to receive her...and he also wanted her to find the surprise he'd left in the closet of her suite.

So when she appeared an hour or so later, it

was in the gown he'd provided, an artfully draped dress in exactly the correct shade of green to bring out all the forest hues of her eyes...and to show off a figure that was usually hidden by her utilitarian outfits of sweaters and jeans.

Because the nights were chilly, he'd also summoned a shawl of soft wool in shades of green and blue to protect her bare shoulders and arms as she walked over here, and she wore it now, only removing it once he'd closed the door to the restaurant behind her.

"Dressing for dinner," she said as she hung the shawl on the coat rack at the entrance. "How...old school."

Omar only shook his head. "While I understand that your usual attire is practical, it does not show you to your best advantage, my love."

She went on her tiptoes—teetering slightly in the heels he'd also provided—and placed a kiss against his cheek. "All right, jeans and boots aren't exactly appropriate for going to the Academy Awards. But while I love the dress, I'm not sure I'm a fan of these shoes."

He sent her a sly smile. "Then I suppose you can take them off. I will admit that your bare feet are much lovelier."

That comment made her grin in return, although she also bent down to remove the delicate sling-backs so she could set them at the base of the coat rack. "Much better," she said. "So...what's on the menu tonight?"

"A surprise," he said.

"Not something from the Campos menu?"

Her green eyes were sparkling, and he could tell she was doing her best to act as though there was nothing more to worry about than what he was serving her that night.

"As I said, a surprise."

She chuckled but refrained from comment as he guided her to the same table where they had eaten the night before. This evening, though, he hadn't worried about appearing extravagant, and therefore flowers hung from the wrought-iron chandeliers and bedecked every table, while candles flickered from all available surfaces.

"It looks like a fairyland in here," Olivia commented, seating herself in the chair he'd pulled out for her. "Or maybe someone's fancy wedding."

Djinn did not precisely participate in that very human custom, but he still thought they could consider this their wedding night, now that he'd made her his Chosen. In their case, however, there was no need to worry about death parting them.

No, he would be with Olivia forever, and was very glad of that.

He took the chair to her left. Immediately, a bottle of champagne in a standing ice bucket appeared in the space between them, and bowls of lobster bisque materialized at each place setting.

"Champagne?" she said. "Now it really feels like a wedding."

She did not, however, inquire as to the occasion, telling Omar she understood very well what all this was about. Although he could not count himself an expert in opening champagne bottles, he nudged this one along with his powers and was gratified to see the cork go shooting upward into the rafters before it fell to the floor a moment later with a barely perceptible thud.

The bubbly fluid showed no signs of overflowing, luckily, and he went ahead and filled the flutes that had also appeared at the same time as the champagne itself. Olivia took her glass and lifted it, then asked, "What are we toasting?"

"You," he said simply, and she shook her head, her lustrous hair falling in enticing waves around her bare shoulders.

"I'm not sure I want to toast myself," she replied with a smile. "Let's just toast the two of us."

"A good idea."

They touched glasses and drank. Unlike his brothers, he was not a connoisseur of fine wines, but he had heard somewhere that Cristal was among the best champagnes, so that was what he had summoned this evening.

"God, that's good," Olivia said.

"You have never had it?"

A chuckle. "Considering a bottle cost about the same as a week of rent, no."

He wondered then how difficult her life had been, how many privations she'd had to suffer before the Heat came along and changed the world forever. The few comments she'd made regarding her past had painted a fairly bleak picture.

However, he did not want to ask questions about that now, not when they were doing their best to have a pleasant evening together. It was enough for him to know that whatever poverty and want had marred her childhood and life as an adult, they were nothing she needed to worry about now.

Of course, she was facing a danger far more immediate tomorrow.

"I wish you did not have to do this," he said.

Being a perceptive woman, she did not pretend to misunderstand what he was saying.

"I'm not looking forward to it, either," she responded, then set down her glass of champagne so she could pick up a spoon. "But it's something that needs to be done. Maybe at some point, the elders would step in, but that's not guaranteed, right?"

"Nothing regarding the elders is 'guaranteed,'" he said, retrieving his spoon and helping himself to a mouthful of lobster bisque. "They do things according to their own whim and also do their best to avoid interfering until it is absolutely necessary. That is why I think they are waiting to see if we can solve this problem on our own without any intervention on their part."

"Makes me wonder what they're good for."

Omar gazed back at her, at the frank expression in those shimmering green eyes, and reminded himself that she still knew very little of djinn culture or history. "They are good for a great many things. I suppose you could view them as a guardrail, designed to keep us in place if we veer too far out of line. However, they are not a governing body in the way you might be more familiar with, and they are certainly not the djinn equivalent of the police."

At once, Olivia set down her spoon and reached over to touch his hand. "Sorry, that was probably tactless of me. I suppose I'm just feeling frustrated. It would be so much easier if the elders just appeared out of nowhere and sent Khalim back to the outer circles where he belongs."

"It would," Omar agreed. Unfortunately, he doubted the elders would deliver the desired *deus ex machina*. In this situation, the Santa Fe djinn and he and Olivia would be working on their own. "But your plan is a good one. Now all we can do is wait and hope that Khalim is desperate enough to approach Martine again. It is all well and good to set out some bait, but if the animal we are trying to catch does not take it, then we will have to start over with a different plan."

Rather than look downcast at this comment, Olivia only lifted her chin and gazed off to their left, roughly in the direction where Santa Fe was located. She was silent for a moment, then spoke.

"Oh, I think he'll take the bait. He won't be able to stop himself."

Chapter 20

OVER THE REST OF DINNER, THEY WORKED out the plan, then confirmed it with Aamir, who told Omar he would manage the rest of the details. A chunk of the stone would be borrowed by several of the male Chosen in Santa Fe, who would also ferry it to the house in Cedar Crest Olivia had selected as her supposed home base. It was actually a place she'd considered living in, big and luxurious and nothing she would ever have been able to afford in real life, although she'd eventually decided against it because the house simply wasn't self-sustaining in a way the farm had been, with its solar panels and well and large propane tank.

But she remembered it well enough, and was able to give the address and description to Omar, who passed it along to Aamir. The al-Qadir brothers would travel to the general store on

Highway 14, since it was an easy landmark to find, and also only a quarter-mile or so to the house they would be using as the honey pot. That would place the store outside the field of effect of the stone the two Chosen had placed in the home, but close enough that it would be an easy walk.

Despite the ecstatic lovemaking she and Omar had shared after their dinner, Olivia found it hard to sleep that night. It seemed their plan was strong enough, but she still kept waking up and forcing herself to roll over into a different position in an attempt to fall back into slumber, her mind racing, trying to poke holes in the scheme, doing her best to think of every contingency in case Khalim surprised her.

There was also the possibility that he would smell a rat, and wouldn't show up at all.

Eventually, though, she slept in the later hours of the night, and woke up to shimmering sunlight beyond the filmy curtains that covered the window of their suite.

Omar leaned over and pressed a kiss against her cheek. "I will not ask if you slept well, my love, for I can tell you were restless."

"I'm sorry if I kept you awake," she replied, pushing herself up to a sitting position.

He sat up as well, the sheets falling away from his well-muscled torso. Desire stirred in her...but worry was stronger.

"It is not so much that I was awake, but that I was able to sense you were." His fingers found hers and stroked them gently. "I understand your concern, but I think everything will be fine. My brothers and I will be there to protect you. Khalim will be quite outnumbered."

Intellectually, Olivia knew that. Even so, her brain kept wanting to manufacture all sorts of terrible contingencies.

She wouldn't burden Omar with her worries, though. While this might have been uncharted territory for all of them, it didn't change the simple truth that it would be three djinn against one, and no matter how cunning Khalim might be, he wouldn't be able to overcome the sheer force of their numbers.

"Yes, he will," she said, making sure she sounded firm and confident, and as if she'd never harbored any doubts that they would emerge victorious. "So, let's have some breakfast and get this party started."

Omar knew Olivia was doing her best to hide her worries from him, so he didn't attempt to weary her with constant reassurances. No, he summoned a hearty breakfast in bed for both of them, since he knew they needed to be ready to go at a moment's notice, and afterward, while they shared a shower to save time, they did not attempt to liven it up with some impromptu lovemaking.

Later, though...after this was all done...they would have to make up for lost time.

It was a good thing they had made such haste, for only a short time after they'd emerged from the shower and gotten dressed, he heard Aamir's voice in his head.

Khalim approached Martine on her morning ride, just as we had hoped. She confessed to him that Olivia had gone back to Cedar Crest, and he promptly disappeared after that.

Then we do not have a moment to lose, Omar replied. *I will meet you at the general store, as we planned.*

I will let Jamal know.

Aamir broke off the contact then, but since the necessary information had already been conveyed, there was no reason to keep speaking to one another. Omar glanced over at Olivia, who had just pulled her heavy dark hair into a sturdy barrette, and said, "It is time."

She swallowed, but then her chin went up and she nodded. "Then let's do this."

He went to her and placed his arms around her waist, then blinked them to the general store she had shown him in her mind the day before. At once, they emerged in the rather shabby confines of the shop, its numerous bare shelves a testimony to all the quiet raiding she'd done during the years she'd lived in Cedar Crest.

Immediately afterward, Jamal and Aamir appeared as well. "Aidan and David have remained in the area," Aamir said, naming the two Chosen who had planted the stone in the house where they had set their trap, "but not so close that Khalim should be able to detect their presence. However, I doubt we will need their assistance."

No, Omar saw no need for their intervention, not when he had his two brothers with him. It was true that Aidan harbored a particular grudge against the rogue djinn, for it was Khalim who had cut the human's face open, leaving him with scars he would wear until the end of his days, but still, one angry human was no match for a djinn.

"That is good to know," Omar said, and left it there. He looked over at Olivia. "Are you ready?"

"Sure," she replied, and her tone was steady, betraying nothing of the worry he knew she must be experiencing at that moment.

He went to her and kissed her very gently on the cheek. "It will be fine," he told her. "Just remember that Jamal and Aamir and I will be close, and that we will not allow any harm to come to you."

Once he was finished speaking, he summoned a backpack filled with supplies—energy bars, a small bag of sugar, a few cans of food—to make it seem as though she had gone out foraging, just in case she came upon Khalim while walking to the house. Omar hoped that would not be the case, and that she would be safely inside before the other djinn found her, but they could not count upon such an eventuality.

Olivia took the backpack and settled it on one shoulder. "Okay, I'm heading out. Remember, it's 223 Oak Grove Lane."

"I remember," Omar replied. No, the image of the house she had shown him the night before—a sprawling one-story home with a swimming pool and extensive gardens—was now engraved in his mind, along with the image of the streets that surrounded it. The neighborhood was one of large plots of land and equally large homes, most of them bordered with trees, which would make a covert approach a bit easier. He and his brothers would have to rely on stealth, for they would not be able to blink themselves directly there, thanks to the power-nullifying qualities of the stone Miles Odekirk had loaned them.

She managed a smile and a small wave, then turned and walked out of the general store and began heading south on Highway 14. Omar couldn't help thinking she looked very small and exposed as she strode away from them, and wondered what would happen if Khalim materialized then and there, in a place where all of them had possession of their powers.

But he did not, and soon enough, Olivia disappeared around a curve of the highway. Omar turned to his brothers.

"It is time."

She was all too glad to get off the highway and onto the feeder road that led into the expensive neighborhood where her destination was located. At least here most of the properties had trees ringing them, affording her a little more privacy, even though she still felt as though every unfriendly eye on the planet could spy her making her way along the narrow street, backpack hanging from one shoulder.

Well, no one would probably fault her for shooting a cautious glance upward every once in a while to make sure no djinn were descending upon her. But the sky remained clear except for a couple of hawks circling far above, so she continued to forge ahead, hoping she would make it to the house before being accosted. Not that she would necessarily be any safer once she was indoors, but something about having a roof over her head still felt better.

As it turned out, she reached her destination

without incident and let herself inside right away. It felt strange to be in here after so much time had elapsed, since even her last foraging expedition to this particular house had been nearly a year ago. However, nothing about the place seemed to have materially changed...well, except that it was obvious that the same men who'd hidden the stone here in one of the drawers in the coffee table in the living room had given the rooms a quick dusting so the house wouldn't look so abandoned.

But it was still a large ranch-style home, with vaulted ceilings and multiple fireplaces and furniture she knew had once been very expensive. Not for the first time, she wondered who had lived here, or in any of the high-dollar homes in the neighborhood. Probably lawyers or doctors or executives who worked in Albuquerque but wanted to come back to country life, since the commute wouldn't have been that bad, maybe thirty minutes or so.

Not that it really mattered now. They were long gone, along with most of humanity.

Since she wasn't sure what else she should do, she headed into the kitchen, figuring she could unload her backpack there and keep up the façade that she'd been living here all along and had only ventured out to get more supplies. It was a big space, with taupe cabinets and expensive stone countertops that she didn't think were granite, maybe marble or dolomite or soapstone, like she'd seen on shows about high-end kitchen remodels.

Not that it mattered, except she liked the feel of the room despite its obvious luxury. Maybe she could have Omar make her a kitchen like this one when they settled on a house.

Yes, that was better. It felt good to think about what sort of home they would have together. Something in Santa Fe, she assumed, since it sounded as though that was where all the djinn in New Mexico settled with their Chosen. She was a little iffier on that idea, just because she felt more comfortable at Los Poblanos, even though it was a resort and not a house. But they'd fallen in love there, made love there, and that had turned it into home for her.

Thinking about the future—even one in Santa Fe—was much better than dwelling on where and when Khalim might appear.

If he even showed up at all. Omar and his brothers had sounded fairly certain that he would, but Olivia still found herself doubtful. Would the rogue djinn really be able to sense her presence here, out of all the houses in Cedar Crest?

Well, she'd worry about that when she had to, if this dragged on and on with no sign of her pursuer. They'd come up with this plan, and they'd come up with another one if necessary.

She placed the last can of vegetables in the

pantry and emerged, only to go stock still in shock. Standing near the kitchen entrance was Khalim, an ugly smile pulling at his mouth.

"Hello, Olivia," he said. "I'm so happy to find you at home."

Omar and Jamal and Aamir had not taken the same road into the neighborhood that Olivia had followed, wanting to make sure they kept far enough away from her that Khalim would have no chance of seeing them if he happened to intercept her before she reached the house. Instead, they had materialized as close as they dared, then took the much rougher path that bordered the development, one Omar guessed had been designed as a walking trail but had become completely overgrown in the years since the Dying.

None of them spoke, which he thought was just as well. He did not want to discuss the alteration in his relationship with Olivia, and neither did he feel inclined to explore contingency after contingency. They would reach the property and get the lay of the land, and decide what to do after that, depending on what they encountered.

However, after they'd walked for about five minutes, Jamal remarked, "My powers are gone. We must be getting close."

Aamir nodded, even as Omar paused to see if he could cause even the slightest of earth tremors. Nothing at all, which meant his brother was correct.

"Good," he said. While it was somewhat disconcerting still to recognize that he could not tap into the powers that had been his almost since birth, this was nothing like having one of those terrible devices acting on him. He still felt fully himself, not weak and useless. "Then we must take even greater care."

Luckily, whoever had created this development had seen fit to plant many trees along this path, so it was not difficult to maintain their cover as they moved closer and closer to the home they were pretending was Olivia's. A few more yards, and there was the low stone wall that surrounded the property.

All three of them easily climbed over it and moved closer. Not a moment too soon, for Omar heard her voice then, carrying clearly through a window that should not have been open at this season, even on a sunny day such as this one.

"Stay away from me!"

At once, Omar bolted from their hiding place in the shrubs, Aamir and Jamal fast on his heels. A set of French doors opened onto the patio, and he headed for them, hoping they were unlocked, wondering what he would do if they were not.

They did not yield when he tried to turn the handle.

"Here," Aamir said, hefting an iron patio chair. "There is no point in stealth now."

No, there wasn't. His only concern was speed.

He took the chair from his brother and hurled it through the French doors, shattering the glass and sending it flying in all directions. That was no matter, though, since they were all wearing heavy boots and could ignore the dangerous debris.

The three of them hurried through the remnants of the door. Omar looked around frantically and saw the living room was empty. Olivia's voice had come from somewhere off to the left, though, and he moved in that direction, his brothers flanking him.

Sure enough, Olivia and Khalim stood in the kitchen. He held her tightly by the bicep but did not seem to have committed any other acts upon her person. And when he saw the three al-Qadir brothers burst into the room, he only tightened his grasp, enough so that she let out a gasp.

"Omar," Khalim said pleasantly, as though they had just encountered one another at a favorite coffee house or tavern, "Jamal, Aamir. How nice to see you. Did you require assistance with something?"

"I need you to let go of that woman," Omar returned. His blood boiled to see him manhandling

Olivia in such a way, but he knew he needed to be careful here lest the rogue djinn cause her even worse pain.

Khalim lifted a surprised eyebrow. "This woman?" he said. "Why, is she a particular pet of yours? I thought you had no use for humans."

Not so long ago, he did not. Now, though, Omar knew the woman straining against Khalim's ugly grasp was the most important person in the world to him.

And he knew there was only one thing he could say to make the other djinn release her.

"She is my Chosen," he said, making sure the syllables rang out loud and distinct, so there could be no mistaking what he had said. "And that means she is off limits to you, Khalim."

Rather than let Olivia go, however, the other djinn only laughed. "You have taken a Chosen, Omar? You, whose only goal was to rid this world of its human filth? I will admire the boldness of your gambit, but you cannot expect me to believe such a thing."

"It is true," Aamir said, stepping forward. "A surprise to all of us, but this woman is Omar's Chosen...and you know the penalty for harming a human who was been bound to a djinn."

This argument seemed to have very little effect, for Khalim chuckled again. "I have been sentenced to the outer circles and have escaped. Do you really believe I care about such consequences? I will take what I wish from this world, and that is this woman."

Omar glanced at his brothers, and both Aamir and Jamal gave the subtlest of nods. It seemed clear enough the time for debate was over.

But before any of them could step forward, Khalim let go of Olivia and pushed her behind him —just as he raised his hands and a wall of fire appeared in front of him.

What the devil?

Their powers were blocked. He and his brothers had tested their abilities and had confirmed they did not have the use of them.

Except....

Omar sent his power into the earth, and the floor beneath them shook. Only a little, but enough to tell him that he also had had his gifts returned. How, he had no idea, but that was a puzzle to be solved later, after they had subdued Khalim and rescued Olivia.

Jamal and Aamir also seemed to have realized the stone was no longer blocking their powers, for Aamir summoned his own flame, darker and stronger than Khalim's, overtaking the wall of fire and consuming it so that it was soon gone. And although Omar and Jamal both knew they would have to be careful about invoking the power of the earth so that the house would not collapse around them, they still did their best to send the ground immediately beneath Khalim's feet into spasms so he was thrown violently about and nearly fell to his knees.

Sensing his weakness, Olivia backed away further. Her eyes met Omar's, and a very small smile touched her mouth before she bolted from the kitchen. Where she was going, he had no clue, but he thought it a very good idea to have her somewhere else rather than the spot where a battle was raging amongst the four djinn.

Khalim recovered himself enough to throw a fireball in Omar's direction, one he could not dodge completely. It hit his shoulder and he cursed, although he would not allow himself to stagger and lose his balance, and forced himself to ignore the searing pain in his flesh. The wound would heal soon enough, and he needed to focus on subduing the djinn who had dared to lay hands on the woman he loved.

The floor shuddered again, the wooden planks beneath their feet beginning to splinter from the repeated abuse. Aamir flung a fireball of his own, and although it could not truly hurt Khalim, who was also a creature of fire, it distracted him enough for Jamal to send another shockwave through the floor, one that almost made their adversary lose his footing.

Almost, but not quite.

And then Olivia was at the entrance to the kitchen, a gun very similar to the one she'd shot him with only a few days ago hefted in one hand. She lifted it, aiming at Khalim.

Oh, no. He could not allow her to do that. Not because he didn't believe that Khalim should be blasted from this world, but because he did not want her to carry the burden of killing another living being.

He, however, had plenty of blood on his hands.

A single thought, and the shotgun was yanked from Olivia's grasp and flew across the room into Omar's waiting arms. He lifted the gun, quickly parsing how it worked, and then pulled the trigger.

The blast caught Khalim in the chest, knocking him to the floor in a way their earth tremors had not. His eyes widened in anger and pain...and then narrowed.

Not much time. Not when he was probably already beginning to heal.

Omar lifted the gun and squeezed the trigger again. The blast caught the rogue djinn in the head, and the resulting damage ensured that he would never rise again.

"Well done, brother," Aamir said, sounding slightly breathless. A lift of his hand, and flames roared across the dead djinn's body, leaving only ash behind.

Olivia ran to Omar and threw her arms around

him, even as he lowered the shotgun to the shattered floor. "You didn't have to do that," she whispered, and he held her tightly against him, wanting to feel every inch of her, needing to reassure himself that she truly was safe and unharmed.

"Oh, yes, I did," he said.

Miles Odekirk's voice emerged from the speaker of the radio in Zahrias and Julia's home. "I'll need to perform more tests, but as far as I've been able to tell, something about being exposed to our atmosphere has created an oxidizing effect in the stones, neutralizing their effects. It seems this is not a process that happens all at once, which is why it was not immediately detectable."

"That would have been good to know in advance," Omar grumbled, but because he'd uttered the words mostly under his breath, Olivia didn't think the two-way radio picked them up.

"Thank you for the clarification," Zahrias replied. "We did retrieve the specimen from the house in Cedar Crest, so we will return it to you the next time a group from Los Alamos visits here."

Which, Olivia guessed, wouldn't be too long from now, with the threat from Khalim now neutralized. She still couldn't quite believe he was dead. Yes, she'd grabbed the shotgun from the hall closet—she'd found it when she first explored the house years earlier and had decided to leave it where it was, since she already had a gun at the farm—and had fully intended to blow the horrible djinn's head off, but Omar, not wanting her to carry the burden of his death on her shoulders, had done the deed instead. Maybe she would have been able to handle it, or maybe not.

Now, though, she wouldn't have to worry about her hypothetical guilt...or Khalim. He was gone for good.

After that last exchange, Zahrias ended the call with Miles. Now he turned back toward the waiting group—Omar and Olivia, Jamal and Aamir, his partner Julia—and said, "I have heard it is your turn for congratulations, Omar. It is good that you will now be a part of our community, and close to your brothers."

Yes, that would probably be for the best. The al-Qadir brothers were no longer separated by a feud over having a Chosen, so they could be together again.

Why did that prospect not make her as happy as she should be?

Judging by his expression, Omar didn't look too thrilled, either. They hadn't had a chance to sit down and talk things through, but had returned to Santa Fe immediately after Khalim was vanquished.

Olivia didn't know for sure what had happened to Aidan and David, the two Chosen who had been hanging around in Cedar Crest in case additional help was needed, although she guessed that Julia or someone else here in town had radioed them to come home.

But before Omar could respond to Zahrias' comment, three djinn appeared in the room, two men and a woman with red hair even brighter than that of Jamal's Chosen.

Or at least, Olivia assumed they were djinn. From the way Omar and his brothers and even Zahrias straightened, she got the feeling they might be a little bit more than that.

"Elders," Zahrias said, confirming her suspicions. "How may we be of assistance?"

"It is you who were of assistance," said the taller of the two male djinn. He had a few hints of gray in his night-dark hair, a sign of age Olivia hadn't seen in any of the elementals who lived in Santa Fe. "For you have rid the world of Khalim al-Usar, and that is no small thing."

"Our apologies for not intervening sooner," the female elder put in. "But he did not settle in any one place long enough for us to locate him. However, it seems you were able to catch him in the end."

Not without a few scary moments in between. Olivia didn't think she would ever forget the way the air felt as though it had been sucked out of her lungs when he appeared in the kitchen of the house in Cedar Crest, or his horrible grip on her arm. She was sure he must have left bruises...except that she didn't wound easily anymore, not now that she was Omar's Chosen.

"We did," Zahrias said. "And now all is well. We were discussing Omar al-Qadir's new home here in Santa Fe, for he has taken a Chosen of his own and will need to settle among us."

The female djinn's gaze moved to Omar. "It seems that you are not quite as happy with this conclusion as one might expect."

"I am happy in my Chosen," Omar returned, his chin up and his stare unflinching. Olivia didn't know whether all djinn were okay with meeting an elder's gaze head-on like that, but it seemed her partner didn't have a problem with it. "But I do question the need to live here in Santa Fe."

"You do not wish to reside near your brothers?" asked the third djinn, the one who hadn't spoken yet. He seemed younger than the other male djinn, handsome and dark-haired, with a serious expression.

"It is more that I wish to live in a place that has stolen my heart," Omar replied. "While we were hiding from Khalim al-Usar, Olivia Raskin and I took refuge in a place called Los Poblanos, located in Albuquerque. I have many plans for making it fruitful again, and it seems my energy would be better spent there than here in Santa Fe."

"But you must reside in a community of djinn and Chosen," the elder with the gray-streaked hair said. "That is how we've decreed it must be done."

"Not always," Omar responded without missing a beat. "For I know that you allowed a similar arrangement involving Nasim al-Jibril and his Chosen not so long ago."

This revelation appeared to be news to the Santa Fe djinn, although Olivia could have sworn the younger male elder's expression had turned almost sheepish.

"It is true," he allowed. "But that was a special case."

"I would argue that this case is just as special," Omar said. "For if it is important that Nasim and his partner should tend the vines at their home in Napa, then I would argue it is equally important for Olivia and I to make Los Poblanos a productive farm again. The situations seem equal to me."

The three elders exchanged glances, although none of them spoke. Or maybe they were communicating mentally, the way Omar could do with her and with his brothers.

It seemed that must have been the case, because after a moment the eldest elder said, "Very well. You may go to live at this place called Los Poblanos. It will be safe enough, with Khalim al-Usar no longer a threat and the outer circles strengthened so such a thing will never happen again."

"Exactly what *did* happen?" Olivia asked, surprising herself a little with her boldness.

The female djinn sent her a smile that wasn't quite indulgent. "A ripple that affected many planes. It will not be repeated."

And the three of them disappeared just as precipitously as they'd arrived.

Olivia blinked, but the djinn present didn't seem too off balance, as if they were used to the way the elders popped in and out of places according to their own whims. "So...what now?" she asked, and Omar smiled, even as he bent down to kiss her on the cheek.

"We go home, my love," he replied.

Chapter 21

SO MANY THINGS TO DO, CHIEF AMONG them remodeling the guest accommodations at Los Poblanos so that the entire structure was now one enormous house, with multiple bedrooms and bathrooms and a kitchen just as spacious and well-appointed as the commercial version connected to Campo. The bar, though, Omar left completely untouched, for he knew Olivia loved it just as it was, and to be honest, he could not think of any real improvements that were required there.

The two of them also looked over the records they found in the former resort's business offices, the ones that detailed what had been grown where, and they also made plans for the coming spring, plans that included reducing the size of the lavender fields so they might produce more edible crops. Through all this, Olivia appeared engaged enough, but from time to time, Omar caught a faraway, almost anxious look in her eyes, and he guessed easily enough what she must be thinking.

Yes, they were both safe and happy here, but she couldn't help worrying about the animals she'd left behind at the farm in Cedar Crest, despite his assurances that they would be just fine on their own.

That was why he thought he would surprise her, and one morning several days after they'd come to live at Los Poblanos, he told her he wanted to visit his brothers for a few hours in Santa Fe. A calculated risk, for he knew she might ask to tag along, but to his relief, she appeared content to remain at the house in front of the fire with the book she'd been reading.

Because while he could of course blink himself anywhere he wanted in a fraction of a second, and could summon almost anything they required to make their lives there more comfortable, those sorts of tricks did not extend to sending other living beings to and fro as he pleased. No, that would require some actual effort.

He blinked himself away from Los Poblanos and back to the Miller farm in Cedar Crest. All looked very much as it had been when he and Olivia had left, the house with its white siding and tin roof still sitting in the open fields that surrounded it and its barn a hundred paces or so to the rear. Even so, something about the place felt forlorn in a way it hadn't when Olivia lived here, as though her absence had drained it of any energy or vitality it once had possessed.

Even so, the place was not as lifeless as it had seemed at first glance. Movement just beyond the barn made him focus his gaze in that direction, and a moment later, the two goats she'd named Billie and Willie moved out of the shadow of the structure so they could focus on nibbling a promising patch of grass.

Excellent.

Although he would have to move the goats using mortal methods, he'd still been able to conjure a truck and trailer that would allow him to transport them back to Los Poblanos. Now that the vehicles were close by, he summoned a bin full of feed inside the trailer, and at once the goats trotted over, their little beards wagging with interest as they mounted the ramp.

Simple enough.

A single thought was sufficient to close the trailer's rear gate and fasten it firmly in place. One of the goats let out an annoyed little bray at being confined in such a way, but then it decided the pellets that had been provided were much more important, and it began to munch away next to its companion.

Now that was settled, Omar knew he had to

focus on much more elusive quarry. His gaze scanned the barnyard and the open land beyond, but he didn't notice any obvious signs of movement.

Where was that cat?

He decided he would look inside the house first, just in case Olivia's erstwhile feline companion had decided to remain there even after she was gone. However, a quick survey of the farmhouse's various rooms proved it was just as empty as it looked.

Muttering under his breath, Omar headed down the stairs and once more glanced around the farm. Nothing immediately stood out to him, except....

There was the barn, a rich, rusty red against the frost-yellowed landscape. Perhaps it, too, would be empty, but it did appear to be the most obvious place to look now that he'd proved to himself the house was empty.

Stride purposeful, he walked inside the barn and glanced around. Even though the day outside was bright enough, in here it was quite dim, with the darkness here and there pierced by a slender beam of sunlight as it slipped through the slats that made up the walls.

But djinn eyes were keener than those of a human, and almost at once, he saw the black and white shape crouched up in the loft, its narrowed green eyes staring down at him.

Clearly, the cat was not too happy that he had taken its mistress away.

Well, Omar was here to remedy the situation. And while his powers would not allow him to blink the cat to Los Poblanos, that didn't mean he couldn't still use them to dislodge the slit-eyed feline from its perch.

A single thought, and the cat lifted into the air and came drifting down into his arms, where it let out a hiss and promptly scratched at his forearm. Luckily, the heavy linen of his sleeve provided some protection, but the pain was still annoying enough for him to mutter a curse under his breath.

Good thing that scratch would heal itself in an eye blink.

With the cat still wriggling in his arms, he marched grimly out of the barn and seated himself behind the wheel of the truck he had summoned to haul the trailer. Once he deposited the cat on the passenger seat, it sat up and sent him a baleful green glance, but appeared intelligent enough to realize that, with all the windows closed and the doors locked, there wasn't much point in trying to get away.

He allowed himself a moment of relief. Even so, he thought it was going to be a very long drive back to Albuquerque.

Olivia set down her book and glanced at her watch. Maybe time didn't mean as much in a world where you didn't have to be at work at eight o'clock in the morning and there weren't any doctor's appointments that needed to be kept, but still, she figured it didn't hurt to keep track of things. As far as she could tell, Omar had been gone for at least two hours, possibly a little more. He hadn't said why he needed to visit his brothers today and she hadn't asked, and yet now she couldn't help wondering what was keeping him away for so long.

Restless, she got up from her chair and went out on the porch. From somewhere off in the distance, she thought she heard the rumble of an approaching engine, something that sounded loud and growly like a diesel truck...but that was crazy, wasn't it? She and Omar were the only two people living in the entire Albuquerque metro area, and there was no reason in the world why he'd need to be driving that kind of vehicle.

However, those inner denials had to be immediately tossed to the wayside, because in the next moment, a large silver truck hauling a small livestock trailer came down the lane that led to their home's front entrance, and a minute or so after that, it stopped right in front of the wide steps that led up to the door.

Omar emerged from the truck's cab, looking mighty pleased with himself.

Wait, was that Zorro in his arms?

She came hurrying down the steps, and he grinned at her before handing over a writhing cat, who looked less than pleased at being uprooted from the only home he'd ever known and driven fifty or so miles to an unfamiliar place.

"I thought you were missing him."

"I was," she replied, and bent so she could press a kiss in between Zorro's flattened ears. However, since she knew he wasn't a fan of displays of affection, she immediately set him down after that, and he hurried into the house, tail flicking with indignation.

Then she looked back at Omar.

"How did you know I was worried about him?"

"Because I know you, my love," he replied, leaning down so he could touch his lips to hers. "I did not want you to go through this life thinking we had abandoned the cat who'd been your companion these past four years."

"And the trailer?" she asked next, although she thought she already knew the answer.

"Your goats, of course," Omar said. "We should let them out, I think. They were starting to sound rather cranky the last leg of the journey."

She could imagine. Although he hadn't gone

into any detail, she had to believe the drive here would have been difficult even for a djinn, since he would have had to expend a lot of energy zapping abandoned vehicles out of the way just so he could keep heading steadily toward his destination.

And he'd done all that so he could bring Zorro and the goats home.

Smiling, she followed him to the rear of the trailer, where he undid the latch. Billie and Willie didn't even wait for Omar to drop the ramp, and instead bounded out of the trailer and onto the drive as soon as they knew they were free. At once, they headed to the overgrown lawn on the other side of the drive and began cropping away at it, and the djinn she loved glanced over at her, a grin of his own brightening his face.

"They seem very happy," he said, and she nodded.

"I think they're going to really like it here." She reached over so she could take his hand, hoping that something in the pressure from her fingers would let him know how much she loved him for what he'd just done.

"It would seem so." Omar paused there, then glanced down at her, dark eyes gleaming in the sunlight. "Is there anything else you need? For you know I will bring it to you, even if I must go to the ends of the earth."

Olivia didn't even have to stop to think. She went on her tiptoes to kiss his cheek.

"No," she said firmly. Omar had given his heart to her, and she knew she could never ask for anything more.

"I have everything I could ever need right here."

The End

The Djinn Wars series concludes with *Mistaken*.

Also by Christine Pope

THE WITCHES OF MINGUS MOUNTAIN

(Paranormal Romance)

Stolen Time

Borrowed Time (January 2025)

Killing Time (February 2025)

———

THE DJINN WARS

(Paranormal Romance)

Chosen

Taken

Fallen

Broken

Forsaken

Forbidden

Awoken

Illuminated

Stolen

Forgotten

Driven

Unspoken

Hidden

Written

Given

Mistaken

FAMILIAR SPIRITS*

(Cozy Mystery/Paranormal Romance)

Spells and Spaniels

Cauldrons and Cats

Hexes and Hedgehogs

Charms and Chihuahuas

Runes and Ravens

LATTES AND LEVITATION*

(Cozy Mystery/Paranormal Romance)

Caffeine Before Curses

Muffins After Magic

Pastries and Prophecies

Eclairs and Ectoplasm

Sugar Skulls and Specters

Wedding Cakes and Wishes

HEDGEWITCH FOR HIRE*

(Cozy Mystery/Paranormal Romance)

Grave Mistake

Social Medium

Household Demons

Perpetual Potion

Jingle Spells

Wandering Monsters

Uninvited Ghosts

Prophet Motive

Ballroom Bits

Spell Check

Brew Confessions

Charm School

UNEXPECTED MAGIC*

(Urban Fantasy/Paranormal Romance)

Found Objects

Finders, Keepers

PROJECT DEMON HUNTERS*

(Paranormal Romance)

Unquiet Souls

Unbound Spirits

Unholy Ground

Unseen Voices

Unmarked Graves

Unbroken Vows

THE DEVIL YOU KNOW*

(Paranormal Romance)

Sympathy for the Devil

Charmed, I'm Sure

A Wing and a Prayer

Wish Upon a Star

THE WITCHES OF CANYON ROAD*

(Paranormal Romance)

Hidden Gifts

Darker Paths

Mysterious Ways

A Canyon Road Christmas

Demon Born

An Ill Wind

Higher Ground

Haunted Hearts

THE WITCHES OF CLEOPATRA HILL*

(Paranormal Romance)

Darkangel

Darknight

Darkmoon

Sympathetic Magic

Protector

Spellbound

A Cleopatra Hill Christmas

Impractical Magic

Strange Magic

The Arrangement

Defender

Bad Blood

Deep Magic

Darktide

THE WATCHERS TRILOGY*

(Paranormal Romance)

Falling Dark

Dead of Night

Rising Dawn

THE SEDONA FILES*

(Paranormal/Science Fiction Romance)

Bad Vibrations

Desert Hearts

Angel Fire

Star Crossed

Falling Angels

Enemy Mine

TALES OF THE LATTER KINGDOMS*

(Fantasy Romance)

All Fall Down

Dragon Rose

Binding Spell

Ashes of Roses

One Thousand Nights

Threads of Gold

The Wolf of Harrow Hall

Moon Dance

The Song of the Thrush

THE GAIAN CONSORTIUM SERIES*

(Science Fiction Romance)

Beast (free prequel novella)

Blood Will Tell

Breath of Life

The Gaia Gambit

The Mandala Maneuver

The Titan Trap

The Zhore Deception

The Refugee Ruse

STANDALONE TITLES

Hearts on Fire (Paranormal Romance)

Taking Dictation (Contemporary Romance)

Golden Heart (Gaslamp Fantasy Romance)

Night Music: A Modern Reimagining of The Phantom
of the Opera (Contemporary Romance)

Ghost Dance: A Sequel to Gaston Leroux's The
Phantom of the Opera (Historical Mystery/Romance)

Flight Before Christmas (Fantasy Romance)

* Indicates a completed series

About the Author

USA Today bestselling author Christine Pope has been writing stories ever since she commandeered her family's Smith-Corona typewriter back in grade school. Her work includes paranormal romance, fantasy romance, and science fiction/space opera romance. She makes her home in Arizona.

Christine Pope on the Web:
www.christinepope.com

facebook.com/ChristinePopeAuthor
youtube.com/@ChristinePopeAuthor